THE LAST LEAVES FALLING

THE LAST LEAVES FALLING

SARAH BENWELL

Definitions

THE LAST LEAVES FALLING
A DEFINITIONS BOOK 978 1 909 53122 2

First published in Great Britain by Definitions,
an imprint of Random House Children's Publishers UK
A Penguin Random House Company

This edition published 2015

1 3 5 7 9 10 8 6 4 2

Penguin Random House is committed to a sustainable future for
our business, our readers and our planet. This book is made from
Forest Stewardship Council® certified paper.

Set in Zurich BT Light 10.4pt/15pt

Definitions are published by Random House Children's Publishers UK,
61–63 Uxbridge Road, London W5 5SA

www.**randomhousechildrens**.co.uk
www.**totallyrandombooks**.co.uk
www.**randomhouse**.co.uk

Addresses for companies within The Random House Group Limited
can be found at: www.randomhouse.co.uk/offices.htm

THE RANDOM HOUSE GROUP Limited Reg. No. 954009

A CIP catalogue record for this book is available from the British Library.

Printed and bound by CPI Group (UK) Ltd, Croydon, CR0 4YY

For Malcolm, and for Mark –
I wish you were both here to see this

Glossary of Terms

Bah-Ba – affectionate name for grandmother (obaasan)

bakeneko – catlike supernatural creature

Benzaiten – Japanese Buddhist goddess; goddess of everything that flows, including the arts

bonsai – 'tray plantings'; miniature trees, cultivated in pots. The art of bonsai is complex and revered

gagaku – ancient Japanese court/dance music

jūnihitoe – traditional, elegant, complex kimono; the 'twelve layer robe' (although it's not always twelve layers)

Ojiisan – grandfather

Otosan – father

Okaasan – mother

racoon dog – indigenous East Asian canid species, named for its resemblance to a racoon (to which it is not closely related)

sake – alcoholic beverage made from fermented rice

-san – a suffix to names, which indicates respect. A little bit like 'sir' or 'ma'am'

yūrei – ghosts or supernatural creatures

......A Note on Names

The use of names and honorifics in Japanese is complex and steeped in respect. People will often use full names or the suffix –*san* in everyday conversation, and there are different names for (for instance) *your* grandfather, and someone else's. It may also be useful to know that in Japanese, names follow the pattern: family name, given name (e.g. Benwell Sarah).

The names and honorifics in this book nod towards these patterns, but do not entirely follow them, because the complexities are lost in translation and can be confusing or overly formal and *different* to foreign ears. And ultimately, this story is about a group of teenagers not so very different from ourselves.

USERNAME		UPLOAD A
TAG-LINE		PROFILE
AGE	GENDER	PIC NOW

INTERESTS

If you could be anything in the world, what would you be?

I stare at the cursor blinking expectantly at the top of the page.

Who do I want to be?

There are so many choices; honest, funny, brave. A superhero with a tragic past and bright, mysterious future; with superstrength or telekinetic powers. I could be anyone and they would never know.

People say that is the problem with the internet; paedophiles, murderers, conmen, the internet makes it all too easy to hide. But I like it.

I type 'SamuraiMan' into the first box, then my fingers come to rest against the keys again. I know I'm overthinking this, but it has to be right. Put all these boxes together and you'll have a picture: a picture of *me*.

Outside the computer, nobody sees Abe Sora any more, they only see the boy who looks weird, the boy who cannot walk, the boy who needs assistance.

The boy who's going to die.

At first, they thought that the aching in my legs was flu and nothing more, but the weakness grew, and one day, out on the baseball field, I fell. My legs stopped working. The tests seemed to go on for ever. Nobody knew what was wrong with me. They probed and prodded and asked a million questions. Every theory proved wrong, every disease and condition crossed off the list, until finally they found an answer.

I knew as soon as we opened the door. The doctor gestured to the empty seats, his face so serious, and I *knew*. They say that a warrior must always be mindful of death, but I never imagined that it would find me like that, in a white room with strip lights buzzing overhead.

'The good news is we *have* a diagnosis,' he said quietly. 'Amyotrophic Lateral Sclerosis.'

My mother shifted her chair a little closer, curled her fingers around my balled fist then said slowly, deliberately, 'What is that?'

'That's the bad news,' he sighed. He was staring somewhere between us, as though he could not bear to look at us.

I remember thinking, *Is what I have so terrible that he cannot even stand to say it? Will looking at me make him sick too?* I imagined germs flowing from my fingertips, infecting everything I touched. I tried to pull away from Mama's grasp, but her fingers were tight with fear.

I glanced across at her, watched her eyes desperately searching the doctor's face for clues. She looked tired. I noticed it for the first time that day. She has been tired ever since.

'It's rare,' the doctor continued. 'That's why a diagnosis took so long; it is not something you would expect to find in someone your son's age.'

My mother did not wait for him to continue, and when she spoke her voice was hurried, desperate. 'But what *is* it?'

The doctor stared over my right shoulder as he recited symptoms, using big words which meant nothing to me then – *atrophy* and *fasciculations*, then *neurodegeneration* – in what should, I'm sure, have been a reassuring tone.

His words rushed at me full force and then receded, like the flow of waves. 'Gradual deterioration . . . limited movement. No cure . . . average prognosis of two years, but in some cases it is more, or less . . . I am sorry.'

No cure. And since then, even to my mother, I have been the boy who's going to die; but here, here I can be anything.

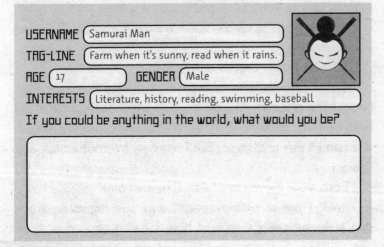

USERNAME (Samurai Man)

TAG-LINE (Farm when it's sunny, read when it rains.)

AGE (17)   GENDER (Male)

INTERESTS (Literature, history, reading, swimming, baseball)

If you could be anything in the world, what would you be?

Anything?

My mother's voice interrupts my thoughts, calling, 'Coming!' as she shuffles down the hallway. I hear the latch and the soft creak of the door, polite voices, too quiet for me to recognize.

Who *is* it?

I glance at the clock, as if that will hold the answers, even though neither my mother nor I have very many visitors these days. It's . . . difficult. Embarrassing. No one wants to be around us any more.

I listen for any sign of who the visitor might be; a cough, a laugh, the rhythm of familiar steps. Nothing. I can't tell.

I wish they'd go away.

Holding my breath at every sign of company has become almost a ritual. Every time I hear the door, the telephone, a stranger's voice I wonder, who else is going to know my shame? Who else will stare, not knowing what to say?

Finally, the door closes and my mother's gentle footsteps move back along the hall. I rest my head against the monitor of my computer and breathe a long sigh of relief as the cool glass spreads its calm across my skin. They've gone. I'm safe.

'Sora?' Mother knocks at my door.

'Uhh,' I groan, turning my face towards the door. The cool of the glass shifts a little. I imagine that the cold is an iceberg, that I'm alone in a desert of ice where everything is clear and fresh and quiet. But I am not; my mother speaks again.

'Sora, your friends are here. Can we come in?'

'We?' I panic, sitting upright and pushing away from my desk, suddenly aware of how small my room is, how intrusive the large wheels of my chair are in this little space. There is nowhere to hide.

Who would visit unannounced? I never really had friends at school, more like acquaintances. People you could joke with in the classroom, but no one special. I preferred my own company and the quiet of the library, especially in the last months.

'Sora?'

I grunt, and the door slides open. My mother smiles at me and steps aside, ushering in the school's baseball captain, Tomo, and a girl I think I might have seen in the corridors of school, hunched below a cello case. I squint at her. Yes. Just before I left she caused a ruckus, leaving her first chair in the orchestra to start a rock band. They look odd together, short and tall, gutsy and clean-cut, the musician and the jock, but she's clinging to him tightly.

What are they *doing* here? Neither of them has ever been to my home before. We're not friends; we've barely even spoken.

They stand in the doorway for a moment, exchange glances. And I know: someone *made* them come. And neither of them wants to be alone with me. The cripple. The sick. The dying.

'Hey,' I say.

'Hi,' they say in unison, still not stepping over the threshold.

For a moment we just stare at each other, until I cannot stand it any longer.

'Come in, make yourselves at home.' I force myself to smile as I speak.

They step forward, one step, two.

'This is Reiko.' Tomo shrugs himself from her grip.

I gesture to the bed, with its neatly turned sheets. She sits, fiddling nervously with her plaits, but Tomo paces, swinging his arm like he's warming up to pitch a ball.

He stops and stares at the wall above my bed, the poster of Katsuhiro Maekawa, pitcher for the Tigers in the 2004 match against the Yankees. Below that, the shelf with my catcher's mitt, my limited edition silver bat, the ball signed by half the current team. And my baseball cards. Most of them are kept neatly in folders, organized by team and season. One, however, showing the face of Yoshio Yoshida, sits alone on the shelf looking out at me. It is a duplicate; he's safely stored away with the rest of his team as well, but I like to think that he is watching over me.

'Wow!' Tomo nods towards the ball which takes pride of place beside Yoshio. 'Is that Tomoaki's signature in the middle there?'

I nod. The signature is barely recognizable; wonky and left-handed. Tomoaki Kanemoto had smiled at me and signed the ball even after playing through the game with a torn cartilage. That day, every boy in the bleachers learned about determination.

He frowns at it for a moment, squinting. 'Is this from 2004? *That* game?' he asks, eyes wide.

I nod again.

Games like that are not forgotten. Every pair of eyes is glued to the action, every heart longing to be down there on that green, soaking up the glory.

Tomo might actually make it there one day. He's good. I always wished that I could pitch like him.

'Awesome!' he says. 'You know, you should come to a ga—' He stops, his eyes now on my chair. 'Well, y'know. If you find the time.'

'Yeah, maybe. Thanks.' I have no intention of watching the high school games, the team I should be on. I will never step onto the field or sit in the bleachers and cheer again. I know it, and Tomo knows it, and an awkward silence eats up all the air again.

'Actually, that's why I'm here.'

'Oh?'

'Yeah.' He shoves his hands into his pockets. 'Coach wants to dedicate the season to you.'

'To *me*?' I was only ever a B-team, after-school-club player.

'Uh-huh. He thinks, er . . . he thinks it might inspire people. Remind them what they have . . . sorry.'

I'm glad he has the decency to look ashamed.

'Anyway. He sent me to tell you, and to invite you to the last game of the season. If you want. He thought you might do a speech. To motivate the others.'

What does one say to that? I am not a circus lion. I can feel an angry heat rising up my neck. It should not matter what the people of my past think. But it does.

I am nothing but the sick boy.

The unfortunate.

A puppet.

It is always like this. And suddenly a hundred awkward pity-moments flood my synapses, hit me all at once. Tomo and his girlfriend need to leave now; I need my room back. But as the seconds tick by, neither of them move, they just stare, and suddenly there is not enough air in here for three of us and I want them to leave *right now*.

I swallow hard, try not to sound desperate as I say, 'I'm sorry, I am very tired.'

'Oh. Of course.' Tomo nods curtly and shuffles to the door.

Reiko gets up to follow, but she stops halfway. 'We've missed you in class.' Her eyes shine too brightly, as though she's going to cry. 'All of us. Hayashi-san is organizing everyone to sign a card.' She falters. 'We'd have brought it today, but a few people were absent and we know they'd want to send their thoughts.'

I do not want to think about my classmates, sitting at their desks as though everything is normal. Has someone taken my seat, or is it empty, a reminder that last term there was one more eager student? I look away from Reiko's heavy gaze, tap the mousepad so my computer whirrs to life. 'Thank you. I'm OK.'

She stays just for a second, then sighs and follows Tomo out. I hear them walk down the hallway, thank my mother. And as the door clicks shut behind them, I breathe.

Slowly, the air clears, and after a few minutes alone I turn back to the boxes on my screen.

If you could be anything in the world, what would you be?

I imagine myself passing Tomo in the hallway, sliding clumsily into fourth base, sitting in a classroom without thirty-five sets of eyes on me.

Healthy.

But then I think, *I'm more than that. I* want *more than that.* So I write:

> I would like to be a professor when I grow up. Does that count?
> Or are you looking for something more abstract? In which case, I
> should like to be a fountain pen, expensive, elegant, belonging to a
> writer of beautiful calligraphy, or novels, recording truth and wonder
> for the years to come.

I am not exactly lying. I would love to spend my days in lecture halls until my hair is as white as the chalk dust floating through the air. I just . . . will never get the chance. But they did not ask me that.

I read the words again from start to finish and try to picture what someone else would see; what do I look like to a stranger? But even I struggle to see myself without this disease.

At the bottom of the screen are two buttons, *save* and *post*. My finger hovers over *post* but those shocked, sad faces from the school halls and the streets flash right before my eyes, judging me, and I do not click. I can't. I'm not ready.

2

My mother and I sit on either side of the table and eat in silence. She steals glances at me over her bowl of noodles, and I hope she does not see the tremor in my fingers. It is new, and I do not want her to know, yet. Once she sees it, she will do what all good mothers would, and fuss, but I want more time to do the little things myself.

I catch her eye, and she smiles her oh-so-tired smile. It is me who's done this to her, and I hate it. I wish that I could turn back time, change something, take her hand and run and run and run in another direction so that ALS can't find us.

She's curious, I know, but it takes her a moment to ask about my visitors. 'I don't think I have met your friends before.'

'No.'

'They seemed nice.'

I nod, picking up my chopsticks.

'Will they come again? Perhaps you should invite them for a meal.'

'They are very busy, Mama. I do not think they'll have the time.'

She hides it well, but I imagine I can see the longing in her eyes. I should be busy too.

'Perhaps we *should* apply to that other school.'

That 'other' school is a place for children who have disabilities. I am *not* a special student. I don't need help to tie my laces, yet, or to read, or manage my emotions.

Even if I am around for long enough, no one graduating from a special school will get a place at university.

We declined. But now I think my mother's having second thoughts.

'Are you going past the library tomorrow?' I ask, to change the subject.

'I could.'

'Great. If I write you a list, could you pick me up a couple of books? I can study on my own, Mama. You don't need to worry.'

'You know, we could go to the library together. Or the park? We could go for ice cream?'

I shake my head, and she sighs.

'Well, you have a session with Doctor Kobayashi to-morrow, don't forget.'

I nod. I can avoid the park, social trips and errands, but weekly meetings with my counsellor are compulsory, part of the terminal package. Every week, instead of going to extra classes alongside my peers, my mother drives me to the hospital and I sit for one stifling hour in that airless room, watching the seconds tick by until she will drive me home again. Doctor Kobayashi seems pleasant enough, but I do not know what to say to her. That I'm scared? That I wish it was someone else sitting in this chair? That I don't deserve this?

If I were a child, I'd cry. I'd scream. I'd throw my Hanshin Tigers baseball through the window as hard as I could.

But I'm not, and I cannot say these things.

I am so tired that my eyes itch, but every time I close them, fragments of the day flash into view. The look of pity on Reiko's face as she leaves. Tomo, in his baseball uniform, sliding into fourth base. An empty desk. A bustling classroom filled with people who don't fit into the real world. The lines around my mother's eyes.

When I can't stand it any longer, I swivel my hips so that my legs flop out of bed, and I sit, haul myself into my chair, and turn on the computer.

It is late. My mother is probably in bed asleep by now, but I listen tentatively for a moment anyway, before I type into the search bar:

 Amyotrophic Lateral Sclerosis prognosis

The first page of results is all highlighted blue; all sites I've visited before. It doesn't matter, I need to read it again. Somehow seeing it written down makes it easier to process, as though I've unloaded part of the burden from my brain onto the screen.

I click on the first link, a simple wiki page.

> Amyotrophic Lateral Sclerosis is a progressive neurodegenerative disease, usually presenting in patients over 50. The disease is always fatal, with most affected patients dying of respiratory compromise after 2-3 years.

The bit that always gets me, every time, is 'over 50'. I have an old man's disease. The doctors tell me that there are others, that I am not the only young sufferer or the youngest. But they cannot show me anyone else except sick old men leaving behind their grown-up children.

And if it is so rare, why me? Jealousy is an ugly emotion. It is not the warrior way. But I will never be that old man, never have children to sit upon my knee and teach about the way of things. And it is not only me I'm jealous for. I try not to think of my mother left alone, exhausted from two years of physical and emotional strain.

I try not to think of everything that comes between now and then, or rather to think of it, but as though it won't be happening to me. Because although my brain works fine, eventually I will be exactly like the kids at the disabled school. Unable to button up my shirt or raise a spoon of food up to my mouth. Unable to master the simplest of skills.

It has started already. The aching in my hands, the intermittent trembling. Subtle now, but not for long. Months, perhaps, if I am lucky.

Legs, hands, arms, one by one they will give up on me.

If this were the olden days, I'd take a trusted friend and a sword out into the yard and perform the last ritual. Quick and final. No mess except the blood to sluice away. But it is not; we don't operate by that code any more, and no one speaks of the honour which flows through our veins. And I am stuck inside this failing body.

3

Doctor Kobayashi's office is on the third floor. You can see the tops of the trees through the window, laughing gently in the breeze; a stark contrast to the clean white walls of the hospital.

In here, the air is still, and there is nothing to laugh about. Doctor Kobayashi has placed a bonsai on the glass-topped table. Intended, I imagine, to calm her patients: a touch of green, a symbol of the essence of life. The cycle in perfect miniature.

Tiny yellow leaves spill across the table between us like curls of caramel. Nothing lasts for ever.

She watches me, her expression unreadable.

Judging me. They always do. Everyone.

Finally, she breaks the silence. 'Have you had a good week?'

I shrug, stare at the table rather than look at her. I know she wants me to speak, but I don't know what to say.

She cannot help me anyway.

To:	S...
From:	KyoToTeenz
Subject:	Welcome To KyoToTeenz (:

Dear *SamuraiMan*,

Congratulations and welcome on becoming a member! We hope you will be very happy here.

Some features include:

Open forums – discuss anything and everything with the KyoToTeenz community.

Contacts – add your friends to a list; find their posts with ease.

Private chat – some things you don't want to share. Private chat lets you talk only to the people who you want to see.

Ready to jump in? Your username and password will be with you shortly.

I flick through my emails one by one: a 20% sale on textbooks, and a message which reads:

**WE THINK YOU WOULD LIKE THESE MAGAZINES:
TRY ONE FREE TODAY.**

Then this:

I read it again, because I cannot quite believe what it seems to be asking, and then quickly press delete. My heartbeat's pounding in my fingertips as though I have just handled stolen yen; if my mother saw this, she would take my computer into the street and burn it, ban me from the internet until the end of days.

But now she'll never know.

I stare at the unopened messages before me, more offers and one more from KyoToTeenz; nothing to suggest what I've just read. I'm safe.

5

'How are you today?'

I shrug, barely, trying not to think about this morning's physiotherapy and my awful performance on the walking bars. Last month I had been able to shuffle awkwardly down that runway, half using my legs. Today, they were bent and cramped and useless, and for the first time, my wheelchair felt like freedom.

'It's difficult for me to help you if you will not talk to me.' Doctor Kobayashi sighs a practised little sigh which I am sure is meant to lay just the right amount of guilt.

I stare hard at the bonsai. It is almost bare now, only a few leaves clinging to the branches, and the yellow curls which spread across the desk at our last meeting have gone, swept into a garbage can somewhere.

She tries again. 'How have things been since our last appointment?'

I do not answer. For a while she sits, studying me, then she breaks the silence. 'Your hand is shaking.'

I want to turn away, to hide my hands in the folds of my sweatshirt. To deny it. But there's no denying what is in plain sight. I nod. She cannot gather anything from one small gesture, right?

'That's new. I'm . . . it must be difficult.'

I've heard those two words so often these past few months that it surprises me when she does not say them. And I'm grateful. *Sorry* does nothing.

I nod. 'Sometimes.'

A tiny flicker of a smile crosses her face, and she waits, expectant.

I wish I could retract my words, suck the sound back into my mouth and stay silent. But now it's out there, and she's waiting for more.

And she didn't say those two terrible words.

'Sometimes I—' And then I stop, because I don't know what to say. I take a deep breath. 'What will happen to me?'

'You mean your symptoms? Didn't your neurologist explain all that?'

I blink the Google images away, of end-stage patients, all pillows and trachea tubes and desperate eyes. Trapped.

I shake my head. 'No, I mean—'

What *do* I mean?

She watches me, waits, but I do not have the words.

'Life is full of mysteries,' she says sadly. 'Things which are only answered in the doing. I cannot tell you what it will be like, only that many have gone before you.'

We sit, neither of us saying anything, but it's different now.

I listen to my breath, strong, unlaboured. I let the instinctive rise and fall of it calm me. I do not have to think about that yet; in, out, in – it happens automatically.

The clock ticks by, counting the seconds, and I breathe, letting myself just *be*.

Is this what it will be like?

Not if the textbooks and search pages are right. It will be ugly.

'It's not dignified.' The words are out before I hear them in my head, and they sound bitter.

'No,' she says. 'The body rarely is . . . The *mind,* however, *that* you can control. That's where you keep your dignity.'

She sounds so sure. Profound. And yet . . .

'I don't know how.'

The clock is fast approaching the hour; two minutes left, but Doctor Kobayashi does not hurry. She sits, watching me, and for a moment there's a question in her eyes, then she shakes it away, apparently satisfied. 'OK.'

She stands, crosses over to the bookshelves behind her desk, and pulls down a slender volume.

'Here.' She presses the book into my hands. 'I want you to borrow this.'

Making sure my bedroom door is firmly closed first, I pull the book from my backpack. The deep grey paper of the cover is soft and warm. Inviting. Calm.

I hold it for a moment before my eyes slide across the title. *Death Poems: Last Words of the Samurai.*

6

I blink, surprised for a moment by the bold black print, no different from any other book. These are words of age and wisdom from the best of men, not written with a delicate brush, but typed onto a screen so long after they were first formed. Still wanted.

I skip over the long introduction; I will read it later, but right now I want *their* words, I need the stillness and the gravity of men who knew The Way. At the first poem I stop, let my fingers glide over the page to feel the words before I raise the book to read.

> *I cannot mourn, for I have lived*
> *a life*
> *of mountain air and cherry blossoms, steel, and honour.*
> > *(Tadamichi, 1874)*

I feel the words float around me, settle on my skin and then sink slowly into me. It is a while before I turn the page.

> *On journey long*
> *I stop to rest and watch*
> *the end of days.*
> > *(Kaida, 1825)*

I imagine leaning on the gate at the end of days, looking back, the sun warming my face.

I turn the page.

The whistle of the sword, sings;
smiles 'neath silver sun,
frees me with a final kiss.
          (Okimoto, 1902)

I feel a breath of cool, fresh air across my arms, gentle and welcome.

I read and I read, one after the other until the words and feelings tumble through me, indistinct and beautiful.

And then my fingers rest upon the final page.

Words
are mere distraction –
Death is death.
 (Tokaido, 1795)

ヿ

All through dinner I'm distracted by the echoes of the samurai and I barely hear my mother's attempts at conversation. Finally, she sets down her bowl and, reaching out to me, asks, 'Are you all right?'

I nod. 'I was just thinking about something I read, that's all. I'm sorry.'

She smiles her bemused, proud smile, and I want to be with her instead of with those words. I try to push them aside and focus on the last of our meal.

'This is delicious,' I say, slurping down the last of the salty prawn broth.

She bows her head, an almost invisible movement, accepting the compliment. Almost invisible, but I see it, just as I see the sadness just beneath that smile.

I'm sorry, I want to say. *I'm sorry.*

I almost show my mother the poems that night. I want to. I want to place them in her hands the way Doctor Kobayashi put them into mine. I want the words to swirl around her head and quieten the storm. But that would mean explaining where they came from. It would mean broaching that awful phrase, *I am going to die*, and I don't think I am ready.

8

The words of the samurai hang in the air like the memory of heavy rain. I feel different somehow, as though the poetry has washed away a layer of pity and despair. But there is one poem which rises above the others, whining like a summertime mosquito:

The orange tea moth;
only witness to my faultless
victories.

I sit with a history book open but ignored, trying to make sense of it.

The orange tea moth . . .

And then I realize. All I am now is a failing body; a boy without an ending, who will not achieve. And even if I did, who would see it?

Not even the moth.

Soon after I was diagnosed I heard my grandfather, distant and distorted, talking to my mother on the phone. 'It is not right, a boy sitting alone all day. He should be out catching the world.'

I thought him foolish then. The world is difficult to catch if you cannot run after it. But maybe he's right after all.

With his voice in my head, my fingers move the cursor across my screen and click open the web browser; they sift through recent pages until I find myself logging in to the KyoToTeenz network and staring at the profile I created days before.

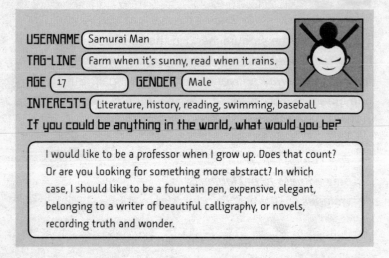

USERNAME (Samurai Man)
TAG-LINE (Farm when it's sunny, read when it rains.)
AGE (17)   GENDER (Male)
INTERESTS (Literature, history, reading, swimming, baseball)
If you could be anything in the world, what would you be?

> I would like to be a professor when I grow up. Does that count? Or are you looking for something more abstract? In which case, I should like to be a fountain pen, expensive, elegant, belonging to a writer of beautiful calligraphy, or novels, recording truth and wonder.

There it is. The boy I'd like to be. The boy I *am*, beneath it all.

POST

For three whole seconds I stare at the message 'Post Successful'. I almost hit return, delete my entry, but I force my hands steady. I want this. I don't want to be alone.

To distract myself, I scroll down the list of open chatrooms. There's HomeworkChatz, and CollegeWorriez, and below that StReSsBuStInG, OMGAnime, and ILoveArnie-Schwarzenegger. I log in to the first one, MondayTalk, an open forum, and watch the conversation unfold.

Vixeninety6: OK, no, but I would think about it, and I don't see why you can't live out the fantasy and love BOTH bands. It's not like they're real boys you're ever going to meet.

GuitarGirl1: She might! She might go to a concert and be asked backstage. One of them might ask her to MARRY HIM.

Vixeninety6: Oooooh.

GuitarGirl1: Yes, Bamboo, we do. Meekkat, u so pretty. And fun!

RaindropsOnKittens: Kitty and a Hot Boy sitting in a tree . . .

ChopstixChopstixChopstix: Hush!

ChopstixChopstixChopstix: You lot are so uncultured. It's not about the boys, it is about the music.

GuitarGirl1: Noooo, music IS about boys. And thrum. It's alllll about the thrum.

Ace101: Sorry to interrupt, but has anyone ELSE been getting mail from the SClub?

Ace101: It's creeping me out.

ChopstixChopstixChopstix: Thrum? Really?

Ace101: (also hi!)

MadSkillz: Nooooo, what mails?

KyoToQueen: Yes. Me too.

BambooPanda: Yes!

Ace101: Ugh, lucky, Mad. It's a suicide petition thing. For disaffected youth like us :(

Ace101: Glad I'm not alone though.

TandemRide: Me :/

Chocol8pocky: Hiiiiii guys! Whatcha talkin' about?

BambooPanda: Me. It's HORRIBLE. I mean, who DOES that?

BambooPanda: It's like they've got no hope or something.

TandemRide: Hi Choco. This suicide email everyone's been getting. A mass organized thing.

Chocol8pocky: Who came up with THAT plan? What's the point? No one's going to change the world if they're dead right?

TandemRide: Oh I don't know. It could work, with the shock factor. It might make people think.

TandemRide: I'm not saying it's a GOOD idea . . . Just interesting.

MadSkillz: Oh come on! It might be fun. (jk)

BambooPanda: Fun? FUN?! You're sick! It's horrible and sad and NOBODY should join them. None of you be thinking about it! *glares*

Ace101: Panda's right, it's STUPID.

ShinigamiFanBoy: HAVEN'T YOU SEEN JISATSU CIRCLE? O_O

MadSkillz: OK, OK, I was just trying to lighten the mood. I'm sorry!

KittyL<3ve: Aieee! I came top! All that studying WORKED!

KittyL<3ve: (hi everyone, what's going on?)

MadSkillz: *bows* Congratulations, KittyL<3ve 😊 Was that for your Nglish test?

KittyL<3ve: Thank you! Yes! But it is English.

MadSkillz: Just this email thing. Nothing. It's depressing anyway, and I'm not helping, apparently. Save me from myself, let's talk about youuuu.

MadSkillz: Haha, typo! No wonder I am always beat.

Ace101: I'll help you study, Madskillz!

MadSkillz: Sure, I'll be right over, Chika ;)

Ace101: Bring soda!

ShinigamiFanBoy: Madskillz, what are these Mad Skills?

MadSkillz: Haahahaha, they are secret, Shinigami — If I tell you, I reveal my identity, and then I have to kill you. Wouldn't want that. Ace — Cola, or Coffee?

ShinigamiFanBoy: Come on dude, what's spoken in chatroom stays in chatroom!

Ace101: Coffee, plz Madskillz. Always coffee.

KittyL<3ve: :-o Ace101, surely not always?

Ace101: ALWAYZZZ

SUSHIKING: Hi guys!

ShinigamiFanBoy: Hi, Sushi!

Ace101: Hi Sushi!

MadSkillz: Hey, SUSHIKING. How's it?

SUSHIKING: Good thanks, Mad. Did you SEE the Tigers play?

KittyL<3ve: Hi Sushi. I was just leaving. Gotta study. Look after this lot.

MadSkillz: Hah, gotta keep up the streak, hey Kitty? Laters.

KittyL<3ve: Totally. Bye guys!

I watch the words appear, one line at a time, listening in to these normal conversations. I talked like this, once.

I almost join them. My fingers hover over the keys, as I think the word 'hello', over and over, but I cannot bring myself to type it. I do not know what would come next.

So I sit there, a voyeur on normal lives, and in my little room, in my chair, alone, I enjoy their company.

There's a knock at my door.

'Time for your medications, Sora.' My mother walks in and places a glass of water and a handful of pills gently on the desk beside me. 'Do you need some help to get ready for bed?'

'No thanks. I can manage.' I may be growing weaker, but I can still undress myself.

She sighs, then kisses the top of my head. 'Goodnight, then.'

'Night, Mama.'

She pads out quietly, closing the door behind her. And there's a pause; I know she's standing there, waiting, as though she does not know whether I can really manage. It is several minutes before she walks away.

Reluctantly, I switch off the computer monitor and scoop up the tablets – all in one go. It's better to get it over with. As they hit the back of my throat, I raise the glass and pour half of the water in behind them. I swallow, hard. Done.

At first, I imagined this cocktail of drugs working miracles, sewing up the broken parts of me. But this is no cure, it merely buys me time, alleviates some of the pain. I *wish* it were a cure.

My head aches, dully, as though I've thought too much

today. My mother is right, it's time for bed. I spin my chair around to face my clothes drawers, pull out an oversized T-shirt and wheel myself across to the bed.

I turn down the duvet so I won't have to caterpillar my way under it, and lay the shirt out flat across the end of the mattress. Then, with one arm on the bed and the other on the arm of my chair, I heave my weight up and over, swaying briefly on my feet as I turn. I land with a heavy *plumph* upon the bed, breathless from that one movement.

Useless body.

The worst bit done, I let my breath slow and the shaking in my arms and legs subside before I reach up to pull the shirt I'm wearing up over my head.

It's another T-shirt. I've given up wearing buttoned shirts. I do not think my mother's noticed yet, but it will not be long. It won't be long before she bustles in here morning and night to help me with all the tricky things. Buttons and zips first. Then this, the simple act of pulling off a shirt. At first she'll do it because she wants to make things easier, but then because she has to.

I imagine her fingers, too close as she rids me of my jeans. Her perfume, sweet and sharp at once, clouding the room, settling on my skin and in my hair.

She should not have to do this.

And she doesn't, yet.

Having changed my shirt, there's one more thing. Jeans. I force the buttons open with my thumb. It's awkward, but I manage; one, two, three, four. I push the top of my jeans down, edging the fabric beneath my buttocks so that if I were to stand, the jeans would fall, and then, shifting my weight from left to right, left to right, I work them down a little at a time. Left – tug, right – tug, left – tug, right – until the waistband hangs around my knees. I let go and my jeans fall to the floor. Sometime in the night my mother will come in and fold them neatly over my chair, or put them in the laundry pile.

I scoot back into the centre of my double bed and swing my legs around and, finally, lean back until my head hits the pillow.

The fabric is soft and cool against my cheek, and I inhale the freshness of it as every muscle in my body sighs with relief, and I relax.

Sleep, so comes the end
of a long and winding day.
Sleep, for now it ends.

9

The next morning, I wake early. The sun has not yet risen, and the light which filters through the slats of the window-blinds is dim and grey. My room is steeped in shadows.

I could reach out and switch on the lamp, slowly get myself up out of bed, but instead I lie here, staring at the grey space above me, let it wash over me. It is a long time since I've heard the apartment this quiet. My mother wakes with the first crow and switches on the radio before she bustles in, opening the blinds and offering a hand to help me up, and most nights she sits with the TV long after I have gone to bed. But now, all I hear is my own breath.

I wonder whether anybody else is up this early. The road-sweepers, perhaps, and early-morning traders? If I wheeled myself outside, I bet I could get all the way to the Imperial Park before I saw another soul. But it is warm and safe, cocooned in the softness of my sheets, and there's no chance of gawking strangers, full of pity and repulsion.

Instead, I close my eyes, focus on my breathing, and try to imagine the oxygen travelling through me: trachea, bronchii, bronchioles, alveoli, then into the bloodstream, whooshing from my heart to my toes and back up again. One minute per cycle. In, out, up, down.

Breath and blood. Life. It's mine, and I do not want to waste it.

As a gentle pinkish light begins to rise, banishing the shadow, my mother's alarm clock sounds: a tinny, desperate cockerel. Two minutes later I hear the mattress creak as she gets out of bed. My thinking time is up; the day's begun.

I'm going to make this one count.

'Mama, do you have time for the park this morning?'

My mother looks up from her toast in surprise.

'I thought maybe we could stop for tea at the café stand before my appointment.'

She blinks at me, then smiles. 'Of course! Are you sure? There will be lots of people on a day like this.'

'I'm sure.'

She was right, the park is full. Everywhere I look there are love-birds holding hands and children running up and down the paths, trailing kites which will not fly in today's light breeze.

I'm sure people are staring, but the sunlight dances through the leaves of overhanging trees, and the air is clean and my mother smiles as we stand in line for tea, and today, I do not care.

I hold our paper cups as she pushes my chair until we find a spot down a smaller path which is a little quieter. There is a bench beneath a red-leafed maple tree, overlooking a small stream.

She parks my chair beside the bench, and we sit, sipping at the bitter green liquid.

'This is nice,' I say.

'Yes.'

'The leaves will be changing soon. We should come back to watch them.'

She nods.

'Mama?'

'Yes?'

I take a deep breath, and look into her eyes. 'Thank you.'

'For what?'

Confusion clouds her eyes as she looks back at me. Confusion and sadness and pride. I want to say, *For everything. For giving up your life, for the appointments and the early mornings and late nights, for the worry and the sadness and for never giving up.* But as I open my mouth to form the words a group of thirty or so schoolkids appears, marching towards us, laughing, and the words stick in my throat. 'The tea,' I say instead.

She pulls her gaze away, then reaches over and squeezes my free hand. 'I *love* you, Sora.'

'I know.'

We sit a while longer, listening to the shrieks of joy and rustling of the leaves around us, until Mama stands, handing me her empty cup.

'Come on. We'll be late.'

The outer doors to the hospital slide open, and the gases of a thousand sick drift out into the street. Hot, sweaty body smells, sharp disinfectant and that strange, sweet scent of medication. I try not to breathe as we cross the threshold, but you can't not breathe for that long, and before we even pass the information desk I have to gasp in great lungfuls of warm, rancid air.

The hallways all look the same, and if it weren't for the big blue signs and brightly painted arrows, you could get lost for days. To get to Paediatrics, you have to go along to the East Wing, then up in the lift and back the way you came along the upper floor, past the general wards.

My mother is silent. I can almost feel the tension in her shoulders as she pushes me along; she does not like it in here any more than I do. I wish that I could make it to the hospital alone so that she did not have to come.

Downstairs, it's quiet, full of people waiting in nervous silence, shifting in their seats uncomfortably every time a name is called out by a nurse. But when the elevator doors swing open at our floor, the gentle squeak of wheels on polished lino is lost to other noises – people talking and the clattering of bowls and cutlery.

Lunch time?

Yes. An overcooked-rice aroma greets us halfway down the hall: starchy and sour.

'Hey, Mama,' I say quietly, so that she has to lean over to hear me. 'I'm glad *you* know how to cook.'

'Hush,' she whispers, but she sounds as though she's smiling.

Nobody else seems to mind the smell, though. In every room people are eating happily, although one woman is shouting at the top of her lungs that her jello isn't right: '*It doesn't wobble! How on earth can that be right?*'

I peer into the ward as we pass, and there are three nurses around her bed, trying to calm her down.

Halfway down the last corridor before you round the corner into the bright muralled Paediatrics, there's a ward I've never seen into before. The doors are always locked, with frosted glass instead of clear. But today, the doors are open.

It's quiet, though, with none of the everyday noise of the other wards.

My stomach knots as we approach, but I cannot help but look.

It only takes a second to go past the doorway, but I still see them halfway down the hall. Three elderly gentlemen surrounded by wires and monitors, each as thin as paper-covered skeletons. The man in the nearest bed lies with his neck at an unnatural angle, his mouth open a little. And his glassy eyes stare right past me.

It's like they are all already dead, hanging around the hospital so they can feed, turn unsuspecting victims into one of them. I shudder. I can't help it. And then I realize something even worse.

I just saw my future.

I won't be white-haired like those men, but I'll be just as frail, just as *stuck* as they are. Just as creepy.

Will anybody visit me, or will I scare them all away?

As we wait in the hallway for Dr Kobayashi, I wonder about the old man. Who was he? Does he have kids or grandkids who care for him? Who visit him at weekends? Or is he all alone?

Perhaps he was a businessman with no time to start a family. Or maybe he has children who spend every evening telling him the latest stories from the office. Perhaps he survived Hiroshima. Or maybe he flew to America on business and fell in love with a beautiful film star.

Yes. He fell in love with a Hollywood actress and she moved back to Japan. They had three beautiful babies, and every weekend they would all go out to the lake to fish. And his children went to university, and had families of their own: grandchildren who paint pictures to pin up by his bed-side. Yes.

Except the walls around his bed were bare.

* * *

'It must be tough for you.'

I wonder how the bonsai tree can stand it in here, in this heat, this airless room.

Doctor Kobayashi tries again. 'I noticed the young people are all back at school today, for the autumn term.'

I shrug, try not to remember the happy crowd of girls and boys carrying satchels through the park.

Soon after the consultant had said those two awful words, *no cure*, my mother and I sat in another too-small room, on the wrong side of the desk, and my school principal frowned down at us over steepled fingers.

'I'm sorry,' he said. 'We're simply not equipped to deal with it.'

'But Kouchou-sensai, he's a bright boy. And he studies hard. It would be such a waste.'

His frown deepened, and he studied my face before he spoke.

I wondered whether he was counting the days I had left, calculating the value of high school if it does not lead to university, and what I could *possibly* offer now.

I raised my eyes to meet his. *I want to be here*, I tried to transmit to him with nothing but my gaze. *I want to learn everything whilst I still can.*

'Well,' he sighs, 'I'm afraid we do not have the budget for adaptations to the building. I suggest you contact the Sunshine School, try to get your son admitted there, but in the meantime, whilst he can still get to his classrooms, Sora is welcome to stay.'

Three months, two crutches and one walking frame later, and the time had come; I could no longer manage the hallways, and he did not want me littering his school with difficulties.

'I know you wanted to go back.' Doctor Kobayashi's voice is gentler now. 'I'm sorry.'

I stare harder at the tree, cannot look at her as I say, 'The principal was right, it would be impractical.'

She nods, and is quiet for a moment. Watching me until I cannot stand it any longer.

'Thank you for the book. It was very kind.' I reach into my bag and pull out the thin grey volume.

'You've read them all?'

I nod.

'What did you think?'

It wasn't really what I thought, more like what I *felt.* But I don't know how to put it into words.

'They were beautiful.'

Silence.

She's still watching me.

'You know, everything dies, Sora. Eventually.'

Er . . . I nod, because I don't know what to say.

'Everyone. Some people sooner than others, and that isn't fair, but it's a fact of life.'

I study the tiny branches before me. How old is this tree? How many patients has it seen? *Stopped* seeing?

'The samurai . . . they knew this. You can see it in their words, right? What matters is not how much time you have, but how you use it.'

I . . . guess.

I nod again, wait for her to continue, but she seems to be waiting for me. I hold the book out to her. 'Thank you.

I liked it. Very much.' I bow.

She rests a hand upon the cover, gently pushes the book back towards me. 'Keep it for a while longer. You might find a need for them again.'

'Thank you.'

She waits whilst I slide the book back into my bag, and I feel her watching me. The shakes are not too bad today, but a rucksack zipper is small, dependent on the right degree of pressure, and I have to concentrate to coordinate the movements.

I wonder if she notices.

When I look up, book finally packed away, Doctor Kobayashi folds her hands into her lap decisively, and smiles.

'What do you want out of life, Sora?'

What? I think I might have recoiled, physically flinched at her words; but if I did, she does not show it. There's no indignation in her eyes.

'I mean, what do you *really* want?' She reaches across the table, squeezes my hand. 'Because we can make things happen, you and I; use your time wisely.'

'What do you mean?'

'There's a group of people who arrange for . . . they grant wishes. And I think you're the perfect candidate.'

'Wishes?'

She nods.

'Like what?'

'Well, some people go on holiday, all over the world. They hunt tigers on safari, or go to the Olympics and meet their country's fastest runner. Some people skydive, or get a tattoo, or record an album. Anything, really. You think of it, they make it happen.'

Final wishes. One last glorious race across the battlefield. Even the suggestion makes me feel uncomfortable.

'Can I think about it?'

'Of course. Talk it over with your mother.' She hands me a sheet of paper. 'This'll get you started.'

I fold it without looking at the words, and push it into a pocket. I do not want to read it here.

'Thanks.'

There are five minutes left, and Doctor Kobayashi keeps on talking about how it works, but I do not hear a word because I'm thinking, *What will be my dying wish?*

* * *

IDEAS SHEET

Wish
4
LIFE

I wish to have _____

_____

_____

I wish to go _____

_____

_____

I wish to meet _____

_____

_____

I wish to be _____

_____

_____

I've read through the list several times; I can't seem to stop, yet with each 'I wish' I can feel the anger bubble like thick black tar in my chest. I wish to *have*. I wish to *be*. I wish, I wish, I wish. But they cannot grant me anything I really want.

I wish to have a *life*.

I wish to go to university, to work, to go to a Tigers game against the Yankees in twenty or thirty years' time.

I wish to meet my *grandchildren*, and feed them ice cream until they're sick.

I wish to be young and free and not in this wheelchair.

I hate everything about this sheet. The leading phrases, cheerful logo, even their *name*. Wish4Life? Really? It is as if they're saying, 'You are going to die. The best you can do is *wish* for life.'

It's insensitive and horrible and . . . It's. Not. Fair. I want to mash the sheet into a ball and drop it in the trash. Or burn it. Tear it up into a hundred thousand pieces and let them fly out from my window like rancid hateful snow or the saddest cherry blossoms. But . . .

But Doctor Kobayashi has been kind. She means well. And she thinks that this will help. I can't throw that away. So instead, I fold the paper back in half and slide it between the covers of a textbook I will never read again. Hidden. Gone.

I have not mentioned Wish4Life to Mama yet. I can't. I know that we could use it; go on vacation to the mountains or New York, or get a hoist put in above my bed, without my mother having to work the extra hours to pay for one. But it feels like a cheat wishing for these things. Things I do not really want.

Besides, the last time Mama and I wished for anything

was when I first got sick. We went to the temple and we wished with all our hearts that it was just the flu, just growing pains, just my imagination.

I do not want to stir those memories. I won't.

..... 1◻

After a while, looking at the wish sheet makes my head ache, so I turn on the computer in search of something light and cheerful.

I scroll down the list of open chatrooms, past StReSsBuStInG, Parents!No and ComicFreakz. Halfway down, I see that ILoveArnieSchwarzenegger is open, and I click.

TerminateExterminate: but WHY move to politics? I mean, his talents, his *real* talents are on the screen.

Arnie4Eva: *shrug*

TerminateExterminate:: What, you don't think so?

Arnie4Eva: Yeah, but maybe he just got bored.

TerminateExterminate: Bored? Of a metal endoskeleton? How?!

MisterSenator: I'LL BE BACK

Arnie4Eva: I dunno, like, I like history, but sometimes I want to do science instead, y'know? If I had to do one thing all the time I'd go mad.

TerminateExterminate: I *suppose.*

MisterSenator: I'LL BE BACK

Arnie4Eva:: And he must've been good at politics too. He was re-elected.

MisterSenator: I'LL BE BACK

TerminateExterminate: By people that elected *George Bush.*

MisterSenator: I'LL BE BACK
MisterSenator: I'LL BE BACK

MisterSenator: I'LL BE BACK

Arnie4Eva:: *shrug*

TerminateExterminate:: Shut UP, Senator.

MisterSenator: hehe

TerminateExterminate: Not funny dude. Not remotely funny.

TerminateExterminate: Anyway, Arnie4Eva, he was *better* at acting, obviously. The Terminator will be preserved for ever.

Arnie4Eva:: nothing lasts for ever

MisterSenator: Hahahahahahahaaaaa

Arnie4Eva:: what?

MisterSenator: That's pretty funny, coming from a girl whose tag is Arnie FOR EVER!!!!!

TerminateExterminate: Hah, yes. And anyway, it *will*. It's preserved in the US National Film Registry. It's THAT GOOD.

MisterSenator: Yeah, so good that it has the BEST CATCHPHRASE EVER . . . I'LL BE BACK.

Arnie4Eva:: Don't start that again.

I log out and scan down the list again. Seeing *SkoolWorries: for All Your Academic Concerns,* I can't help thinking of the crowd of children in the park, and the classmates I have left behind. I wonder if any of *them* are logged in tonight.

I click on 'room stats': 147 participants. Maybe I can spot someone I know, guess who they are from their username or the things they talk about, and if not, there are enough people in there that I can lose myself amongst the crowd.

For a moment I cannot follow anything, there are so many conversations going on at once, but then I start to pick out different strands of it. There's this:

ShinigamiFanBoy: Has anyone else from 3C done the classics essay yet? I need ideas!

TandemRide: Sorry, Shini.

ShinigamiFanBoy: Anyone?

TandemRide: >>>>@ >> *TUMBLEWEED*

ShinigamiFanBoy: fine, I'll do it myself then. Anyone done the MATH assignment? ;)

TandemRide: Eeee, one of these days, Shini. One of these days.

ShinigamiFanBoy: One of these days what? 0_0

TandemRide: You'll see.

Bluebird_79b: Some of us don't try to pass our work to others, Fanßoy!

ShinigamiFanBoy: Yeah, and look where that gets you. ;)

Bluebird_79b: *siiiiiigh* maybe he has a point. There is a mountain of textbooks waiting for me, but I love you guys so much I don't want to leeeeeave.

KyotoQueen: *sigh* me too. How is there SO MUCH homework already? It's only the first week. Waaah!

Bluebird_79b: I know. :(

ShinigamiFanBoy: I hear ya!

0100110101100101: Agree!

And this:

Meekkat: Will somebody sit with me at lunch? I hate being the new girl.

BambooPanda: I'll sit with you Meekkat. What school u go to?

Meekkat: International.

BambooPanda: Oh. Sorry ☹

BambooPanda: I'm sure you'll make friends really quickly. Introduce yourself to someone who looks nice at lunch?

Meekkat: I'm too shy!

BambooPanda: ☹ Who goes to International? Someone let Meekkat join them tomorrow? It SUX being the new girl.

Meekkat: Aw, thanks Panda. You're so kind.

BambooPanda: Not at all ☺

GuitarGirl1: You can sit with us, Meekkat. We're in the second year and starting a band. You play an instrument?

Meekkat: Um, no.

GuitarGirl1: That's OK. You can be a groupie. OHHH! GROUPIE!!! <3

Meekkat: What are you called?

GuitarGirl1: We haven't picked a name yet. Any ideas? No wait, we can discuss it AT LUNCH. Yay! Meet me in the courtyard, I'll have my guitar.

BambooPanda: Successful matchmaking of the friendship variety! Yessss!

And this:

BlossomInDecember: We're going out for FroYo after school to celebrate. Who's coming?

BITTERnGREEN: Meeeeee!

LikesEmWithSparkle: Me ☺

WindUpBird: Me!

I watch the conversations unfold, one line at a time, piece them together like a jigsaw puzzle where someone put a dozen pictures into the same box. I'm imagining WindUpBird and BlossomInDecember meeting over pumpkin-flavoured frozen yoghurt when *BRrRrRrRrRrRrRrR*, a flashing dialogue box appears at the bottom of my screen. It reads: *You have a Private Message from MonkECMonkEDo*. My stomach jolts with fear; nobody's supposed to notice me!

What do I do? I can't just ignore it, can I?

Can I?

BRrRrRrRrRrRrR the box flashes again.

No, apparently not.

I scroll up the chatroom conversations, looking for the name. Making sure she's real, and it's not a virus trap. MonkECMonkEDo says: Strawberry flavour. With lemon sprinkles.

I do not scroll further up to see what should be strawberry.

BRrRrRrRrRrRrR

OK, OK!

I click, and the box expands.

Hi, SamuraiMan. Welcome to KyoToTeenz :)
Hello?
Are you there?

What do I say?

OK, never mind. I just wanted to say hi. I'm not a creep, btw, I just . . . I like to see who's signed up to the forum and welcome people.
It can be a bit terrifying when it's busy.
I hope you jump in though, everybody's really nice.
OK byeee!

In the background, MonkECMonkEDo also joins in the conversation:

MonkECMonkEDo: *I have to go too.*

KyotoQueen: What, now? U just got here!

MonkECMonkEDo: *My parents are home. I have to study.*

KyotoQueen: Tell them you're studying in your room.

MonkECMonkEDo: *I wish! Byeeee! xx*

And she is gone.

11

I cannot stay online. I've been seen. Compromised. And I don't know what to do.

But before I go, I just have to:

<click>

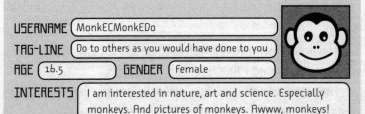

USERNAME MonkECMonkEDo

TAG-LINE Do to others as you would have done to you

AGE 16.5 GENDER Female

INTERESTS I am interested in nature, art and science. Especially monkeys. And pictures of monkeys. Awww, monkeys!

If you could be anything in the world, what would you be?

More than anything, I want to draw the things that make me happy. And I want to work for Masashi Ando or Hayao Miyazaki. I'll do anything, even make the tea or run messages until my feet fall off. Are you listening Miyazaki-san? ANYTHIIIIIING!

x <3 x

Dear Ojiisan,

I am doing well. The city is ready for autumn now; the sun sets gold, just tempting the trees to join it. Have the forktails flown through yet, or are they late again this year? Has Bah-Ba deemed it cold enough for honey cake?

And how do you talk to girls? I can't send that. Can I?
No.

My grandfather and I used to talk about *everything,* but somehow I can't. Once, we talked of grades and universities and far-flung places. Now all I have to report is the latest ache or shaking muscle, and we don't say much at all.

Hope you are well,
Your grandson, Abe Sora

'Sora!'

I look up from my half-full dish of salty miso, and see my mother has already finished. 'Sorry, Mama.'

She lays her chopsticks carefully across her bowl then rests her chin on her hands, leans towards me. 'Are you all right?'

'Yes.' I nod. I hope she cannot see my thoughts – of Ojiisan and MonkEC – I do not even know exactly what they are, and they would only make her sad.

She studies my face for a moment but says nothing.

'There's a letter for Ojiisan in the hall,' I say, to change the subject. 'Will you post it?'

'You don't *have* to write to him.' She frowns. 'He has a phone.'

I shrug. 'He likes them.'

I do too. I like the sense that our conversations can withstand time and distance and still reach each other. But my mother is forever on her smartphone, plugged into the latest news, emails at her fingertips in seconds, and she does not understand.

'You're so like him, you know?'

'Ojiisan?'

'Yes. The pair of you are like two peas' – she pauses, and for a second her frown disappears – 'two nature-loving peas. Sometimes I think you were both carved right out of an old tree trunk or dug out of the earth.'

'Mama, I was born right here. In the city. In the hospital, with you.'

She almost smiles. 'Quite a day that was.'

I've heard the story a thousand times. How Ojiisan and Bah-Ba faced the big tall buildings of the city trying to reach their daughter, to be there for the birth, but the big city travel-gods thwarted their attempts and in the end it was just the two of us. Mama and me. Just the way it's always been.

My father, who whisked Mama away from the countryside, whisked himself away from her, long before I came.

But we don't really talk about him. We don't need him. We're a perfect team.

'Mama . . . how did Ojiisan get lost that day? The trains are labelled. And they do not wander off.'

There it is again, that almost smile. 'That's not the way your grandfather would tell it.' No. Wilful trains with feet, he'd say. Dragon-bellied transport. Mama shrugs. 'The city befuddles him. Too much going on and not enough sky.' I can almost hear the words, unspoken this time: *two peas*. And for a moment I think we might talk about the endless summers we spent every year at Ojiisan and Bah-Ba's, underneath that open sky, or all the other things she sees in both of us. But she rolls her eyes, and starts to clear away the dishes, and the conversation's over.

12

To:	S . . .
From:	TheSClub
Subject:	The Club Needs You.

Fellow Students!

Have you been **depressed** lately? Parents **nagging** you about **college** or exams? Teachers think you're **worthless**?

IS IT ALL TOO MUCH?

For thousands, it is, and we think it is time to take a stand.
Tell the adults in your life to STOP pushing and taking control.

Join us, for the biggest statement this millennium.
Make your life count.

Click the link below to find more info.

I freeze when I see it, but I can hear my mother shuffling down the hallway to the phone. Like clockwork, every week. She'll be busy for a while. So I read it again, and again, try to guess exactly what they mean, what they stand for.

But there's nothing.

No clue.

The last one is etched into my mind, so clearly that I'm almost sure I am imagining it. *Plans to unite unhappy teenagers in their final moments*, it said. But this one could mean anything. It could be a protest, a petition for less homework.

Maybe it *is*, and I'm remembering something that was never there.

For a second I wish that I hadn't deleted it, but then every muscle in my body tenses at the thought of those awful words just sitting there, waiting to be read, believed, obeyed.

My fingers pause, cursor hovering above the link. I want to see, to know exactly what they're offering. And I don't. I want to run. And before I can make up my mind, Mama shrieks, and as quick as the compulsion to look appeared, it's gone. I hit delete and let myself fall into her conversation:

'Eeeehh! Otosan! You should put some traps down . . . no, I know they're not humane, but . . .'

When I was young, my grandparents' cat was as fierce as a pirate, a scarred and grumbling beast who chased anything and anyone except the family who fed him. Then he grew old and round, and slept all day beside the fire.

He died last winter, and since then, the mice have returned.

I know that mice are nothing more than a nuisance – that at the end of the line, Ojiisan will be laughing at my mother's delicate city manner – but still, for a moment I imagine fat demonic creatures scurrying about inside the walls, waiting to feed on my grandparents at night. I shudder; maybe Mama's right.

'And you wonder why we don't . . . No. I don't mean that. I mean . . .' I've heard this conversation before, although Mama thinks she hides it. 'What he *needs* is doctors, Otosan. Experts. A regiment of relaxation. Not—' She stops. 'I'm sorry. Anyway, there's all those stairs.'

She *is* right about the last part. But I imagine my last

days, colour-coded, timed down to the final seconds, surrounded by not-quite fresh bouquets of flowers and cards from our well-meaning neighbours, and I find myself gasping for the country air.

BRrRrRrRrRrRrR.
What?!
Oh. Chatroom message.
I lay my book down on the duvet and push myself up onto my elbows, swing my legs off the bed.
BRrRrRrRrRrRrR.
Hup! And I'm in my chair, spinning around *BRrRrRrRrRrRrR* to face the desk. All right!
The monitor blinks into life, and there it is:

Hi SamuraiMan! How was your day? I hope I wasn't untoward yesterday. I didn't mean to cause offence. I mean, it's OK if you don't want to talk to me, or anyone. I didn't mean to be so rude. OK – bai!

I read the message again and then I just stare at it. I should reply, but . . .

Um . . . hi.

The cursor blinks after my greeting, and I wait.
And wait.
And wait.

*HI!!! ^_^*

What next?

> Hi :)

I say again, hoping she'll start the conversation going. Then try:

> How are you?

I shrug off the nagging ache in my thighs, ignore the shaking of my fingertips against the keys.

> *I'm fine, thank you.*
> That's good.
> *^_^ so . . . you like literature, huh? Have you been on the lit forums yet?*
> No, not yet.
> *Oooh, you should!*
> *So what's your favourite book?*
> I . . . um . . .
> *Go on, you MUST have one. Not the best or the cleverest, just your favourite.*

I let the cursor blink for a minute, and then:

> I can't pick. They're so different!
> *Ahh, a real bookie, huh? That's cool. I don't read much, except manga. Pictures tell the story so much better.*
> You think? I mean, it's not like I NEVER read manga, but it just . . . it's too easy.

Easy? }}:-S What do you mean?

It's all there for you. I like the way that when it's just the words, they make you think, don't share all their secrets at once, you know?

Ha! You sound like a professor already. I don't want to think when I read, I just want a good story.

Most people do.

You sound disappointed.

No.

OK, not disappointed, then; like an old man. 'In my day, young thing, words *were enough.'*

I am almost offended, but I do not think she means it nastily.

Haha! I'll just go over here and light my pipe.

:D

Anyway, what's your favourite manga?

That's eeeeasy. ONE PIECE. Oh, or Akira. Or FairyTail . . .

See. Not so simple is it?

Hahahaha, no, all right. I'm sorry.

Ai, it's like you're a teacher already, making me think and re-evaluate. You'll make a great *professor.*

I . . . what do I say to that? *I know?* Except *I won't?* I . . .

At the other end of the line, MonkEC is sitting there, fingers on her keyboard, waiting for me to respond . . .

> Thanks. I . . . I should go and study.
>
> *All right :(Me too, I suppose. What are you working on tonight?*

I glance down the spines of the books to my left but I have no idea what everyone is studying this term.

What do I say?

> A little bit of everything, really. You?
>
> *Same. But language comprehension is due in tomorrow, so I had better do that first. Catch ya later?*
>
> Sure! Good luck.
>
> *You too. Byeee! Xx*

I log out, and open up Google in its place.

 Language comprehension topics

I am going to need something to talk about.

13

'Squeeze my hand.'

I squeeze until it hurts, and every muscle from my shoulder to my fingertips feels tight. I visualize the doctor's hand going white beneath my grip, but when I look down, I am barely making a fist, and my hand is shaking like a leaf in winter winds.

Ugh!

'Harder.'

I squeeze my eyes tight shut, as though that will make a difference. I can feel my whole arm trembling with effort.

I open one eye, peek at my fist again.

'Hmm.' The physiotherapist pulls his hand away.

The other hand, my left, is slightly better – which makes no sense because it is my right hand which I use more often – but still, he barely registers my touch.

'It's OK' – I try to force a laugh – 'as long as nobody asks me to open their soda.'

'Hmm,' he says again.

'What's wrong?'

'Have you noticed a difference in your hand-strength since your last appointment?'

'A little. It's not so bad.'

'Mm-hmm.'

I frown questioningly.

'Sora.' He crouches so that our eyes are level, lays his

hand on top of mine. 'I think things are progressing faster than we thought or than we'd like.'

I nod. *I know.*

'I'm sorry.'

I nod again, and he pulls away. 'I'm going to show you some exercises which might help,' he says, his voice suddenly brighter.

I wish I could do that, flick an internal switch and suddenly feel optimistic, but I remember the last time things progressed faster than they all predicted. And I have to ask. 'Doctor?'

'Hmm?'

I hesitate, and when I speak my voice squeaks like a child's. 'How long do you think I've got?'

He shakes his head. 'There's no way to predict that.'

'I know, but . . . a guess?'

'No. I would only get it wrong. I don't want you to think—'

'*Please?* I need – I need to know.'

'I can't. I'm sorry.' There's something in that look. Not sorrow, exactly, but . . . detachment. And I think that's worse.

The physiotherapist's words still echo in my ears as I sit across from Doctor Kobayashi. I wonder whether he's even *allowed* to tell me. Is it protocol? Don't put yourself in that position? Don't risk being the shoulder someone leans on? Being wrong?

I'd tell someone. Even if I had to make an educated guess. But I know what it's like not knowing.

'So, have you thought more about Wish4Life?'

For a second I wonder whether I should rethink, whether

the physiotherapist's silence signifies no time at all and this is my very last chance. But surely he'd have said *that*. Right?

I nod. 'Thank you, but I don't think that I want to use it.'

Shock flickers across her face. 'At all?'

'At all.'

She pushes the air out through her teeth. 'Are you sure? It could be a nice way for your family to spend some time.'

'Thank you, but we're fine. There's nothing that I want . . . I'm sorry.'

I don't think she believes me. 'Well, how about I sit on this for a while. Talk to your mother, have a think, and if you change your mind the wish will be here waiting.'

'There's no way to predict that. I'm sorry.'

'I can't. I'm sorry.'

'I'm sorry. I'm sorry. I'm sorry.'

The shock and pity and non-answers of the day rise up at me as I slide my bedroom door closed. I squeeze my eyes shut and press the heels of my hands hard against them until the dark turns red and white. It does not help. Doctor Kobayashi's confusion plays on loop. *Why would I not take the wish?* As if it were a personal snub, as if her offer isn't good enough.

But I don't want it.

I sit there, in my self-made dark cocoon, wondering how much time I really have to fill.

I feel the weight of my limbs, notice the dull aches and the tremors. Were they this bad a week ago? A month? Six?

It's like growing, I think; it happens all the time and you don't even notice, then suddenly you can reach the top shelf, are as tall as your mother or the boy next door, and they'll let you on the big rides at the fair. Suddenly you find you cannot stand, or hold a cup, or tie your shoes.

Eventually, I let my hands drop and my eyes open, exhausted. I need a break.

As I log in to KyoToTeenz a message flashes up on my screen.

MonkECMonkEDo has saved you in their contacts.
Do you want to add MonkECMonkEDo to your contacts?

She's added me?

Really?

I click 'yes' and lean back in my chair, surprised that my heart is thudding hard against my chest. And then I click on her profile, read through her answers to the inane questions, as if a few words can tell us everything we'd want to know.

I Google 'Masashi Ando art'. I like it. People and yōkai and landscapes side by side, bringing magic to the everyday. I wish that I could step into his worlds and explore further than the pictures will allow, into the cool of the forests or through a maze of high-rise city lights.

They're beautiful.

BRrRrRrRrRrRrR.

I'm pulled back to the real world, and there she is:

HI! (-:
What you doing?
Just looking at Masashi Ando's art.
I <

I know; I'm acting on your recommendation. I can see why!

He's like, a god of illustration or something; a guardian of art.

A disciple of Benzaiten?

Yes, exactly!

And you'd like to work with him?

Gosh, yes! Who wouldn't?!? I mean, look at his work!

So you want to draw? As a career, I mean.

I HAVE to draw. Everything. Everything I see and hear and feel, my pencil wants to make a record.

Do you think that's weird?

No!

I'm glad. Most people do :-/

I think of libraries and dusty lecture halls, and for a moment I can almost smell the books and chalk and rows of wooden desks.

I don't think it's weird at all.

14

BambooPanda: Hiiii (-: How was school, everyone?

0100110101100101: Hi Panda! OK. How was your day?

BaSeBaLlWiNs: We won, we won, we won! ← Er, this. *grin*

MonkECMonkEDo: Good thanks!

MonkECMonkEDo: Whooooo!

BambooPanda: Your team? Baseball?

BaSeBaLlWiNs: YES! We played against the older class from another school, and we won. Wewonwewonwewon!

BambooPanda:: Congratulations! :)

ShinigamiFanBoy: Well at least SOMEONE had a good day.

BambooPanda: You didn't, Shinigami?

MonkECMonkEDo: Aww, what happened Shino?

ShinigamiFanBoy: It just sucked. All day. Maths test, which I forgot to study for.

BaSeBaLlWiNs: That's it? One maths test? :/

BambooPanda: Shhh, Baseball, what kind of attitude is that? Every test makes a difference!

ShinigamiFanBoy: Well you know EXACTLY how to cheer a man up, Bamboo! Thanks!)':

BambooPanda: Oh no! I didn't mean . . . What I mean is that I understand why you're upset.

BaSeBaLlWiNs: Tomorrow is another day, man. It's not like you lost a game or something.

ShinigamiFanBoy: Weeeell . . .

BaSeBaLlWiNs: O_o you didn't, right?!?!?!?!?

ShinigamiFanBoy: *shrugs*

BaSeBaLlWiNs: Tell me you didn't!!!?!!!

BambooPanda: Sheesh; boys! ;)

ShinigamiFanBoy: Not baseball, no.

BaSeBaLlWiNs: What other game IS there?

ShinigamiFanBoy: It's not even a game. But I definitely lost . . .

ShinigamiFanBoy: There's a girl, Yuri. She sits ahead of me in class.

BaSeBaLlWiNs: Ahhh. Some other dude get there first?

ShinigamiFanBoy: uhuh

BaSeBaLlWiNs: All sucks in love and war, my friend.

Hey Samurai!

Oh, hi!

Good day?

Yes. You?

Yeah, I guess so.

KyoToTeenz has become my refuge. After every day of tests and therapy, every history book which reminds me that my future is so short, every stifled conversation with my mother, I log in to the one place where wheelchairs and wishes are no more than a nightmare and the old me still exists.

You guess?

Yeah.

Anything I can help with?

Oh it's nothing really.

Are you sure?

Yeah, thanks. You already ARE helping actually. Talking with you cheers me up 😊

I . . . thanks 😊

Hahahahaha, I totally made you blush, huh?

No!

U-huh. Sure. ;)

No! I was just thinking the same thing, that's all.

Awwww, well now you've made ME blush.

So, what am I distracting you from?

Oh, school stuff, preparing dinner, all the usual. You?

Just reading.

Do you like, spend all your time in a book?

No. I'm talking to you . . .

Apart from that?

Well ;)

(-:

I wish that I could stay online for ever, like a character in one of MonkEC's beloved manga series; that I never had to face the realities beyond the screen, but everything must end, and all too soon she says:

sigh my mother wants to know what I've learnt at school today. I have to go. Sorry!

It's OK, I'll see you later. Bye!

Byeeee! xxx

15

'Thank you, Mama, this looks delicious.'

She stops bustling about the kitchen and sits down. 'I'm glad.'

I take a moment to inhale the steam rising from my bowl – the sweetness of the rice and the saltiness of soy and onions, together with the fresh sea scent of white bream. 'Mmmmm.'

Across the table, Mama does the same, then looks into my eyes and smiles. 'Read anything interesting today?' she asks.

'Not really.' I pull my dish closer and pick up the chopsticks. 'I finished the books from the library yesterday.'

She hesitates, but I know what's coming. 'Will you come with me next time? Choose your own? We could go for dinner too.'

'Maybe.'

We both know that I won't.

'We could stop at the park if you like. Go when it's quiet? The leaves are just starting to turn. You'd like it.'

I imagine the crunch of leaves beneath my tyres, the rustling of branches overhead, the heavy smell of autumn air, and I am tempted. 'Maybe.'

'That's settled then. I don't start work until late tomorrow. We'll go earlier . . . It is not good for you to sit inside all day.'

'Mama!'

She sighs. 'I know, I just wish . . .' She looks down at her dish, snatching up a piece of fish aggressively.

I *know* she only wants what is best for me, but how can she – who will outlive me by so long – know what that is?

I lift a clump of rice up to my mouth. I chew, and swallow, and lift again. Chew, swallow, lift. But what appealed a minute ago drops like lead into my stomach as we eat in silence.

'I'm sorry, Mama.'

She raises her gaze without lifting her head, and studies me. I bring more food up to my lips. 'This is really good.' I force a smile before I pop the food into my mouth and chew.

She almost smiles back, but then her face clouds over and she stares, hard. 'Sora?' she says slowly.

'Yes?'

'Are you . . . are you shaking?'

I lower my chopsticks, carefully placing them upon the table. Every grain of rice inside my stomach thrums with nerves, and I think I'm going to throw up. I let my eyes meet hers and open my mouth to speak. But I cannot say it. I cannot break her heart again.

She nods curtly. 'How bad?'

'They don't know,' I barely whisper.

'When were you going to tell me?'

'I . . .'

'Oh, Sora!' she cries, moving round behind me. She wraps her arms around my shoulders and presses her lips to the top of my head.

And then she straightens up and clears her dish away as though nothing has happened.

'Mama?'

'Yes?' she sniffs.

'It'll be all right.'

'Do you need me to help with anything?' My mother picks up the T-shirt that is neatly folded on my pillow, shakes it out and folds it up again.

She came in with my medications, and has been there since, for ten minutes at least, folding my clothes and watching me as I read.

'No, thanks.'

She glances at the pot of pills beside me. 'You're sure?'

Go. Away.

'Yes. I'm *fine*, Mama. No different than I was before dinner. I can manage.'

She is silent for a moment and then, 'OK. Call out if you need me, OK?'

I nod, putting my book face down on the desk and turning to the computer. I press the power button and stare at the monitor as it warms up, fading out from black to grey to blue. I cannot look at her. I won't.

She sighs a tight little sigh, and I hear her move towards the door.

I double-click the browser icon.

'Goodnight,' she says.

And I breathe a sigh of relief as the door slides closed behind her.

I log in, hoping MonkEC will be there with a smiley face, but she is nowhere to be seen.

I pick up the book I was reading – *A History of Fishing Patterns and Their Effects on the Sea of Japan* – but I cannot concentrate. All the figures float right through my brain and will not stick.

I turn back to the screen.

CONTACTS ONLINE: 0

Still not there.

Idly, I click onto the general forum. At least their chatter will be easier to follow than the habits of yellowfin and sea bream.

BaSeBaLlWiNs: So, Shino, how'd it go with . . . . whoever she is?

ShinigamiFanBoy: Dude, I can't even TALK to her. She's with him, it wouldn't be right.

BaSeBaLlWiNs: Nooooo, tell her! You have to tell her! How can you win if you don't even play?

BambooPanda: Man, he already lost. He shoulda told her faster!

BaSeBaLlWiNs: Noooo! Tell her! Tell her! Tell her! Tell her! ⟵ you have to imagine me chanting this. Tell her! Tell her! :D

ShinigamiFanBoy: Uuuugh, I can't.

BaSeBaLlWiNs: Wimp!

I try to let them carry me away, to delight in the safety of their lives, but all I can think is: *What girl would ever want a boy who cannot feed himself? That's where you're heading.* And: *You'll never be like them.*

AAAAAAAAAAAAAAAAAAAAAAAAAAAAAAAAAAA

I press heavily into the keyboard,

```
AAAAAAAAAAAAAAAAAAAAAAAAAGGHHH!
```

Over and over again, I let the frustration pour out onto the screen.

```
AAAAAAAAAAAAAAAAAAAAAAAAAAAAAAAAAAAAAAAAAAAAAA
AAAAGGGHH
```

Delete.

```
AAAAAAAAAAAAAAAAAAAAAAAAAAAGHHH!
```

Delete.

```
AAAAAAAAAAAAAAAAAAAAAAAAAAAAAAAAAAAAAAAAAAAAAA
AAAAGGGHH!!!!!
```

I stab out each exclamation point and it's almost as good as an actual scream.

```
AAAAAAAAAAAAAAAAAAAAAAAAAAAAAAAAAAAAAAAAAAAAAA
AA-AAAAAAAAAAAAAAAAAAAAAAAAAAAAAAAAAAAAAAAAAA
AAAAAAAAAAAAAAAAAAAAAAAAAAA-AAAAAAAAAAAAAAAA
AAAAAAAAAAAAAAAAAAAAAAAAAAAGGGGGGGGGHHH!!!!
```

Oh. Did I . . . ?
Yes. My angry scream joins the stream of conversation.
I did . . .
Maybe they won't notice.

I hold my breath as I watch the conversation pour onto the screen.

> **BambooPanda:** Nah, he's right, she's made her choice.
> **0100110101100101:** Hi everyone!
> **0100110101100101:** What's this? Are we still arguing about Shino's love life? *Cackles* excellent!

I let the air slink out across my lips, but then:

> **NoFaceBoy: What's up, SamuraiMan? You OK?**
> **BambooPanda:** You OK?

They saw.

Of course they saw.

I can't explain. I can't. How do you explain something like this?

I do not even stick around to properly sign out, just click the browsers shut and push my chair away from the desk.

What will they think of me now?

16

I awake the next day with a chest full of dread.

Do they think that I'm completely mad?

Or rude, for leaving without explanation?

Did they spend an hour imagining all the reasons why I might have screamed? Like, perhaps I was attacked by an angry spider, or a rabid dog. Or I am having a nervous breakdown after a bad night at cram school, or I simply did not like their girl talk.

Do they hate me now?

I'm brooding, convinced the world is over, when Mama slides open the door and announces that we're going to the park and that I should hurry up and dress.

'Just the park, Mama, please. I don't want to go anywhere else.' I know I should be glad of the reminder that there's life out there, and the company and fresh air, but outside there are people. And I don't fare any better with them in real life than I do on the screen.

'Just the park,' she nods.

I hate leaving our apartment, and somehow this morning it is worse. The squeak of rubber tyres upon the shiny floor, giving me away to anyone who cares to hear. The elevator; the chance of being trapped with neighbours who choose to gaze at the ceiling rather than look at me. Even the superintendent with his too-friendly smile.

And it is not much better in the street. People gawp as Mama struggles getting my chair across roads and up onto the pavements; stare over my head and offer her a sympathetic nod.

Poor you, they smile, *such a burden.*

I try to ignore them, but my skin itches with annoyance.

Mama must have noticed too, because halfway there she reaches out to squeeze my shoulder. I imagine her saying to me, 'Hush, it doesn't matter,' the way she would when I was three if I had skinned a knee. And I reach up, squeeze back.

As we pass under the gate into the park, she leans down and whispers in my ear, 'See, isn't it beautiful.'

The leaves of trees on either side of us are the palest shade of yellow green, as though they're shy about their change, trying to hide.

Further up are leaves with deep green centres and rust-coloured borders. And every now and then, the flame of maple dances in the morning breeze.

Mama is right, it's beautiful.

The path is wide and straight, the trees magnificent, and as Mama pushes me along I tilt my chin towards the sky. Branches reach out to each other above my head, glowing against the sun. And then we veer off into the open, across the wooden bridge. She stops in the middle of it, swinging my chair round so that I can see the lake. She leans against the railings beside me.

'One, two, three . . .' she counts. When I was small we had to stop at every bridge we crossed so that I could count the koi below.

'Help me up?'

'Really? Here?'

'Yes! I want to see!'

She glances nervously across the bridge, but offers me a hand. I pull myself up onto my feet and lean over the side.

'Be careful!' she whimpers.

'There's one!' I point out across the water at a fat red carp.

She only hesitates for half a second before she joins in, with a laugh I had not known that I was missing. 'And there! Three, four, five, six!'

'Seven!' I declare, a little too loud for the serene waters. Tourists gawp at us, but suddenly I do not care. 'Eight! Nine!'

We carry on like this until I do not know whether we're counting new fish or ones we've seen before. My arms are tired from holding myself up for so long, and I know my knees are bowed and shaking, but I'm not ready to give up yet.

I stare out at the water, watch the sun bounce off its surface and the fish, some slow and mellow, others skitting to and fro, and catch the multi-coloured scales.

'Look at that one,' I sigh happily. Right below us is a huge fish, glittering gold above a sleek black skin. 'He's been blessed by the lady of the lake. I bet he's the Emperor-fish!'

'Ooooh, he's handsome!' And then Mama looks across at me. 'Come on, you're tired. Let's go.'

She's right, I *am* tired. I let myself fall back into my chair.

'Tea, or ice cream?' Mama asks as we cross the bridge.

'Tea.' There is a chill to the air which fits the season, and I tug at my coat collar.

'Tea it is.'

* * *

We take our tea along a smaller path into denser trees and sit beneath a huge five-needle pine.

I sip, inhaling the woody pine scent and the sharpness of the tea as I replay the bridge-scene in my mind. And I smile all over again.

I wonder whether the Emperor-fish knows that he has an audience, whether he struts up and down the lake just to show off his beautiful skin and make people forget their own.

Can he hear our jangling laughter through the water? I have heard tales from wardens of fish who greet them every day; does he recognize our voices even? And miss us when we're gone? Or do they view time differently, the way I imagine trees do: long and slow.

I imagine the Emperor-fish, two hundred years of age and very wise, watching; watching children grow until they bring their own sons to the bridge to meet him; watching everything we do.

'Mama?'

'Mmm.'

'What do you think happens—'

'When?'

'When we . . . after . . .'

She turns, and I watch as realization paints itself across her face.

'Hush!' Her voice is hard and bright.

'But—'

'No, Sora. This is not the time or the place. Not here, not now.' She tears her gaze away and takes a long sip of her tea, wraps both hands around the cardboard cup and rests it neatly in her lap. Her jaw is set and I know that that's the end of it. She will not answer me.

We sit, the comfortable silence thickened into something suffocating, each of us waiting for the other to finish their tea so we can leave, forget this conversation ever happened and burst out from the shade into the sunlight.

17

Dearest Ojiisan and Bah-Ba,

I am well, and hope that you are too. Mama tells me you have mice joining you at the supper table. She'd have me believe that you are overrun, and the mice have sneers upon their faces and katana tucked into their belts. 'Food, or death?' they'd say, and then they'd laugh whilst they ate all the best cuts.

I think she's probably exaggerating, but I'm rather jealous that they get Bah-Ba's cooking whilst I do not.

I looked up ways to deter mice today. Have you tried peppermint oil? Also, did you know that in many countries people eat mice? And in some, baby mouse wine is supposed to cure you of, well, anything. But if you're going to try the last two, let's keep it between us.

Your mouse-less grandson,
Abe Sora

18

I tried to ask Mama again, over dinner, but she slurped loudly on her noodles and refused to answer. Alone in my room, I turned to the internet.

> 🔍 **What happens when you die?**

282,000,000 results flash up on my screen.

Two hundred and eighty-two million.

I scan down the list, from *What happens when you die: Uncovered*, to *REPENT BEFORE YOUR TIME IS UP!* And *CancerCare: the final stages*. Page after page of theories, rants and questions. Halfway down there is an advertisement shouting, *MEET THE PEOPLE WHO SHOW US THE WAY. WARRIOR FUNERALS, for all your post-life needs. Now offering tours (by appointment only).*

I imagine walking through the dim-lit back rooms where the bodies go, led by a man with a too-wide smile who says, 'And here we have the ovens, one thousand degrees at full blast.'

Weird.

I scroll back up to the top of the page and read the first link.

Along with the meaning of life, 'What's next?' is one of those seemingly unanswerable questions. Seemingly. Does that mean they *have* an answer?

I click on it.

For centuries, people have tried to determine what happens after this life. The Egyptians built vast tombs to house everything their kings could want in future lives. The Mayans lived well so they could get to Tamoanchan. Religious folks will tell you that their god is the only path to heaven or a better self, and everybody else will go to hells unknown, stuck in cycles of pain and suffering. But what's the truth? Who's right? Join the debate below!

No, they do not have the answers.
I try the next link, *We ask, what happens when you die?*

So, your heart and brain have stopped. You're dead. What's next?

Many people hold strong beliefs about what happens after death, but no one really knows. Because the only way to know is to actually *die*. And the dead ain't talking.

Backspace.
Nothing in this millions-strong list looks promising. I don't understand; someone must know something, right?

The old man who lives next door to my grandparents has told me countless times about the ghosts who live up in his attic, but I always thought him mad. He has no proof, except that he hears noises sometimes and will swear that he left out the pepper pot, only to find it neatly placed inside a cupboard.

My grandmother, too, keeps a lantern burning to protect the house from wayward yurei. If they're right, if there are spirits, that means there must be something to move on to. But *what?*

As I close the browser down I think, for half a second, of going to KyoToTeenz and chatting with MonkEC, but I remember yesterday, and my stomach roils. I pick up the samurai *Death Poems* instead, heave myself onto the bed, lean back against the pillows and then let my fingers trail across the paper and *feel* the words before I read them.

Many of the poets talk of death, the act, as a thing which sets them free. They say:

The sword.
And like a bird, I fly.

and:

The final thing,
a gate,
closed on the way out.

and:

Death is death . . .

I like that. The samurai thought deep and wide, and accepted their fate, embraced it. I think, when I have to go, I'd like to go like that.

....19

I sleep with the poetry beneath my pillow in the hope that maybe it will filter through my dreams, allow me to wake up a better person, but the first thought when I awaken is not, *'Honour, valour, focus'* or *'What can I make of today?'* it is, *'Ineedtopeelneedtopeelneedtopee!'* I lie here for five seconds, pondering my next move, but it's clear I'm going to have to get up. Fast.

I push up and back with my hands so that I'm almost sitting up, and swing my legs out of the duvet. Except my arms cannot support my weight, and I fall awkwardly back on the bed. I try again, half crossing my legs as I push, willing myself to make it.

And I'm up. But the intense movement squeezed at my insides and my bladder burns. I concentrate on holding it; imagine the urine flowing back the other way, away from the danger zone. It's better if I do not breathe, hold everything tight and do not move an inch. But the bathroom is across the hall.

I shift my weight tentatively, and I can feel the liquid rushing downwards. I freeze, breathe in, and out again, wait for the urgency to pass, and try again, this time pushing myself up off the bed and swinging around in one swift movement, so that when I fall back I will land in my chair.

Oh.

As I stand, I feel the rush, hot and urgent, and I cannot stop it. Warm wetness streams down the inside of my pants and, as I land, pools in the seat of my wheelchair.

Damn it.

DAMN IT.

It takes an age to transfer back to the bed, strip off and wipe my chair dry, and hot shame courses through me the whole way through the process.

Why didn't I move faster? Wake earlier? Hold it in?

I bet the legendary samurai never pissed themselves.

Stupid!

Finally, I bundle my clothes into the laundry, trying not to think of what my mother will say, and head for the shower.

'You were up early this morning.'

'Mmm.' I try not to look conspicuous as I munch on a slice of thick white toast and berry jam.

'Sleep OK?'

'Yes, thanks.'

'OK.'

Mama shoves a pile of papers into her work satchel, and glances at the clock, then me. She thinks I do not notice, but she does this every morning, wrestling with that awful question: Should she stay at home with her dying son, or go to work and earn a wage to put food on the table.

But this morning she pauses.

She pours herself a coffee and hugs it to her chest. 'Sora, I think we need to talk about the park.'

'No, it's OK, Mama. Anyway, you will be late.' Yesterday I was desperate to talk but now, suddenly, I do not want to. Not yet.

She glances at the clock again, and sighs. 'You're right, I

really have to go. But it's not OK; we'll talk tonight?'

'OK.' I swallow another bite of toast to hide my grimace.

'You'll be OK today, won't you?'

'Of course.'

'OK, good!' She smiles, swallows her coffee in three gulps, and picks up her house keys. 'Listen, I've had an idea. I'll tell you everything tonight.'

I don't like the sound of this *idea*. More hospitals perhaps? Tests? Aerated therapy dreamed up by monks who live in the sea?

But you do not argue with my mother. And besides, she's in a hurry. 'Have a good day!'

'We'll talk when I get back!' she calls out from the hallway, and she's gone.

Once, Mama and I would have left the house together, walked the first two blocks before we parted ways. And we would talk, run through revision for a quiz, or argue gently about what we'd have for tea.

I miss that, and I almost pick up the phone to ask her whether she could get some prawns on her way home. Maybe something sweet for dessert. But she has enough to worry about without me adding extra errands, so I do not. Instead, I pull the soaked boxers and T-shirt from my laundry basket and take them to the sink. At least I can spare her from *this* shame.

As the water runs, splashes against the porcelain, I remember:

Life, runs like water
down the hillside.
Laughing.

Fast. Takes no prisoners.

I plunge the clothes into the water, watch them billow and then sink.

If a warrior had disgraced himself this way, I bet he would not stay on this earth for long.

And I don't want to either. Not like this. I want . . .

I don't know. The half-thought shudders right along my spine, and I taste bitterness against my tongue.

I force myself to swallow. Breathe. Look at myself in the mirror and draw that thought out into something logical and safe.

I do not want to die. No.

But I don't want to end in a puddle of my own waste, gasping for breath like a foul stinking fish.

Back at the computer, with poetry and conflict still ringing in my ears, I seek concrete answers. What can I do? How can I ensure that this is not my ending?

I type 'disgraced samurai' into the search bar, expecting to see accounts of ritual seppuku, of shame turned into honour, but instead, there's this:

Although the notion of dying by the sword is strong, and accurate, it was not the only path. Wounded samurai who could no longer fight might find work around the village or in fields. Many became useful and valued members of society once more.

Useful and valued members of society.

I do not feel useful and valued. But why? If it was good enough for the warriors of old, why do people look at me the way they do? As though I am a burden, or an animal.

Have the rules changed? Am I suddenly less of a person than I might have been in the old days? Of less use in these lesser times of need?

I type *long-term sickness Japan* into the search bar. I know what I have is not long term, but . . . it is not the forty-eight-hour flu. It counts.

There are pages filled with figures about health insurance; I skip over those. I see how Mama tightens her purse every month. I do not need the numbers.

There are statistics comparing Japan with other countries. I don't want to read those, either. What I want is to know why people don't see me for who I am; whether anybody could.

I scroll past *this*: BetterEndings.com, and as I keep scrolling it takes half a second for my thoughts to shift from 'these people acknowledge that the situation's awful', to, 'better than what?' and then I scroll back up, curious, and start to read:

Here at the Better Villa, we aim to make your stay as comfortable as possible, with medical and assistive care to suit your needs.

In Japan some 80% of terminal patients die in hospitals; Better Endings provides a halfway point, allowing the comforts and freedoms of your own home, whilst providing the best possible care.

Consider us as an alternative today!

I suppose it makes sense. As endings go, this place does not look so bad. But there are still guardrails on the beds, and staff in crisp white uniforms, and no matter what the gardens look like or food tastes like, people still go there to die. There are still rasping breaths and body fluids and, I bet, the taste of goodbyes in the air.

What does a Better Ending look like?

When the time comes, Better Endings' staff will do everything in their power to make you and your loved ones comfortable. We have a meditation room and temple, and can provide family lodgings in addition to your own. Further, all visitors have access to our extensive, beautiful grounds and are encouraged to wander the gardens.

You will have the time and space to say goodbye.

And in your final time, our trained medical staff will ensure you have a comfortable and easy passing, without pain or prolonged suffering.

I wonder how they know?

At what point in the rasping, gasping final moments of a person half delirious with discomfort or unconscious from medications, do they know that this is *it*?

Is there a code I have not learned yet? A secret signal?

And do they ever get it wrong?

Does it matter? No matter what you do or where you are, is it ever comfortable or dignified?

I don't know. I wonder what other people think, and I'm halfway through typing the KyoToTeenz address to ask, when . . . Oh. I haven't been back since . . . Will they even talk to me, after I screamed at everyone?

I almost turn away, but it does not seem *right,* somehow.

I can't give up that easily. I inhale slowly, let my fingers steady on the keyboard, and, compiling a list of excuses for my behaviour, I log in.

BRrRrRrRrRrRr.
BRrRrRrRrRrRr.
BRrRrRrRrRrRr.

Before the screen has even loaded, my speakers explode with notification alarms, and then a box announces:

YOU HAVE SEVEN MESSAGES

Great. I imagine seven versions of 'What's wrong with you, moron?' or, 'What kind of samurai loses his cool like that?'

And everyone laughing cruelly at the boy who screamed and ran.

And the moderators asking me, 'Please leave. We're blocking your account.'

But I'm here now, and the noise won't stop until I click.

The first message is from a name I do not know, but I do not open it because below is a whole wall of messages from MonkEC. She's tried to talk to me six times in two days.

I hope nobody's told her what I did.

Nervously, I click on the first one.

> *Hiii! I hope your day was good to you. I had the most BORING lessons, but it's OK because I followed it with art class after school and I spent an HOUR talking to the instructor about animation.*

85

She doesn't know, she doesn't know!

> *Hi!*

> *Are you there? You're usually around by now . . .*

> *Hellooooooo?*

I picture her sitting at her desk in a quiet, empty house, with only the internet for company. And I wasn't there. My fear morphs neatly into guilt, and I wish I did not have to read on.

I open the next one with my eyes half closed, but that does not stop me from seeing the words.

> *OK, so I just looked through the chat logs, because . . . well, I wondered whether you might be ignoring me . . . and I saw what happened. Are you OK Samurai? It feels so weird to call you that, like I don't know you at all. But I think I do. Are you OK? And what should I call you (you can make something up if you don't want to tell me)?*

She . . . she knows? And she's still talking to me?

I stare at her message, a mess of guilt and joy and worry all at once.

Finally, settling on mild relief, I click on the last message.

> *Where are you? I don't know whether I can help you but I need a friend and I wish you were here. Maybe if we talk we can help each other?*
> *Please?*

PS I'm not a stalker – honest!
PPS Don't worry about the other day. Sometimes I feel like screaming at everyone too. (:

REPLY

Hi MonkEC. I'm sorry, I wasn't ignoring you at all. I've just been really busy.

No. That's ridiculous.

Hi MonkEC, I'm sorry if I scared you, I just kind of freaked. I'm OK though. How are you?

Just kind of freaked? You're an idiot, Sora. And that's not a proper answer.

Hi,

I don't think you're a stalker at all, and I'm sorry I haven't been around over the last few days. I have been really busy, and it all got a bit much. Sorry if I had you worried.

Sora (that's my real name by the way, not something I made up).

PS You can talk to me. I'd like that.

I click 'send' before I have a chance to change my mind, and then my eyes are drawn to the last unopened message.

I click.

Hey Man,

I don't think we've spoken before. Probably not, since I'm usually pretty quiet, but I had to ask – are you OK? That was a pretty loud yell, back there.

Anyway, I know what it's like to get lost in the sad, so if you need something, please let me know.

REPLY

I'm OK, but thank you for asking.

They don't hate me.

They don't hate me.

Perhaps I'm not so worthless after all?

Maybe I can really be myself here. *All* of myself, faulty bits included.

I click on 'start new thread' and type: *Friend or Freak: Do you know anyone who is disabled? Seen anyone in the street? How do you think of them? (Help?! I am volunteering at a special school, and am trying to research this for class credit.)*

And then I log off, because I don't want to see the answers pouring in.

..... 20

I check the thread after a few hours, when everyone gets home from classes, hardly daring to look in case I don't like what I see.

My grandmother uses a cane, but that's just because she is old.

I haven't seen anyone with what you'd call a disability. Sorry.

Yeah, I mean, I'm sure they're lovely, but we don't go to the same schools. How would we know?

I wish that I could show them all, scream: *Yes you do; you do know someone, right here, talking to you now.*

But these aren't real answers to my questions. And it could be social suicide. So instead, I sit here worrying, staring at the same three answers, searching for some deeper meaning.

When I find none, my mind wanders back through everything I've read today, and as the sun slides across the sky, I have an idea. Perhaps the wounded warriors weren't *allowed* to become valued members of society, but simply did whatever they could.

My mother will be home soon, that tired look stretched across her face, hiding deeper worries. And today I'm going to surprise her, show her that I'm not completely useless, and she does not always have to worry or unearth new ideas to fix me. I am going to prepare dinner.

But what? Mama always does the cooking – although I

learned a little in home economics – and when she won't be home for lunch she leaves me something wrapped up in the fridge. Which means *I* am out of practice.

I wheel into the kitchen and pull open the cupboards. Immediately the kitchen-smells flood into the room, take me back to childhood, when my mother and I would cook together on the weekends: spices and vinegars and soy, dirt-clod potatoes, rice and beans. I reach into the cupboard and pull things out. Dried shrimp, vinegar, eggs; I pile ingredients onto my lap: garlic, rice – no, not rice, egg noodles are easier. From the refrigerator: green beans, ham, ginger.

As I place the food upon the side, I try to assemble a dish in my head. *This'll work, right?*

I decide it will be easier to prepare everything first, then cook. So I slide open a drawer and pull out a knife, and cutting board, and I begin. I try using the board up on the counter, but when I press down on the board it flips right off the edge into my lap and the knife slips from my grasp and clatters to the floor.

Damn it!

Shaking, I check my skin for knife wounds, but it did not catch me. I breathe. And then I reach down to retrieve the knife, but it's too low, and scuds across the floor as my fingers brush against it. I'll have to leave it there, ask Mama to retrieve it when she's home.

Maybe this is a bad idea. But my mother does everything and I want to surprise her.

I pull a second knife from the drawer, and this time I rest the cutting board across the arms of my chair.

Much better!

I hold the knife steady, feel the weight of it beneath my fingers, imagine the damage it could do. And then slowly, carefully, I slice the tops and tails from the beans. I slide them back onto the counter. Next, garlic. I put three fat cloves flat on the board and squash them. It's easier than cutting. All I need to do is lean my weight upon the flat edge of the blade.

And last, ginger. I love ginger: pickled, steeped in broth, covered in sugar and dried, I do not care. Mama used to say it was a wonder that I looked like a boy at all, since I was mostly made of ginger with all that I'd been eating. But she was just as fond of it as me, and sometimes we would stop by the park on our way home, sit on a bench beneath the trees and devour a whole bag of sugared ginger, just the two of us.

I cut off a small piece at the end and lift the root up to my nose, breathe in the sharp warm spice of it so hard that I think I'm going to sneeze.

I slice the root into thin strips, although they're not as thin as I would like, because I'm too afraid to get my shaking fingers that close to the blade.

Right.

I reach beneath the sink for a large steel pan, dented by a thousand meals, and I place it on the stove. My mother chose this apartment over others for its kitchen, bigger and better equipped than most city rentals. We might have to move, she said, but we do not have to lose our love of food.

But this kitchen wasn't made for me. Now that the pan is on the stove, I cannot reach into it or see inside. Great.

Taking care that the knife I dropped is nowhere near

my feet, I push myself up from the chair. Upright, I lean my waist against the countertop and let it take my weight so that my hands are free. I flick on the 'ignite' switch, listen for the *click click click* before I turn on the gas. Blue flame licks the edges of the pan. I reach for the ceramic bottles Mama keeps beside the stove – oil, soy sauce and sesame. I pull them closer, and then pour the oil into the pan.

I wait a moment, then in go the ginger and garlic, sizzling as they hit the pan. The harshness of their smells disappears in seconds, replaced by a roast-sweetness.

I'd forgotten how much fun cooking can be.

I glance across at my ingredients, neatly laid out. This is *easy*. I'd half expected my legs to give out by now, or my fingers to play dumb, refuse to chop or stir or anything, but this feels *good*.

Shrimps next, then I will add the soy and sesame and beans. Mama will love thi—

'Sora!'

I'd been so engrossed that I did not hear my mother's keys, her sock-clad footsteps.

'Hi.'

'What are you doing? Sit down before you hurt yourself!'

'It's fine, Mama. I'm fine. I'm cooking dinner.'

My mother stares at me, and I stare back. Why isn't she *pleased*?

The mixture in the pan crackles, hisses, burns, and suddenly the sweet smell is black-acrid and my mother rushes over.

'What were you *thinking*, Sora? Of all the stupid, dangerous things!' She lifts the pan, now smoking, from the flame, and steps towards the sink with it. The chopping knife scuds across the floor. 'Oh, Sora!'

Suddenly, my thighs are shaking with the weight of standing, and I cannot maintain it. I let myself fall back into my chair and get out of the way.

'I'm sorry,' I say quietly, and then I flee.

Safely in my room, I grab the pillow from my bed and slam it hard against the mattress, again and again until my arms tire and I cannot swing it any more.

'Sora?'

'Yes?' I try, but I cannot shake the grump out of my voice.

Mama slides open the door and sits down on the bed beside me. 'I'm not angry. I just . . . what were you doing?'

I look away.

'Sora?'

I was *trying* to be nice. She was supposed to be amazed!

'Sora, look at me.' She reaches out, places her hand upon my shoulder. 'Please don't do that again. You might fall, or cut yourself. That knife on the floor – you can't do these things.'

'I was doing *fine*, Mama.'

'No.' She's firmer now. 'I will not risk it. Not in my house!'

I reach back, push on the back wheels of my chair so that I roll away from her and spin round.

'Do you understand, Sora?' she pushes. And I can feel her watching me, waiting for an answer.

The thing is, if I think about it, she is right. If she hadn't walked in, anything could have happened.

She's right, and I hate her for it.

'Sora?'

'Yes, Mama.'

She stands to leave, but pauses at the door. 'I don't mean that you can't cook at all. Just, not by yourself, OK? Maybe we can cook together?'

'No thanks.'

I pick at the chicken noodles on my plate, not hungry.

'You have to eat, Sora.'

I don't answer her. I can't. Why can't she *see*? She does not push it further, but the silence between us sits heavy in the room.

'I was thinking last night . . .' she tries again. 'Maybe you and I need to spend more time together. Go somewhere. Or not; we could spend time in the city, go to the museums.'

But I don't want the city. I don't want to be watched all day. I don't need her hovering.

'It's OK, I know you have to work.'

'No, but I could . . . I could take some time. The boss knows our situation.'

He does?

I suppose that it makes sense. He'll need to know when the time comes. But I do not like that she's talking to strangers about me.

'It's *fine,* Mama. You don't need to.'

And she's gone, pushed away her chair, filling the teapot with fresh water. And I know I should feel bad that I have set her jaw like that and made her run away, but I don't. Why should *she* control everything? It's me who's dying. Me.

I hope that MonkEC has seen my apology, that she isn't too upset with me, because all I want to do right now is talk to her.

> You there?

I wait a moment. Nothing. But I can see that she's online, so I try again.

> Hi MonkEC?

Nothing. Perhaps she has decided she doesn't want to be friends.

I wouldn't blame her really. I can't do anything right.

> *SORA! HIIIII :)*
> *Sorry, I was in the bathroom.*
> *How are you?*
> Fine, thanks.
> Actually, not really.
> *D-: What's wrong?*
> I know I shouldn't speak badly of her, but ARRGH!
> Sometimes I just wish my mother would trust me a little. :(
> *Aww. I know how you feel. I mean, my mother is all about homework and grades, all the time. And she's going on and on and ON about what universities have the best law and engineering programmes and I don't even LIKE that stuff.*
> *I think that's just what they're like. Parents.*
> Your mother doesn't want you to become an artist?
> *It doesn't pay, apparently. I tried to tell her how much Miyazaki's films gross every year, but she just sighs and says 'That's one man, dear. One in a million.'*
> But if it's what you want to do . . . ?

It IS. But she's right I guess. I mean, I want to have a roof over my head, as well.

I just wish she'd take me even a little bit seriously. She won't even look *at my drawings.*

That's awful. I would.

Hahahaha.

No, I'm serious. Could I see?

I don't know . . .

Please?

Maybe someday? I just . . . I want my MAMA to take an interest, but everything I've scanned is old, and rubbish. I'd be so embarrassed.

I'm sure it's NOT rubbish.

Blush it really is.

OK, if you're not comfortable. Just . . . think about it?

Please? I'd like to see. I could be your personal admirer . . .

If it helps, I can't draw at all. Not for all the chocolate in the world.

(-: EVERYONE can draw a little.

Not everyone. Even my stick-men are wonky.

Hahahahaha. OK, I'll think about it.

Thanks :)

So, what's your *mother done today?*

Oh. I'd forgotten all about our argument. How does MonkEC *do* that?

Oh, it's nothing really. The same. Overbearing stuff. I think you must be right – it's what they do.

Yeah. Oh well. One day, we can do it to our own children. :D

Hah, one day!

21

Days later, there is still not much of a response to my forum thread. Perhaps it is simply too uncomfortable to talk about, even here?

But I can't just let it go.

Hey!

Hiiiii :)

How are things?

sigh my research is not going so well.

Why?

Have you seen it?

Nobody is saying what they really think.

It's a difficult question. Maybe nobody really knows what to say or how to say it?

But I NEED to know. How do I get answers? Any ideas?

Maybe . . .

Maybe what you need is not words.

Sorry?

What if what you need is . . . not words?

I don't understand.

Wait here . . .

What is she doing?

How can you ask a question without words?

Finally, she returns, pastes a web address into the conversation.

> *Post this. With the caption 'What's the first thought in your head?'*

It's a photograph. Of a kid in a wheelchair, with a blanket on his knees.

> You're a genius!
> *Hahaha. So kind of you to say so!*

And so I start another thread, *What do you see?* I paste the photograph into the description box, and write beneath it, *What's the first thought in your head? Please be absolutely honest. Thank you.*

> What do you think?
> *Perfect. I bet you'll have a hundred answers before you go to bed!*
> Thanks :)

Thirty seconds later, I see that MonkEC has left the first response.

> **MonkECMonkEDo:** *I'd like to think I wouldn't treat them any different, and my first thought would be 'That blanket looks cosy'.*

Just for a second, I think about turning on my dusty webcam and letting her see. *Look. This is me.* But what if she's lying, or wrong?

So I wait, and I sit here watching a discussion unfold.

LikesEmWithSparkle: That picture makes me sad. Not awful pity sad, just sad that the person has to go through life with difficulty.

WindUpBird: Yeah. It must be TOUGH.

0100110101100101: Honestly? My first thought is: has that kid ever raced that thing? Because, those WHEELS! :D

Ace101: How much do you think the boy understands? Is he like us, and it's just a physical thing? Or is his brain affected too?

LikesEmWithSparkle: O_o oh I hope not, wouldn't that be awful?

NoFaceBoy: Is it poor form to say 'lucky'? I bet that kid doesn't have to study all day, or sit through terrible exams. I bet he gets to sit around all day doing all the things we're not.

I almost answer that. I want to shake him by the shoulders and tell him that I would give anything to have his place inside a classroom, to know that I could go anywhere I wanted, *be* anything I wanted. Be *something*. But I remember that he wrote to me that day, and I cannot shame him. Besides, somebody else has already replied:

LikesEmWithSparkle: I don't think that's lucky at all. What does he DO all day if he doesn't study? And we get an education so we can get jobs. Good jobs. And have a career and a good life and everything. And that poor boy . . . :(

I should feel grateful for this girl, stepping in like that. But I imagine her voice, dripping with compassion, and it grates. What does she know? Why *poor* boy? He could be a famous author or scientist. A genius. How does she know?

But I wanted to hear this. I still do.

So I swallow my anger and read back over people's answers, with as much detachment as I can muster.

Until this:

IamSxy: People like that should fucking die. I mean, what's the point?

What?!

0100110101100101: What?!

LikesEmWithSparkle: Have some heart, you have no idea about him.

IamSxy: No. True, but look, what can he do? He is a vegetable.

0100110101100101: Shut up!

IamSxy: What? Why are you jumping to his defence? YOU don't know him either.

IamSxy: And SERIOUSLY, he should go join that fucking death cult.

0100110101100101: *GO AWAY, PLEASE.*

WindUpBird: No!

LikesEmWithSparkle: That's HORRIBLE!

LikesEmWithSparkle: You can't SAY that stuff. It's AWFUL.

NoFaceBoy: Sparkle's right. You have no idea.

WindUpBird: Yeah. That stupid email is dangerous. NOBODY should be forced into something like that.

IamSxy: Hah! There's too many people draining our resources. They should all do us a favour.

I can't watch any more. Shaking with shock and hurt and anger, I minimize the window and turn my chair away.

Does he really think that?

How can *anybody* think like that?

I'm finished. I can't be part of this.

Except . . . MonkEC. I'd lose our friendship. I can't do that. I won't do that, not for him.

I turn back to the screen.

<IamSxy has been removed from this conversation.>

0100110101100101: Good riddance!

LikesEmWithSparkle: Yesss! Can we talk about something else, please? Come to General Chat?

I make myself look back over the answers, pick out the good ones and read them twice, commit them to memory. It helps, a little.

And when I get to NoFaceBoy's comment about school, I feel almost guilty; he doesn't *know* – how can he? And I wanted honest answers.

I click on 'send private message' and I write:

Hi NoFaceBoy

I just wanted to properly thank you for writing to me the other day. I needed that.

How are you? I hope you're well. You sound a bit fed up.

I'm going to add you as a contact – I hope we can be friends.

SamuraiMan.

PS One day we'll all look back on school as a distant memory.

It is only a minute before I get a message:

NoFaceBoy has added you to their friend list.

22

> **ShinigamiFanBoy:** Guys! Have you seen? We're famous!
>
> **GuitarGirl1:** What? Who?
>
> **TandemRide:** Huh?
>
> **ShinigamiFanBoy:** The news. They're talking about us. Well, not US . . . but.
>
> **TandemRide:** What?
>
> **GuitarGirl1:** Explain? WHO's famous? :-S
>
> **ShinigamiFanBoy:** www.natnews.jp/2647_13a6

There is a pause whilst everybody follows Shinigami's link.

HOW EASILY DOES DEATH ROLL OFF THE TONGUE?

Chatroom moderators across the country have alerted the authorities to a strange trend: young people everywhere are discussing suicide.

Although initially this pattern raised the alarm, the online discussions have been reported to be 'usually trivial', punctuated with emoticons and referencing nothing more than homework worries.

The noble death is an innate part of Japanese culture and a focus for many successful storylines in popular series. Nevertheless, it is rare to see more than a cursory reference, and nothing of this scale has been documented before, leaving the nation's adults asking, *What is happening to the youth of today?*

Panic shudders through me as I remember the words 'Join us, for the biggest statement of the millennium.'

Widespread discussions. That means those emails driving people to take a stand, to vote – for what I am not sure – with their lives, is everywhere.

What would the papers make of the emails, if they knew? Or the act itself?

Would they glorify the deaths of thousands, or would they play it down? And would anything actually change?

I sit here for a while, wondering whether being corralled into death cancels out whatever statement it is that you try to make. I don't know, but it feels wrong. Dangerous. And I'm glad when a message pops up on my screen to drag my thoughts away.

Hi SamuraiMan
Hi!
Is this a good time?
Sure.
:) Oh good. How are you?
Good, thanks. How are you?
Yeah. OK. How's the survey going?

Survey? Oh, yes.

It's OK. I mean, I see this as a longer project – I want to collect as much data as I can before I start compiling.
Wow, you're really taking this project seriously, huh?

Yes. I think it's important to understand the way society thinks, and try to work out why. Otherwise how do we develop as a nation or as people?

Wow. That's deep!

Yeah, well. I . . . know some kids with problems. And I wish they didn't have *our* problems heaped on top.

What do you mean?

Oh, I don't know. I just . . . it's the little things. The staring. Why should anybody have to deal with that?

Yeah. I suppose.

I do not want to talk about this any more. I do not want to justify myself, even in disguise. An awkward silence fills the screen and I realize I befriended NoFace without ever looking at his profile. I know nothing about him except for two brief encounters.

Desperately searching for something to say, I click.

USERNAME (NoFaceBoy)

TAG-LINE ( )

AGE (17)   GENDER (Male)

INTERESTS ( )

If you could be anything in the world, what would you be?

UPLOAD A PROFILE PIC NOW

Somehow, even though I do not know him, I am not surprised.

Mysterious, aren't you? ;)

Huh?

You don't give much away on your profile page.

Yeah, well, those questions are so asinine. Besides, I am a changeable person. I'd have to update all the time. I figure people can just talk to me if they want to know.

Hah, fair enough. So . . . what would you put today?

Um . . . NoFaceBoy, likes movies and popcorn and shoot em up games. Is liable to laugh at everything you say; does not mean this unkindly. :D

Hah, brilliant!

OK, I'm totally stalking you now, since you've seen mine. I'll be right back.

I wait, and as I wait, I realize I am holding my breath.

Will he see through what I wrote? Will he like me? Would he like the *real* me?

Soooo, you really DO like all that serious stuff, huh?

Kind of. I like books, and I like to learn, at least.

Nerd :)

Thanks 8-)

You're welcome.

23

The next few days are good. During the day, I read. I have found a stack of articles on ailing samurai who made something out of their lives, and I plan to read them all. I want to know everything about the blind masseurs and circus freaks. I want, I think, to compare *then* with *now,* and see what's changed: why is it that we're so keen to throw life away?

So in the day, I read, and in the evenings, MonkEC and NoFace come online, and then we laugh.

In one box, I see:

> *I've just spent three hours with my mother poring over photos in American prospectuses. Every page, she said 'Look, Mai. Those labs, that library. Look how happy and hardworking all the students are.'*

I imagine MonkEC sitting at a table, trying to disguise her boredom, shielding a scrap of paper as she surreptitiously attempts to doodle. I imagine her mother, eyes lit with excitement, jabbing at photos with an enthusiastic finger. And I cannot help but chuckle.

And at the same time, in the box beside it, NoFace regales me with tales of late-night battles.

> **So I was nearly there, the map showed the HQ like, two blocks away. It was risky, but OK. I felt goooood.**

> And?
>
> **And then I poked my head around the corner to see whether the path was clear and BOOM. Dead. Head blown clean off.**

I'm not sure what to say to that, if I am honest. Do I sympathize? Congratulate him? Laugh?

> Nooooooo!
>
> **Haha, I know, that is almost exactly what I said! Except I think my exact words might have been 'You stupid, ugly, fish-loving son of a . . .'**

Hah!
I switch back to MonkEC.

> Hey, I just realized . . .
> *What?*
> You just told me your real name :)

I'm waiting for her to respond, when Mama knocks at the bedroom door.

'Sora, can I come in?'

'Yes.'

I switch off the monitor as my mother sidles in.

'Here.' She hands me a pot of tablets, blue and white and berry-red. I expect her to ruffle my hair or squeeze my shoulder and then leave, but she does not. Her hand hovers unsure in the mid-space between us. 'Are you all right?'

'Of course.'

'You're not . . .'

'What?'

She draws in a breath, and pulls a sheet of folded newsprint from her pocket. 'Have you seen this?' She unfolds the paper, rests it on my keyboard.

OPERATION DEATH WISH

Police are investigating rumours of a devastating wave of email spam, willing teenagers to commit funshi, or *indignation death* in a shock mass suicide.

These persuasive emails, which are thought to be targeting young people across the country, rile them up with campaign talk and then direct readers to 'follow the link' for more information. However, the links provided are invalid after a matter of hours and police are as yet unable to trace the source.

Chief Superintendent Yoshima implores anyone with any further information to come forward.

I can feel my mother's eyes searching my face as I read, and my skin prickles with embarrassment and nerves.

'Sora?' she asks when I have finished. 'You're not getting these emails, are you?'

Her voice is a dead weight around my neck. But I cannot tell the truth.

'No.'

She frowns, studies me carefully. 'Are you certain?'

'Yes, Mama. And even if I did, I would never open them. Emails like that could be *anything.*'

Her face stays calm, but I see her hands nervously seek each other out. 'I don't like you being on that thing all day.'

'The internet?' She is such a hypocrite. My mother lives on her computer, phone, tablet.

'Yes. Look what *happens,* Sora. I know you're sensible, but the rest of the world . . . Besides, you shouldn't be hiding away in here. It isn't right. You should be out making the most of' – she catches my eye, and falters – 'the good weather. It will be cold soon.'

I take a deep breath. 'Mama, I'm *fine.* All I am doing is talking to my friends, and studying.'

My mother's knuckles go white beneath her own grip.

'Honestly. I'm—'

She sniffs. 'You're not. This whole thing is anything but fine.' For a moment she stands there, blanched fingers and pursed lips, a statue, and I know she's trying not to cry. But before I can reach out, pull her hands into mine, she's back, all business-face, a wry smile at her lips. 'Right. We're going away.'

'Sorry?'

'You and me. Away. Away from' – she waves a hand, gesturing at the newspaper and computer but maybe meaning something else – 'this. Let's go visit Ojiisan and Bah-Ba.'

We make dinner together. At least, I sit at the table whilst my mother cooks, and every now and then she will hold out a spoon and demand 'Taste!' with half a smile. And by the time our food is on the table everything is almost normal once again.

We talk about Ojiisan and Bah-Ba's place, how happy they will be to see us, how Mama wants to help my grandmother to insulate the attic.

'It's cold up there in winter, and they're not so young these days,' she says, as though it is a perfect explanation.

I must admit, I'm shocked at her decision. My mother left the countryside as soon as she could; fled to the city with my father and never looked back. But I'm glad. I love it there.

And when that topic's dried up, and Mama's promised to make arrangements as soon as she can, we sit in comfortable silence and eat.

'You know,' my mother says, blowing gently on a chunk of hot steaming potato, 'you could invite them round for dinner.'

I frown. 'Who?'

'Your friends.'

'Is this some kind of internet safety thing, Mama? Because I *promise* I have nothing to do with those emails.'

The tips of her chopsticks dip, hang frozen just above the plate. She sighs. 'No . . . it's . . . you spend so much of your time with them. And if there are people in my boy's life, I should like to know them.'

I want to protest. To tell her that it's the internet, it's separate from real life, and that I hardly know anyone yet. But she's wearing that tired face, and she's right: if I'm going to spend my last days or weeks or months sitting on the internet, I owe her that at least.

Hi!
Hi! How are you?
Fine thanks.
I have something to ask you, though.

I cannot believe I'm doing this.
OK . . .

OK . . .
Would you like to come to dinner?
Dinner?

Dinner?

Neither of them answer me.

It's weird. I've scared them off. They'll never talk to me again.

Yes. I know it's weird, but my mother wants to meet my friends.
Your mother?
>.< yes.

Why?
I . . . Promise you won't laugh?

Of course.
My mother wants to meet you.
Huh?

I cannot tell him that my mother is watching me count down the days, that she wants to be a part of everything. I can't tell him that maybe having him and Mai round for dinner will make losing me easier, somehow.

That is not the way to attract friends.

She wants to meet my friends. Apparently I spend too much time in my room, online, and she doesn't believe you exist. Or she thinks you aren't who you say you are, or something. Like one of us is just making you up.
Haha, well, in that case. I, Invisiblor the Faceless and Imaginary, would be delighted to attend.
Are you mocking me?
A little. But my parents think the same thing sometimes, and I'd love to come.

Yes!
Oh. Oh my! He said yes.
What will I hide behind now?

Who else is coming? Or is it just me? Is this a secret way to woo me?
Dork :p
bows
I don't know who else, yet. You're officially my first guest.
:D

I turn my attention back to Mai, still silent.

I'm sorry. Please don't hate me. I'll tell her you can't make it.
We can still be friends, right?
Sorry but I really have to go.
Talk tomorrow?

Great. I've blown it. Lost her. She thinks I am a crazy stalker-murderer.

25

> *The answer's yes!*
>
> *Sorry I rushed off yesterday. I really did have to leave.*
>
> *Also, I was a little worried. You hear stories about people on the internet.*
>
> *But I do want to come. I'd love to meet you. So my answer's yesyesyes (-:*
>
> *Xx*
>
> *PS You better not be some fat creepy dude. I'm giving my friend your address before I come.*

I stare at the screen. My fingertips feel funny. Extra-shaky, somehow.

They both said yes.

I know that I should tell them about me, warn them, but . . .

Thank you for accepting. Now that I have got you trapped, there's something you should know.

Dear friends, I am not quite who you thought.

No, I'm not a creepy stalker. I am worse.

In the end, I do not tell them anything more than the date and time, and our address. I cannot disappoint my mother. And besides, perhaps they'll understand.

I will have to wait and see.

·····26

I spend the next four days trying not to worry, to push the dinner from my mind, but I cannot.

My mother walks around with lighter footsteps, and twice she's asked me if I think her choice of menu – a spicy mapo tofu, and a sticky cheesecake – will suffice. I smile and try to reassure her, but she is like a child waiting for New Year. It is almost enough to excite me as well, but every time I feel bubbles of happiness rising in my chest, I remember it could all go wrong.

The night before their visit, I shrug off MonkEC and NoFace's declarations of excitement, and retreat to bed. My limbs are heavier than usual, and my head hurts with all the possibilities.

What if they take one look at me and they don't know what to say? No. It's fine. I will remind them of our conversations, and the talk will flow. It will be fine.

But what if I spill every mouthful down my front, or knock the tea into their laps? What if—

I slide a hand beneath my pillow and pull out the book of poems, flick through the pages until I find what I am looking for.

Stillness of the night
Heightened by fireflies

I close my eyes and imagine walking in the park, dark,

117

cool air surrounding me, the stars so deep and far away that I can barely see them, but I know that they are there. The wind rustles in the trees, then drops to nothing as I lean against a cherry trunk, and all I can hear is the buzzing of wings as glowbugs flit through blossom.

27

'Where are they?'

'Hush.' Mama leans over and kisses my forehead. 'There is still time. Perhaps they do not want to inconvenience you with an early arrival.'

I glance at the kitchen clock. She's right: there are still seven minutes until seven, and it's only been five minutes since I last looked at the time. How is it crawling at such a snail-pace?

I look over the kitchen table, count the dishes and place-mats and chopsticks. All there. The kitchen smells of spiced warm pork and garlic, silk-fresh tofu and spring onions, which bubble gently on the stove. Everything is ready.

Mama reaches down, fastens the top button of my shirt and brushes imaginary dirt from my shoulders. 'There.' She looks like she is going to cry, but the tightened collar chokes me.

'Mama! They're my friends, it's not an interview.'

I wait until she turns to stir the dinner, and reach up to undo the button. My fat, dead fingers do not want to cooperate, and I'm sure she's going to turn round and see my failure.

Come on, come on! What kind of idiot can't even—
There. Just as Mama turns back.

She stares at my throat, at my dishevelled collar. I shrug apologetically, and she opens her mouth to say something but we are interrupted by a gentle knocking at the door.

They're here!

'You go, Mama. I don't want to keep them waiting.' It takes an age for me to open our front door; my chair gets in the way. But that is not the reason that I want them to see Mama first.

I linger just out of sight as my mother strides happily down the hallway.

The door clicks open.

'Good evening.' My mother sounds excited, and suddenly I question everything: is she too friendly? Will they like the way she smiles? Her food? Our house?

Me?

'Abe-san?'

'Yes.'

I imagine MonkEC and NoFace bowing politely to my mother.

'Oh, thank you.' One of them has handed her a gift. 'Come in. Sora is just—'

Please don't run away, please don't run away. I push my chair out into the hall as my mother steps aside. 'Here.'

Standing in the doorway is a tall boy with a strawberry-red fringe swept across his face so that all you can see is his mouth and half an eye, and a girl wearing a lemon raincoat and ribbons in her hair. They look more real than I'd imagined. Bright and solid.

I think I might throw up.

'Hi,' I say, more weakly than I'd like.

My guests are standing there, wide-eyed, probably as nervous as I am about tonight, and I am *not* being a good host. I swallow hard, ignore the twisting in my gut and wheel closer.

The boy pulls his gaping mouth into a grin, and I am flooded with relief. 'Sora! Way to keep a secret!'

My mother looks at me, confused.

'Mama, this is . . .' Oh. How have I been talking to this boy, invited him into my home and never asked his name?

'Kaito. Dan Kaito.'

She bows to him again, but slips me a look. I know that she heard *secret*.

Our guests slip off their shoes and slide into the company slippers on display by the door. Leaving their shoes, they step inside, and my mother ushers us all down the hall and into the kitchen. Mai hangs back behind NoFace. She does not even look at me.

'Please, sit.' Mama gestures to the table.

I wait until my friends are seated before sliding my chair up to the table. Mama places two heaving pots before us: glistening mapo tofu and fluffy white rice. The pepper in the tofu steam makes my eyes and mouth water in equal measure.

'I trust your journeys were pleasant?' I ask, watching Mama move towards the sink. I wish she'd hurry up so we can start.

'Uh-huh.' Kaito nods. 'Quiet.'

'And yours?' I ask Mai.

She shrugs, staring intently at the table.

'And everything is well? I mean, with you?'

They both nod. Kaito flicks his fringe out of his eyes and smiles encouragingly at me.

Is there pity there? I cannot tell.

'I met Mai in the elevator. When we got out at the same

121

floor I knew it must be her.' He grins across the table, his ears turning slightly pink.

I nod.

And I keep nodding, like an idiot.

What do I say?

My mother is filling up the water jug, and for a moment the only sound is that of water echoing inside the old ceramic jug, changing in pitch as it fills.

I watch my guests, sitting politely, waiting.

What do I do? I have forgotten how to do this.

Finally, my mother joins us, pouring water into each of four glasses and then taking her place.

'Please, help yourselves.'

There is a second of hesitation, before Kaito nods thanks and reaches for the bowl of rice. He ladles a respectful portion into his own dish, then tops it with the spicy meat. Mai follows suit.

Mama fills her own dish and mine, because I cannot reach across the table. I am glad. I do not have the chance to spill the whole meal on the floor.

'This smells delicious, Abe-san.'

'Thank you.' My mother blushes. And then she gives the word, 'Let's eat.'

It *is* delicious. The hot, salted black bean sauce prickles at my tongue, and then it gives way to a softer sweetness, sated by the silken tofu.

I let the first piece of tofu slip down my throat before I break the silence. 'Did you know that mapo tofu translates as "pockmarked-faced lady's tofu", or "leper woman's tofu"?'

Kaito chokes down a mouthful of food, surprised. 'No!'

'Yeah. Legend has it that an old widow-leper was forced

to live outside of town because of her condition, but she lived along a street which traders had to pass through, and to make ends meet she rented out her rooms to workers. They, in turn, would often bring her meat and tofu and request she cook it up for them. Soon, her great cooking was known by travelling businessmen all over, and when they reached the town they'd ask specifically for the pockmarked-faced lady's tofu.'

'Is that true? Or is it some kind of dreadful moral tale?' asks Kaito.

Mai sneaks a sideward stare at me.

Oh! They think I've made it up. A 'people with a handicap can do just fine' tale. Ugh.

I shrug. 'Who knows? The other theory is that the name derives from "numb", because of all the peppercorns.'

Kaito shakes his head in disbelief. 'Where do you learn this stuff?'

'I don't know. I read.'

'Well, you must have a whole library in that head. I haven't even *heard* of a book on the origins of food names.'

'Neither have I. I probably read it on the internet somewhere. Or somebody told me. I don't know.'

'I do.' Mama lays her chopsticks down and smiles. 'Your grandfather told you. He used to joke that he married your grandmother for her skills with food. He'd wink, and kiss her on the cheek and say that *any* woman who could turn out plates like that would find a man, even if they were a leper woman.'

I laugh. If a girl served me food like Bah-Ba's, I'd marry her too.

The rest of dinner passes with barely a word. I try, once

or twice, to start the conversation, but it's awkward. My friends' questions hang over the table, waiting to be asked. Mama glares across the table. I'm the host. I should be making my guests comfortable, making more of an effort. But I don't know what to say. We need to get away from here so that I can explain.

I swallow down my meal as fast as is polite, and wait.

Eventually, Mama says, 'Well, now that we're done, why don't you show your friends to your room?'

I let Mai and Kaito enter first, and close the door behind us. It smells in here, like plastic, medications and stale air. I have not noticed it before.

'Please.' I gesture to the bed, the only place to sit. At least my bed is made today, with fresh, clean sheets straight out of the laundry.

They perch uncertainly, their eyes roving across the room, over the desk and bookshelves and my old world map, and baseball shrine. They are judging me. For everything I am. A stack of books. A yellow Tigers bobble hat hanging from a nail. A wheelchair.

'I'm sorry.'

Kaito draws in his breath. 'Why didn't you tell us?'

Because I didn't want to be that Sora. Because that Sora is weak and useless. Because you're looking at me as though I have webbed feet and three heads.

'I don't know.' Would you have come, if you knew?

He glances at Mai, and for a second I see everything play out exactly the way it has before. Them and me. The normals and the crippled boy. But then he looks away from her and says, 'So, you're a Tigers fan?'

I nod.

'Me too. Sort of. I mean, I like to watch occasionally.' He stands up to get a better view of my display. 'So do you . . . I mean, did you . . . did you play?'

'Just for the school B-team. I wasn't going on to be a star or anything.'

'So did something happen?' Mai's small voice jingles as she talks, almost disguising the weight of the question.

I glance down at my legs.

'What's wrong with you?' she demands.

My stomach lurches, but I have to tell them. Don't I? They've seen my chair. They *know*.

And they're still here.

I don't look up, mumble to my lap. 'I have ALS.'

'What's that?' Her voice is softer now, the jingling turned to velvet.

Kaito sinks back down onto the bed, and they wait for my answer.

I take a deep breath, and force myself to look into their eyes. 'It stands for Amyotrophic Lateral Sclerosis. And it means' – I have to push the words across my lips – 'I'm going to die.'

'You're what?' Kaito mutters to himself, then louder, 'I'm so sorry.'

Mai just stares, her muscles tensed like a sika deer waiting to run. And then she coughs politely and gets to her feet. 'I'm sorry too. I just remembered that I have to be home early. I really have to go.'

She does not even look at me as she strides to the door and pulls it open.

I stare after her, trapped in the familiar. I hear her in the hall, thanking my mother, gathering her things.

Kaito looks from the doorway to me, and back, unsure which of his new friends he should align with.

And I realize that I don't want him to go, but it was stupid, thinking this would work. So I release him. 'You should probably go after her. Make sure she's all right.'

'Thanks, Sora. I *am* sorry,' he says, laying a hand on my shoulder. 'I would have liked to stay.'

And then he's gone.

I expect my mother to come in and lecture me about the proper rules of entertaining and of friendship, tell me how I embarrassed her and was not fair on the others, that she expected better.

But she does not. When my mother brings me my tablets, she does not say a word. And I don't know which is worse.

28

I sleep badly, drifting in and out of dreams of huge ice-caverns which go on and on, where my wheels slip everywhere and I am alone. Completely, utterly alone. And then I am awake in the still-dark with an emptiness sitting heavy on my gut.

I switch on the lamp and heave my body upright, out of bed. I have to apologize to them. Explain.

But when I log in to the site, there is a message waiting for me.

Dear Sora,

I am so sorry that I ran out earlier. Please apologize to your mother as well. I did not mean to be so rude, and I hope you are not terribly upset.

I really didn't mean to leave like that, but I was shocked.

I think I understand why you didn't say anything. I would want to forget too. But I wish that you had told me.

I hope you can forgive me.

Your friend, Mai.

PS Are you really going to die? :(

I click reply immediately.

Yes, I am.

It's OK that you left; I am not offended. Sorry, perhaps, that I did not warn you. It was selfish of me. Although I did try, I just couldn't find the words.

I understand if you don't want to be friends with me after I lied, or if you do not want to be friends with a dead boy. But please, if it is the latter, do not tell me.

Sora. x

I sit back, and sigh. There should be some kind of deal; I should get superpower-wisdom and empathy as an exchange for this body. I wish it worked like that.

I don't expect I'll hear from her again, but at least I have apologized.

Can't sleep? Me neither.
Of COURSE I still want to be friends.
Can you promise me something though?

Really?

Hi.

What?

Can we not do that again?
If you have a secret like that, tell me. It's what friends are for.

No secrets. I think I can do that.

Right. Let's start with this: what is it you have, exactly? I know you said, but I forgot.

Amyotrophic Lateral Sclerosis.

I'll be right back. I'm going to look it up. :)

I wait, watching the cursor blink, ON*off*ON*off*ON*off*,

focusing on the rhythm instead of the words I know she's reading. Progressive. Paralysis. Fatal. ONoffONoffONoffON.

She is gone for quite a while, but just as I think that the words have scared her away, she says:

Do you really have all that? Those symptoms?
Some of them.

I cannot tell her that the rest of them will come, in time. It is written, she will know, if she reads, but I cannot write the words. Not yet.

She barely hesitates.

Which ones?
Do you really want to know? It's . . . I am not a normal boy.
Yes. I guessed that when you appeared in a chair with wheels. :p

---

OK . . .

I give her a moment to change her mind, retreat.

My legs don't really work. And now it's started in my hands, my arms.
When you say 'don't work', what do you mean?
The muscles cramp, they weaken, and they waste away.
They ache a lot, and I can't move. It starts with shaking and weakness, and it just gets worse.
So, it will get worse in your hands too?
Yes.
So . . .
What happens next?

What do you mean?

I mean . . . Oh, I don't know. It isn't FAIR. Why can't someone ELSE be ill?

Someone else?

Someone old, who's already done everything they want to do. It says it's mostly old people, so why do YOU have to get it?)-:

MOSTLY old, not only. Besides, how old is old? Our grandfathers? Our parents?

But you're . . .

I know.

Well, if not someone old, someone horrid then?

Sometimes, I wonder the same thing. Not horrid, exactly, but the undeserving. Why should I be banished from the world when there are people who do not make the best of it?

But I used to read a manga series where a boy is given powers to choose who dies, and I can't read it any more. I would not want that choice.

It doesn't work that way.

How can you be so REASONABLE? It SHOULD. It isn't FAIR.

I know.

But I'm still here.

29

> **DUDE!**
> Hi Kaito.
> **DUDE! Did you know that there's this guy in baseball who had the same thing as you?**

It is two days since the awful dinner, and he has obviously been reading.

> **He's really famous, like, they named the disease after him. And he was really cool.**

Lou Gehrig, of Lou Gehrig's disease, was the first thing I discovered after diagnosis. He gave a famous speech. I tried to watch it once, but I only got as far as 'luckiest man on earth' before my stomach churned uncomfortably and my eyes were hot with rage and wet with tears. I turned it off.

> **And he's not the only one. ALS gets everyone: musicians and scientists, politicians and prize-winning actors.**
> Yeah?
> **Uhuh. So I know it's probably really scary, but maybe it's some sort of secret superpower, and you have to achieve everything because you cannot fail.**

Right. I will conquer the world from my wheelchair,

hooked to bags and beeping monitors. I will conquer the world with my magic laser eyes, the only thing left that I can move myself.

But I do not tell him this, because below the bubbling scorn there is something else.

I have friends who care enough to try.

30

The next day, when she asks how I am doing, I tell Doctor Kobayashi all about my friends.

'That's good,' she says. 'I'm glad that you are sharing this. You're not alone, Sora.'

'I know.' And for the first time in a while, I really mean it.

31

> *How are you today?*
> OK, thank you.
> *Really?*

'Yes,' I type, 'I'm fine. Stop fussing.' But then I remember three words, and a promise: *no more secrets*. So instead, I answer:

> A little shaky, but yes thanks. I'm good.
> :)
> How are you?
> *Oh, you know. I can't stay long. My mother will be home, and today she's quizzing me on college application answers.*
> Have you told her, yet?
> *What?*
> That you won't be going to an engineering school.
> *I couldn't! You should see her face.*

I wish that I could tell her not to ruin everything. That she should live her life, not someone else's. But I don't know how.

Thankfully, that moment, NoFace appears online. Maybe he will have something of use to say.

I slide the mouse across the screen and click on 'add contact to conversation'.

> *Hi Kaito!*
>
> Hey, don't you think she should tell her mother that she's going to be an artist? That it's her DREAM and her DESTINY?
>
> **HI!**
>
> **Oh, I don't know dude, I'm the wrong person to ask.**
>
> *See, it's not so simple ;)*
>
> **Maybe he's right, though. I envy you, Mai.**
>
> *Really?*
>
> **Yeah. Your passion. All I want to do most of the time is hide. I don't want to *do* anything.**
>
> **siiiigh**
>
> *Oh, she's back. Speak to you later?*

Mai does not come back online tonight. I picture her sitting at a kitchen table, leaning her chin in her hands and trying to look interested, reciting key-word phrases and practising her eager smile whilst her mother looks on.

Mama has not mentioned the dinner party once since it occurred. Instead, she just looks at me sadly, and asks whether there are any books I'd like to read this week, and would I like chicken for dinner?

I'm sure she's noticed the clatter of my spoon or chopsticks as they shake against the bowl. I think I've seen her gaze flit to my trembling hands and back, but she says nothing.

I want to ask her what is wrong, but it is not my place as the son. Instead, I try to cheer her up. 'I've been reading up on fairy tales,' I say, as we sit over a meal.

'That's nice.'

'I thought I'd surprise Ojiisan and Bah-Ba with a story over dinner.'

'Hmm.'

'Maybe the one about the demon in the crock pot, or else the story of the little peach boy.'

Mama does not answer.

'Maybe I'll mix the two up, throw them both into a tale at once.'

Three more days until our trip, and I'm getting nervous. I love my grandparents, but . . . Once, we would all have sat upon a picnic rug, in summer, watching the butterflies and letting ice cream dribble down our chins. And now it's almost winter and everything's changed; I cannot trace the familiar patterns we have drawn before.

I wish that I could just turn back the clock, just for this trip; to morph into the growing young man they used to know. And I wish my mother would snap out of it; answer me, look at me, even. Tell me everything will be all right.

But I don't know that it will, and my mother does not lie.

32

> **I'm envious! I wish I could go on holiday, instead of going to school.**
>
> *Me too! How long will you be gone for?*
>
> One week.
>
> *Oh! A whole week! That's for ever!*
>
> Nah. I will be back before any of us even realize.
>
> *:) Have a great time!*
>
> **Don't do anything craaazy!**
>
> Like what?
>
> **Oh I don't know. Hiking through the hills with nothing but a chocolate bar tucked into your pocket. Or staying up all night to learn the waltz.**
>
> That actually sounds like fun.
>
> **Hah! See, it's happening already. You'll come back a changed man, Abe.**

And that is it. My mother folds my clothes into a bag, locks the door, and we are gone.

33

My grandparents live in Sakyo-ku, a northern ward of Kyoto, filled with tall forests and mountains.

We sit in an empty train carriage, my chair rattling against the windows. I stare out through the glass and watch the concrete-cable-sprawl soften into green. I imagine standing up and striding out across the hills, flying out across a bright blue sky.

Mama stares out of the window too, but I do not think she's watching. Her eyes don't flit from tree to tree.

Finally, the tannoy announces our destination and we step off the train. I breathe deep. I like the air up here – it is not as dry as in the city, and it is sweet upon the lungs.

The station master nods as we go by, as though we are old friends. It is like that everywhere. As Mama pushes my chair up the hill to Bah-Ba's house, people greet us with 'good afternoon's and 'pleasant walk's. It is strange, after the busy disregard and scorn of businessmen, and I have to struggle not to set my jaw and look away, to answer in kind.

We get to the top of the hill, Mama puffing with the effort, and there it is: Bah-Ba and Ojiisan's house, a two-storey draughty wooden building, postcard perfect, set against the trees. Ojiisan is sitting on the porch steps waiting.

'Daughter!' he calls out, when he catches sight of us. 'Grandson!'

He strides out, kisses Mama on the cheek and takes her place behind my chair.

'How is my favourite boy?'

I search for the horror in his eyes, but it is not there. I see nothing but happiness. 'Well, thank you, Ojiisan. And you?'

'Grand, Sora. Just grand. Let's get inside; your grand-mother is in the kitchen and she'll be so pleased to see you.'

'Um . . . Ojiisan?'

'Yes, my boy?'

'How am I going to get inside?' I nod towards the four wide steps leading up to the front door.

'Easy!' he says.

I am worried that he's going to try to lift me. My grandfather is big, and strong, but he is old, and I would not want to break him.

'When I heard you were coming, I made you a little something. Wait here.'

He parks me at the bottom of the steps and disappears around the side of the house.

'Mama?'

'I don't know.' She looks as puzzled as I am.

There is a clattering and Ojiisan grunts.

'Perhaps I'd better go and see,' says Mama.

She follows after him, and moments later they return, carrying a huge sheet of wood between them. It has square holes cut into each corner.

'Careful, careful,' Ojiisan directs as they lay the thing flat, up the steps. 'A ramp!' he pronounces, and then he's off again. This time, he returns with an armful of thinner planks which look as though they have been sanded smooth.

'I was not sure whether you were still up on your feet,' he says, 'so I thought I had better build something to hold onto. Just in case.' He winks at me, and in seconds he's erected the finest-looking ramp in history, with a guardrail on each side.

He steps onto it tentatively. It creaks, but it does not give. He walks halfway up and bounces.

'Right. Let's get you inside.'

My grandmother, a tiny woman, is standing on a stool beside the stove when we walk in.

Ojiisan coughs.

'Oh!' she exclaims, startled off her stool. And then she sees us. 'Azami! Sora! You're here!' She wipes her hands on her apron as she crosses the room. She does not have to bend down far as she kisses the top of my head. 'Look at you!'

I blush, although I know she's only saying that because she has to. I look terrible.

'You look tired, Azami.'

'I'm fine, Mother. It is only that hill.'

My grandmother draws her lips tight, as though she's trying not to say something. And I picture my mother's face, worried, willing Bah-Ba not to push the question any further.

'Bah-Ba,' I say, to distract her, 'where am I going to sleep?'

When I was young, I used to love pulling down the ladders which led to the attic space. Bah-Ba would roll out a mattress up there, beneath the skylight, and every night I'd fall asleep flying with the stars.

I won't be climbing any ladders this time.

'I'll make you up a bed down here,' she smiles.

'Come on, champ, let's leave the women to finish

dinner and discuss their women-things.'

As Ojiisan wheels me out onto the porch, I imagine Mama resting her head on my grandmother's shoulder and letting out a sigh. I imagine whispered, sorrowed voices, sympathy: *Oh my, how frail he looks*, and *I can't do this, Mama*.

But then Ojiisan sits on a tree-stump stool beside me, pulls my head out of that room and into something else, out here. The boys' club.

'I am glad you're here, Sora.'

'Why?'

He waggles his bottle-brush brows mischievously and beneath them his eyes gleam, 'I think we have a bakeneko.'

'Oh!' I gasp, playing along. 'Really?'

'Yes.'

I scan the yard. 'I do not see it.' But I imagine a shapeshifting monster-cat prowling through the trees, and shudder.

'You wouldn't, would you?'

'I suppose not. So, what makes you suspect one?'

'Your grandmother keeps hearing noises. Yowling in the kitchen after dark. But when I go to look, there's nothing.'

'Okaaay.'

'And there are the bones.'

'Bones?'

'Yes. On the porch. Once or twice a week your grandmother or I will come out here to drink our morning tea, and there they are. Bones.'

I hesitate, not sure I want to know. 'What *kind* of bones?'

'Birds, mostly. Big birds, picked clean, and with the heads gone.'

Ugh! 'That is disgusting!'

Ojiisan chuckles. 'It is, isn't it? Although we should be grateful that they're clean.'

'Do you really think it is a bakeneko?'

'Oh, undoubtedly.' He shrugs seriously, but his eyes still have that brightness to them.

'But . . . couldn't it be a racoon dog? Or something else?'

'It's a bakeneko. I am sure of it.'

I nod. 'So how can I help?'

'Your grandmother and I, we think it moved in after old Ten died.'

I nod. That makes sense; cats are territorial.

'So we thought, the best way to get rid of it would be to introduce another cat.'

'And you thought I could help choose?'

Ojiisan grins. 'You did such a good job choosing Ten. Do you remember how we used to sit and watch him stalk the dragonflies across the yard.'

'For hours! Yes!'

'That's settled, then. Your grandmother will be pleased.'

I imagine Bah-Ba sitting by the kitchen stove, a kitten curled upon her lap. And I am glad that we have come.

Staying with my grandparents is like stepping back in time. Although they have electricity, when it comes to dinner we sit down to eat by lamplight, which casts a gentle glow across the room. Bah-Ba has left the door ajar, so that the autumn breeze can join us at the table, and the lanterns flicker gently in the sweet night air.

'I hope you are hungry, Sora,' Bah-Ba says, as she puts a plate before me. 'It's your favourite.'

I look down at my plate, and I am five years old again, my legs swinging miles from the floor. I breathe in the smell of a thousand memories.

'Thanks, Bah-Ba.'

Bah-Ba used to make me omuraisu every time I came to visit. Fluffy rice, peas and carrots, sometimes ham, all stirred up with ketchup and wrapped in the thinnest, lightest omelette in the world. Nobody makes omuraisu like my Bah-Ba.

Mama frowns. 'I hope you have gone lightly with the ketchup.'

Not a chance. Bah-Ba likes it just the same as me.

Bah-Ba slides a dish in front of Mama, and Ojiisan, and then sits without a word.

'All right. Let's eat.'

Five-year-old me does not need to be told twice. I shovel in a mouthful bigger than is probably polite, and grin across the table at my grandmother. 'It's great. Thank you!' I mumble, mouth still full.

Halfway through a meal silent with hungry mouths, Bah-Ba says, 'So, how are you feeling, Sora?'

I wish they had not asked me that. I do not want to lie.

'All right.'

It's true. Comparatively.

She nods. 'That's good. So what has my grandson been doing with himself?'

My grandparents lean in expectantly.

I wish I could tell them that I had been top of the class for the entire semester, that I was looking to study abroad and start a life full of adventures that would make her proud. I wish I could tell Ojiisan that I'd been climbing hills, flying kites across the meadows, sliding into fourth base. 'Reading, mostly.'

Ojiisan's eyebrows knit above sad eyes for a moment, then he leans back and takes pity on me. 'So,' he says loudly, 'I have been telling Sora all about our little problem.'

'Problem?' Mama's voice is racked with worry.

'We have a bakeneko.'

'A bakeneko?'

'Yes, my girl. It's haunting us.'

'A *bakeneko*?' Mama does not believe in ghosts and spirits.

'Yes.' He stares defiantly, but his eyes twinkle in the lamplight. 'We need another cat to scare him off.'

Bah-Ba stands to clear the dishes to the sink. 'If I have to clear up one more carcass from the front steps, we might be knocking on your door to stay. So, Sora, will you help us choose a champion cat?'

'Yes! When?'

'I thought we could go down to the shelter in the morning.'

I wake up in the dark, and the wind reminds me where I am. It has snuck in through the cracks and waltzes across the room, caressing everything it touches like a drunken lord. I shiver, snuggle deeper down beneath the blankets. The house creaks. When I was small, I used to wake up to the wind and the noise of wood shrinking from the cold, terrified that the whole building would collapse on top of me. But now it just reminds me that I'm home.

It is strange being down here though, with no stars, no moon peeking in at me. I wonder about getting out of bed, wrapping myself in a blanket and slipping out onto the porch. It is cold, and my limbs are lead, but the air outside is sweet. Just as I have made up my mind and shrugged off the heavy blankets, the wind yowls.

I know it is the wind, but still, what if Ojiisan was right and there's a bakeneko on the doorstep? I picture a huge cat-thing with pointed ears and giant fangs looming shadowlike above the door, just waiting for me to cross the threshold.

Would it tear my limbs apart right there, leaving bloodstains for my grandparents to find when they step out for morning tea?

Or would it carry me away to a far corner of the garden where it will not be disturbed?

Or perhaps the bakeneko hunts like any household cat and it would pounce, then let me go, then pounce again until it tires.

No. It's cold, and my limbs are lead, and there is always tomorrow for admiring the moon, when the wind has dropped and it is warmer.

And there is a cat asleep beside the hearth.

34

Bah-Ba stops at the ARK shelter gates. I twist round in my chair so that I can see her. 'What's wrong?'

'Oh, nothing. I was just praying to the universe that the perfect cat for us is in here, waiting.'

'He is.'

'All right, then. Let's go.'

'Good morning, madam.' The receptionist talks over my head at Bah-Ba. 'What can we do for you today?'

'We're looking for a cat.'

'Oh, great. Are you looking to adopt today?'

We nod.

'Excellent. We just need to check a few things first. Do you have your paperwork? We need—'

Bah-Ba hands over a stack of papers – proof of address and photos of the house, everything the shelter needs to see that she and Ojiisan have the perfect kitten paradise ready and waiting.

The woman flicks through the documents, chewing on her bottom lip, nodding as though she's ticking off a mental checklist.

'And you've had cats before?' she asks, still reading.

'Oh yes. Always. Old Ten lasted fourteen years with us.'

'I'm sorry,' says the woman. 'It's always hard. But maybe we have a replacement . . . or another feline friend . . . for you today.' She stops reading, taps the edge of the papers on the desk to straighten them, then nods. 'All right. I'll double-check whilst you go meet the residents, but I think that's all in order. Would you like to come this way?' And she steps out from behind the desk and shows us through a door.

As we push through the door, I expect the smell of hopelessness. I expect bony, balding creatures, staring at us with sad eyes and yowling through cage bars. But there is none of that. In the first cage, two young tabby cats are curled up in one ball, only their four ears giving them away. In the next, a tiny scrap of ginger wrestles with a fluffy mouse.

Bah-Ba pushes me along the corridor slowly, taking in each cage as we go.

'See anyone you like?' I ask.

'Oh, I don't know,' she half whispers. 'They're all lovely. How do you choose?'

Most of them ignore us, snoozing on cushioned mats or hiding in boxes. The smaller ones tumble over one another, all stubby tails and enthusiastic teeth. They remind me of children charging about with wooden katana. Do cats have an imagination too?

Grrrowl, I'm a TIGER. A pirate tiger! I'm gonna get you!

Yeah? Well, I'm a two-legs! NOTHING CAN DEFEAT ME! Rarrr!

A few cats pace their cages, up and down the glass, and up again. I wish that we could free them all.

But Bah-Ba is only looking for one. And there is nothing to distinguish between them.

And then Bah-Ba stops. 'Look!' She points excitedly.

A rugged grey cat sits in the middle of his cage, upright and proud. His left ear is half gone, and he has a bald scratch across his nose. And he watches us with one open eye as green as the first spring leaves.

Bah-Ba moves closer to the cage, to read the information tacked up beside it. *'Cat Twenty-three. Male,'* she reads aloud, *'approximately three years old. I have a ferociously playful side; no mouse or socked feet can escape me, but I'd like a warm lap too.'*

Cat Twenty-three tilts his head, as though he's listening to Bah-Ba's voice. She stops, and presses her fingers up against the cage. He leans towards her, and I swear I hear him purring through the glass.

'Hello,' she whispers.

We take Cat Twenty-three home with us. He is quiet all the way, except when we go past the fish market, when he pokes his paws out through the door and yowls.

Bah-Ba leans over my shoulder to croon, 'OK, OK, there will be something nice for you at home.'

Back at the house, Mama and Ojiisan attempt to poke their noses up against the bars and bestow their welcome on him, tell the cat how handsome he is, and promise that he's landed on his feet, but my grandmother quickly pushes them away.

'Let the poor thing settle.'

She places the carrier beneath the kitchen table so that she can guard him from their baby-talk whilst she prepares the lunch.

Cat Twenty-three peers out with interest, his nose and

whiskers working overtime. My grandmother lifts fresh blue prawns out of the fridge and pushes one into the basket. The cat swallows it whole and then looks hungrily for more, but Bah-Ba has already bustled off. And when she starts to sing to the rhythm of her chopping knife, the cat curls up and goes to sleep.

35

Most cats seek the dark spaces when they're somewhere new, but not Cat Twenty-three. Freed from his cage, the first thing he did was jump up onto Ojiisan's knee, and claim the old man as his own. Now, two days later, you would never guess that this house had ever been without a loud grey cat.

When Ojiisan walks, or sits down for his breakfast, the cat appears from nowhere. *Mwong!* he says, and stretches up to say hello.

'Good morning, young man.' Ojiisan rubs the cat between the ears. 'And how are you this morning?'

Mwong! 'Very well, thank you. Now, how about some breakfast?'

Cat Twenty-three hops up onto Ojiisan's lap with a *Mrrrp,* and sits, his head peeking up over the table as my grandmother slides a plate of rice balls in front of them.

My mother wanders in, her hair dripping down her back. She helps herself to coffee then sits at the table.

'How did you sleep, Azami?'

'Well, thank you.'

'No more bakeneko bothering your dreams, you see.' He nods, stroking the creature on his lap.

Mama smiles. 'I'm glad. Maybe he'll get rid of the mice now too.'

'There was one dead by the hearth this morning,' Bah-Ba says, finally sitting down to join us.

Mama shudders. 'Mother!'

'What, dear?'

'Talk of dead things, at the table?'

'Oh hush, it is no different to the chicken on your plate at dinner.'

'Yes it is! Those things have diseases. And they're still, y'know . . .'

'Still what?'

'Furry. And you can see their eyes.'

'This one had its head off. I expect the young man ate it.'

'Eurgh!'

I slide a glance at Ojiisan. His mouth is clamped tight, and I can see from his shoulders that he's trying not to laugh at the pair of them.

'Maybe we should skin the rest of it? Put it in a stew?'

'Mother!'

I imagine tiny paws reaching up from the middle of a soup dish, tails hanging over the side like wayward noodles. And Mama's face, green with disgust. And I cannot help it. I feel the laughter rising up my chest, tugging at my lips. At first it's just a little giggle, but it sets Ojiisan off, snorting as he tries to hold it in, and I am done for.

Mama and Bah-Ba stare at us with daggers in their eyes, but then my grandmother chuckles, and finally Mama's waterfall laugh joins in.

Cat Twenty-three looks up at us, bemused.

36

Somehow, I can't sleep through till dawn in this house. It's as if the new day calls to me from its slumber, drags me up to meet it. It is still dark when I wake. I like it, though. The air is quiet and still, and friendly now the wind has passed, and I find myself wanting to get out of bed and out into the yard to watch the sun rise.

I pull on a sweatshirt, settle in my chair, and yank a blanket from the bed to drape across my knees.

This morning Mama is already up, sitting in the kitchen in the dark, hunched over a glowing screen and muttering, 'Oh, come *on*.'

I cough gently so as not to startle her.

'Oh, Sora!' She starts, and freezes with an index finger millimetres from her touch-screen. 'Hi.'

'Working?' It is not lost on me that Mama brought us here to get away from everything, and yet . . .

'Ehh . . . not really. Trying to. I can't get reception up here, though. Anything could be happening in the office and I'd never know. And what if the hospital tries to make appointments?'

'Mama!'

'Listen, I was thinking. When we get back, there's a doctor. He's American—'

'We're on *vacation*.'

'I *know*, but life doesn't stop just because—' She sighs, and pushes her tablet across the table, away. 'You're right.

And your grandmother will be up soon. What d'you say we make some tea, surprise her.'

She lifts the heavy iron kettle to the stove, and rifles through the pantry. She pulls down a bag of oily black tea leaves and scoops them out into the bottom of the pot, scattering a few leaves on the worktop as she goes.

'Ehhh, why doesn't she just use bags?'

'Because they're cheating,' Bah-Ba laughs, scolding as she wanders in, still in her nightgown. She takes the pot from Mama and inspects the contents. 'Use a bag and you're robbing yourself of the *experience*.'

Mama rolls her eyes.

'Besides. The leaves move around this way. It tastes better.'

'And takes twice as long to brew and longer still to clean up all the mess.'

'What's your hurry, little hare?'

'Ugh, don't call me that.'

Bah-Ba smiles. 'Don't rush, that's all. Time isn't going to pass you by.'

And then her eyes fall on me, and she goes quiet.

'Tea.' She nods, that same 'new topic' gesture Mama has, then glances at the clock on the wall. I don't know why. It has not worked for years. 'Who's hungry?'

Later that day, as the sky turns grey, I sit out on the porch alone. I love my grandparents, and their home, but after four days I long for my computer.

My grandparents have tried so hard, including me in trips to the store and the shelter, cracking jokes. Bestowing kisses which, were I not in this chair, I might have shied away from.

But there are things unsaid. I see their furtive glances, and I hear the things they do not ask. *How much time does he have? Will we see him again? What if we break the crippled boy?*

The secret silence is exhausting.

I want to go online and scream and scream until my lungs run dry. I want to talk to MonkEC and NoFace, tell them how my legs ache from the damp air, and how they itch to run up the already snow-capped hills. How the attic calls to me, and the bathroom here is awkward. And I want to share the good things too: to send them a picture of Cat Twenty-three, to tell them all about the bakeneko and delicious food, and ask them whether *they* believe in spirits.

And I want to escape into their worlds as well. What have they been doing in my absence? Has Mai stood up to her mother yet, insisted that she is going to try to carve out a career as a super-animator? And Kaito, has he reached the final level of his game without blowing up the girl he's supposed to rescue? Or has he thrown his console through the window?

I love it here, I do, but it is a sort of limbo-house where nothing ever changes, and all the things I used to love are out of reach.

When I was small, my grandfather and I would spend hours in the yard, pitching baseballs. I caught my first ball out there, and I was so proud that I lapped the garden twice before I ran into his arms. I think we spent the whole summer outside. Bah-Ba would bring us iced green tea onto the porch and we would gulp it down and then go back for more.

And when it got too dark to play, we'd lie on our backs

and watch the moths try to hit the moon down from the sky.

I close my eyes, imagine spreading my arms out like an aeroplane and running, weaving back and forth, then leaping for a ball, hitting wood to leather and racing to the finish.

'What're you doing, champ?'

I open my eyes to see Ojiisan stamping up the porch steps. It must be too dark now to work.

'Just thinking.'

He sits beside me, resting one arm on the edge of my chair, and sighs. 'You do a lot of that, these days, I expect.'

I nod.

He stares out at the shadowed grass, and I wonder whether he's remembering the baseball summer too.

We sit, listening to Mama and Bah-Ba clattering about inside, and the darkness deepens.

'It's cold tonight,' he says.

'Yes.'

'About as cold as your grandmother's electric refrigerator, I should think.'

'How can you tell?'

'My knees. They creak whenever it drops below six. And there aren't any crickets tonight.'

It's true; the yard is deadly silent, even though it is still early autumn.

I listen harder, until my grandfather breaks the silence, grunting as he gets to his feet. 'Come on. Let's go.'

'Where?'

'A man needs to walk with his grandson at least once every visit.'

'Now? But it's dark!'

'So?' He grabs the handles of my chair and starts off down the ramp.

Out in the yard, the air is damp, and already smells like bonfires mixed with dewy grass, as though the seasons cannot quite decide who the night belongs to.

Ojiisan pushes me out awkwardly across the grass. The wheels don't like it, sinking into the uneven ground, making him push and pull and lift to get me moving, but he does not stop.

'Did I ever tell you that a cricket knows the temperature exactly?' His voice only gives away the slightest hint of breathlessness.

'Yes!' And I recite, 'Count his chirps for fifteen seconds, and add thirty-seven. It works every time. Except when it's too cold and they don't sing at all.'

'Good boy.' He concentrates on walking for a while, and then asks, 'Does it hurt?'

'What?'

'All of it. The illness.'

'Not really.' And then, because I cannot lie to Ojiisan. 'A little. Sometimes. Mostly I just wish that I could still do things.'

Ojiisan sighs. 'It sounds a lot like getting old.'

Soon we've reached the end of the yard, where the tall pines stand, and we turn back.

In the middle of the grass, Ojiisan stops. 'Look up.'

I lean back, crane my neck as far as it will go. The moon is nothing but a sliver, but the sky is clear and lit with stars. You do not see them in the city, not like this.

'It's beautiful.'

'Count them?'

I cast my eyes across the pin-pricked sky. They're everywhere, big and small and bright and dull, a whirling mist of light.

'Impossible.'

'Try.'

'I can't. There are too many.'

Ojiisan is quiet for long enough that I tilt my head further back, to look at him. He looks different, upside down in the nearly-black; papery, and old. Finally, almost in a whisper, he says, 'So many of them will be burned and gone before we even notice them.' He snaps his gaze down from the sky to me. 'Dinner. I bet they're almost ready.' And grabbing my chair he starts towards the house.

I imagine tiny baby stars, miles from anyone or anything, desperate for attention, and I tilt my head back once again, but the walk is bumpy, and I cannot focus and their lights merge into one.

'Ojiisan?'

'Hm?'

'What happens to the stars, when they die?'

He does not answer.

'Ojiisan?'

'I don't know.' His voice sounds stretched and strange, and I don't believe him; my grandfather knows *everything*. But I don't know why he'd lie.

37

'Call us. Any time. And come back soon.'

'You could always come to us, you know.'

Bah-Ba grimaces. 'Old folks like us, we belong out here, Azami.' But then she looks from Mama to me, and sighs. '. . . Perhaps.'

'Yes, well. You're always welcome. Please.' And then, 'We should be going, we don't want to miss the train.'

'Goodbye, Ojiisan. Bye, Bah-Ba. Thank you.'

Ojiisan nods curtly. 'Look after your mother.'

'I will.'

'Write,' he adds.

'I will!'

And Mama starts us down the hill. Halfway down, I twist in my chair and look back. My grandparents are still there, standing by the gate, watching us go.

...38

Twilight's setting in by the time we turn into our street. I'd forgotten how the streetlights make the sky look sickly, nothing like the deep blue of the unlit countryside.

The superintendent grins, bowing low.

'Abe Azami! And the young master! Fine trip, I hope?'

'Yes!' my mother answers, though her voice is tired and breathy from getting me back home.

'I'm glad. It's good to see you.'

'You too!'

The elevator lurches upward, taking too long to reach our floor.

Come on come on come on.

We stop outside our door. Mama pulls her handbag from the handles of my chair, and rifles for her keys.

I imagine my computer humming gently on the desk, waiting for me to return.

Come on come on come on.

Finally, she finds them, puts the key into the lock, and turns.

'Right,' she breathes, pushing the door open wide. 'Will you be all right for a minute. I want to check the mailbox, then I'll come and help you to unpack your things.'

'It's OK, Mama. I can manage.'

'Are you sure?'

Yes. My friends are down the hall, and I want to be alone with them.

My fingers feel heavy on the keyboard, as though they have forgotten what to do.

BRrRrRrRrRrRrR.

YOU HAVE THREE MESSAGES

Hi, man!

I know you're away, and you probably won't get this yet but EEEEEEEEEEEEEEEEEEEEEEEEEEEEE! I BEAT HIM, the top boss guy. Shot him in the head, and IBEATHIMIBEATHIMIBEATHIM. Which, actually, is pretty weird. Like, there's this hole in my days. What do I strive for now?

Anyway, hope you're having a zinging trip. Speak soon.

Duuuuude!

I found my new thing, the thing to replace Sergeant Asswipe and his renegade soldiers. And it's SO MUCH BETTER.

Another game? I hear you say. Another game with guns and hiding behind rocks to throw grenades?

I'm home, I'm home! Come online, I want to see!

I click on the last message.

Come Baaaaaack.

You've both left me and I'm lonely. Who'm I supposed to talk to now? D-:

Both left him?

Where is Mai? She's always online, every day.

Hi Kaito!

I'm BACK! Tell me all about this wondrous new obsession!

The trip was wonderful but I've missed you both so much. I need to talk to you IMMEDIATELY :D

HIIIIIII! (-: You're BACK! HELLOOOO!

Yes! Hello!

How was it? Tell me EVERYTHING.

It was wonderful to see my grandparents. And the air up there is lovely.

The air? That . . . doesn't sound very exciting. Where were the gunfights? The girls? The wild adventure?

Hahaha, I was with my mother, and my elderly grandparents . . .

Although there was one thing . . .

What what what?

Well, there was a small, teensy run-in with a BAKENEKO!

O_O

Bakeneko???

Cat demon.

Yeah, I know, but WHAT Happened? Did it jump out from the bushes and try to maul you? Did you slice off its head with . . . wait, I don't even know what the weapon of choice is when you're fighting spirits.

You got a mystical katana?

No, no, and no.

Did it move all the food into different cupboards?

Or swallow the neighbours whole?

Are you going to stop guessing and be quiet so I can tell you?

YES. *clamps lips firmly shut* *ties hands behind back*

All right.

So, my grandfather SWEARS that since their cat died, they've been haunted by a bakeneko. It crept into their dreams at night, and laid half-eaten mice up on the porch.

O_O In their DREAMS? That's nasty stuff!

Isn't it? Every night.

And? Did you see it too?

I heard it. It woke me up. It was like the sound of a hundred tortured wolves, and the roar of hurricanes.

>_<

What did you do?

We found the one thing which can beat a bakeneko.

???

A cat.

We got him from the shelter. An old tom, with so much personality that no spirit cat would DARE to come anywhere near his territory.

A cat?

Yes!

Cats are cool, I guess.

It would've been cooler if you'd sliced his head off with a sword.

Hahaha, speaking of . . . what is this THING you discovered?

Thing?

Oh, THE THING.

Sooooooo, I tried all these games, but they just didn't stick, I couldn't focus.

That doesn't sound like you.

I know! Anyway, I decided I want something new, and I thought 'What would Sora do?' and I thought 'BOOKS'. So I went online and looked for 'best books of the year' and to be honest I was a bit lost, but halfway down the page was a manual on DIY Web design. And like, I love this place, and it would be SO COOL to be able to make something of my own one day.

And it's really hard, there's so much to remember, but it MAKES THINGS HAPPEN. I can make things happen with my fingertips!

Short: I'm learning code. I'm going to make WEBSITES, man. Check me OUT.

That's BRILLIANT!

I can't wait to see.

Ooooh, it's a long way off yet.

Yeah, but still, when you're ready.

:D

You have GOT to tell Mai the bakeneko story. She would LOVE it.

Yes. Where is she?

I don't know, man. The day after you left, she had to rush off, said her mother had 'big news' and she hasn't been back since.

Big news?

Yeah. But what can be so big you do not want to share it with your friends?

I can think of one thing.

I hid it from *them* for as long as I could.

But . . . knowing what she knows, she'd tell us, right?

I don't know. Whatever it is, I'm sure she'll tell us when she's ready.

Yeah I hope so. I don't know. I'm worried, man.

Don't be. She's probably just making up a test score or something, doesn't want our sweet voices distracting her.

Yeah. Maybe. I hope you're right.

Me too.

Hi Mai,

I'm back! And I have STORIES.

I missed you.

Sora.

PS hope your week has been amazing.

Have you seen her?

No :(

:(I thought she might come back when you returned. I thought maybe she needed a holiday too, or she was waiting until the gleesome-threesome could get back together.

I don't know. I don't know why she's gone, or where. But I've left her a message.

She'll come back. I know she will.

Yeah? :(

Dearest Ojiisan,

Did you know that no two star deaths are the same? When they run out of energy they collapse, but how that happens is different, depending on how big they are and what's around them. And we're finding out more every day. Here's a printout of some of JAXA's programmes. Aren't they brilliant?

I wonder what it would be like up there. Exciting, I guess, but I think I'd miss the trees. Would you go, if you had the chance? If they offered you a place in a shuttle to the moon, or Mars or . . . to explore?

Oh, also, the dust and debris and gas left behind provide everything needed for new stars and planets to occur. I like that. Maybe you would find a whole new galaxy!

Grandson first, space-explorer second,
Abe Sora

Hey NoFace!

How's it going?

Yeah, OK, I spent lunch in the IT rooms today. I'm trying out my HTML. It's only the beginning, but it's COOL.

:D I'm glad.

Read anything good today?

Not really.

D-: Geek-boy, not interested in books? :p

Ha. No. I'm tired, that's all. I feel as though I've run a hundred miles by the time I get up in the mornings.

:(Is that a ALS thing?

I don't know. It could be.

:(

What do you think MonkEC is doing right now?

Perhaps . . . drawing kittens in the margins of her school book. Making a flick-book, one page at a time.

Hah, yeah.

Have you ever seen her work?

No. She never wanted to share. Have you?

No. I'd like to though. I bet she's talented.

Yeah.

She's cute too.

Is she? Last time I saw her, she left fairly abruptly, and I was too nervous to notice much of anything.

Yeah.

0_o

What?

I just realized . . .

If she's not at the computer, she's NOT MonkEC. At all. It's like she's stripped a part of her away.

* * *

Hey man, any news?

No.

She does not answer messages, or start up conversations. We have not even seen one single trace of her in any of the chatrooms. It's like she's vanished from the internet completely.

But why?

It's strange, without her. Kaito and I talk well enough, but our jokes are few and deadened, as though we are in mourning.

I suppose, in some small way, we are.

To:	S ...
From:	TheSClub
Subject:	The Club Needs You

Whatever your troubles, The SClub has the answer.

Join us, and your problems will be over.
Join us, and you'll help us to end problems
all across the nation.

She wouldn't, would she?
Never. Not Mai.
No.

44

'Wake up, Sora. It's late.'

I groan, and open my eyes. Mama has let in the sun, and it is too warm, my blankets too heavy, and yet my head is heavier, my limbs dead weight, and I do not want to move.

'Come on,' she says, and I groan again.

Mama sits beside me and reaches a hand to my forehead. 'Are you feeling all right?'

No.

My mattress is wet sand, sticking, clinging, pulling me under.

'Mmhmm.'

'Well then, hurry up. You're wasting away the sunlight.' She gets up to leave, and I try to heave myself upright, but my arms and legs do not respond.

What's happening?

I can feel the sheets beneath my palms. It should be easy.

I push again, harder this time. I can feel my hands pressed against the softness of the mattress, feel my muscles tense, but I am still lying here.

Is this it?

Am I stuck like this for ever?

A bedridden lump with nothing to look at but the whorls of plaster on the ceiling.

I almost cry out, but I catch the sound before it leaves my throat. I can't, not until I'm sure. Maybe it's all in my imagination and there's nothing worth worrying my mother with.

I lie here for a minute, counting the seconds between breathing in and out again, forcing the panic out across my lips with every exhalation.

And then I try again, this time digging in my heels as well, for extra leverage.

Nothing.

I'm stuck. It's happening. I can't get up.

'Mama!' I try to keep the shaking from my voice, but it's no use. 'Mama, I can't—'

She's back in my room in seconds.

'What is it?'

'Help?' I try to gesture to my useless body, the bed, the whole mess. My arm flails, and a desperate cry escapes my lips.

And she's here, smoothing the hair back from my forehead, and squeezing my hand as though our lives depend on it.

Perhaps they do.

'Hush,' she whispers, 'hush. We'll do this, it's all right.'

And then she's sliding an arm beneath me and she's lifting, pulling me up.

And even though I'm flooded with relief that I'm not stuck here for eternity, I am also angry, and ashamed, and I cannot look at her.

45

'Can I ask you something?'

Doctor Kobayashi thinks before she answers. 'Yes.'

Ever since this morning, one lone image haunts me; it hangs behind my eyes, and every time I blink, it's there. I need to get rid of it, but I do not know whether she'll help me.

'Those men, in the ward around the corner, the one that's locked.' I pause, watch her face for a reaction, but there is none. 'What's wrong with them?'

'I don't know, Sora.'

How can she not know? She works here!

'None of my patients are in that ward.'

'But you must have some idea.'

'That room is a palliative care ward. Those men are very sick. Dying. That is all I know, I promise you.'

'Are they allowed visitors?'

'Yes.'

I swallow hard, push away my fear. 'Can you do something for me?'

'Are you sure about this?' Doctor Kobayashi asks. 'Really sure? It could be . . . difficult.'

I stare at the heavy frosted glass, the locked door in front of us. 'Yes.'

'All right.' She punches numbers into the lock and pushes the door open. 'I will be right out here.'

My arms work better now that I'm awake, and the

hospital floors are smooth and flat, and I push myself into the room. It smells different to the corridor, more like hot wet cabbage than pine cleaner.

'His name is Yamada-san,' Doctor Kobayashi whispers after me.

There he is. Somebody has pulled the curtains around the other beds and the nurses, although I'm sure they can't be far, are not in sight. We are alone.

Even from across the room, I can see his Adam's apple bobbing in his paper neck every time he swallows. I can see the painful heaving of his chest sucking in air.

I have to do this.

I wheel up to the foot of his bed, and his eyes, deep and dark and more alive, up close, flicker recognition of my presence.

'Good morning, Yamada-san.'

His eyes rove, and his mouth makes wide, uncoordinated movements, letting out a rasp of air.

I flinch. Is he angry? Sad? Pleased?

My heart hammers out a warning, and I want to flee, but he is looking at me, waiting, and he does not seem to be trying to yell at me. So I continue, 'I thought perhaps you'd like a little company.'

He blinks slowly. I will take that as a yes.

I move around to the left side of his bed, and grasp his hand.

'I'm Sora.'

He half nods, once, and then lets his head flop to the side so that he can see me.

I feel as though his eyes are boring straight into my heart, my mind, my soul. And I want to pull away, but I am too afraid even for that. I stare back, helpless. Terrified.

And then his eyes stop searching and he smiles, an awkward, gaping smile from a face that doesn't work, but it softens everything, and I find that I am smiling at him in return.

We sit together for what feels like an eternity. I listen to his breathing, long drawn-out gasps, a rattling deep inside his chest, and then the eager respite of exhalation. I watch his mouth and throat and torso work to get the oxygen he needs, and I wish that I could breathe my own air into him, to make it easier for just a moment.

I do not want to break the almost-peace, but there's something that I came to do, and I do not think Doctor Kobayashi will let us sit for ever.

'I . . . may I ask you something? Please.'

He blinks acceptance, and suddenly I have a thousand questions, not just one. Who are you? What is it you did, before? Where are your family? How do you tell the nurses if you need to scratch your nose?

Does it hurt?

Are you afraid?

I don't know which is most important, which to choose. My brain aches with the pressure. What if I ask the wrong thing? Waste my chance? Offend him? And why would he answer me anyway? I am a stranger.

But I've started now, and I have to ask him something. Fast.

'Are you all right?' The words come out in one rushed breath, but the question is polite, and safe, and all he has to do is blink yes, or nod, and we are both home free.

But he does not nod. He looks at me, and looks, and

then his eyes take on a fierceness I've never seen before, and his jaw works in wild, desperate circles as he tries to gain control, force unused muscles to make words, and his breathing gets faster, louder, desperate. For a moment I think maybe I should call for help. And then, in one harsh breath, he wheezes out his answer, emptying his lungs:

'No.'

I left as quickly as I could, gulped in the fresh, cool air of the corridor, blinked in the bright, safe light.

No?

No.

One tiny word. And I feel as though the world has dropped from underneath me.

He was supposed to give me answers, tell me that everything will be all right, that it was worth it.

Doctor Kobayashi does not say a word as we go back to her office.

My mother, lost in her own thoughts, sits on a bright plastic chair, her hands crossed neatly in her lap, waiting for the end of my appointment. She's worried. I can see it in the lines across her face.

And the world drops further away.

ShinigamiFanBoy: Are you guys sapping my time? Is this some evil science-fiction masterplan?

Bluebird_796: What?

ShinigamiFanBoy: This week! Where did it go? I feel as though it only just began.

MadSkillz: I agree! SOMEBODY must be behind this!

MadSkillz: Who is it???

MadSkillz: It's you, isn't it?

Bluebird_796: Argh, I know! How are we supposed to get top marks, meet for ice cream, go shopping, AND take over the world? :(

GuitarGirl1: Who? Me? 0:-) It's not me, I promise, I didn't steal your times!

Even here, in the virtual land of candy bars and kittens, I cannot escape. Every time I close my eyes, I see his face, hear his rasping voice, over and over again.

I want more time.

Except, I don't. Not if my time will be spent like that.

TandemRide: Oh come on guys, it's fiiiiiiine, you just need a schedule.

ShinigamiFanBoy: O_o

TandemRide: It's true. Set your week out in blocks of time, so you know what you should be doing, and if you stick to it . . . :-)

MadSkillz: We unlock the bonus hours? :D

6 a.m.–7 a.m.: Lie in bed, wait for sunrise.

7–7.30 a.m.: Stare at ceiling.

7.30–8 a.m.: Breakfast. Fail to eat/choke.

8 a.m.–12 p.m.: Stare at ceiling.

I picture the words, stark, monotonous, arranged in neat boxes, colour-coded and adorned with cheerful stickers. And I want to vomit.

Hey Sora!

How was your day?

Pretty horrible, actually, but can we please talk about something else?

Sure . . . Wanna see my new webpage?

YES!

It's really basic, and it probably doesn't look like much, but I built it myself!

www.oneboysfavourites.co.jp

I click on the link.

There's nothing much there. A red banner, with big, chunky title-text and bold headings. Things that would take two minutes on BlogThis.

It looks great! Well done.

Really?

Yes! I wouldn't know where to start unless someone'd done all the actual work for me.

:) Thanks. I'll learn how to do the fancy stuff. But it's hard. Like, learning a new language – several, all at once.

178

She what?

She's back?

I want to click 'accept' but my arm feels strange. Numb.

I want to ask her where she's been. To throw my virtual arms around her and never let go, and to shake her, turn my back and storm away.

And before I can work out which impulse is stronger, Kaito must have let her in, because she's there, in front of me.

It could be good news. Maybe she's been busy crafting a portfolio, applied for an apprenticeship with a studio, been accepted. Any news is better face to face, with treats to celebrate. But . . . as we make plans for the weekend, I read over her words again, and worry creeps into my brain. Maybe it is just my day, casting monstrous shadows over everything I see, but I can't help feeling there's more to it than that and something's wrong.

'There she is.'

The All America Café is full, buzzing with the clink of glasses and excited conversations, and there are people everywhere, but I pick out Mai easily from the crowds. She is sitting in a booth all by herself, absently stirring a tall-glassed drink with a straw.

'Are you sure you'll be all right?'

'Yes.'

'I could stay, at another table. Just in case.'

'No, Mama. It's fine.'

The lines across my mother's forehead give away her feelings, but she nods, and pushes me towards the table. A waitress scoots out of the way as we approach, gives my mother the sympathetic smile. I wish I could do this by myself, at least, but my arms don't have the strength.

Mai looks up and waves shyly.

'Hi,' I say, as Mama parks my chair at the end of the table. 'You remember my mother?'

'Abe-san.' Mai bows her head. 'I trust that you are well.'

'Yes. Thank you.' My mother sidesteps, so she's facing me, and says, 'I won't be far. If you need anything—'

'*Yes*, Mama.'

Her fingers rest against my arm, just for a second, and then she's gone.

I grin at Mai, relieved. 'Hi,' I say again, and then,

because her eyes are trailing after my mother, 'Sorry. She *had* to come.'

'It's OK.' Her voice is small, and she ducks her head, looking at me over thick black eyelashes. 'How are you?'

'All right, thanks. You?'

'I don't think your mother has forgiven me for the last time we met.'

'It's not that. She just worries about leaving me.'

Mai glances at my chair, my hands limply resting in my lap. 'How are you really?'

'It's getting worse. But I'm managing.'

She looks away, her eyes betraying the guilt, pity. And then, 'Shall I order you something?'

She can't wait to get away. 'Please.'

'What would you like? Coffee? Milkshake? Ice cream?'

I twist my head and shoulders to look at the menu which hangs over the bar. 'Root beer float, please?'

Mai's nose wrinkles.

'What?'

'Root beer? It tastes like medicine.'

'As someone who takes rather a lot of medications, I can promise it doesn't.'

Shock passes across her face as she tries to work out whether I am serious. I smile wider, and she visibly deflates, then grins at me. 'Be right back.'

I let the hubbub re-enter my consciousness and relax me: the twang of American guitars playing through the jukebox, the laughter, the whirr of milkshake blenders. I inhale the smell of fabricated joy – sugared, greasy, leather-seated joy.

'Heeeeey, man.' Kaito slips into the seat beside me, and slinks down so low that his head is level with the table.

'Hi. Mai has just gone to the bar. She won't be long.'

'Yeah. I saw her on the way over. So how are things?'

'OK, thanks. You?'

'Yeah. We should meet like this more often. I mean, the chatroom's great, but there's *milkshake* here!'

'It *is* nice.'

He picks up a drinks mat and taps out a rhythm against the table's edge. He's staring into nothing, completely at ease. My foot joins in – nothing moves, but I can feel the muscles dancing underneath my skin.

'Have you been in here before?'

'No. You?'

'No. I like it, though.'

'Me too. It smells like fun.' I hear the words leaving my mouth, and they sound so stupid. As though I have never been anywhere, or spoken to another human being before. 'I mean—'

'Yeah. The Americans get some things really right. Not all things, but this – *this* is brilliant.'

'What's brilliant?' Mai asks, returning with two glasses in hand. 'Root beer for you' – she places it in front of me – 'and a strawberry-mint milkshake.' She slides it across the table and Kaito catches it, raises the straw to his lips.

'Wait wait wait!' she squeals. He stops dead. 'A toast! To us, the – what did you call us? The Gleesome Threesome.'

'To us!'

Kaito slurps loudly. 'You know, I think our name could use some work.'

Mai giggles. 'I am *so* glad you're both here. Now, Sora, tell me alllll about your holiday!'

I recount the tale of the bakeneko and Cat Twenty-three,

and Mai gasps and giggles in all the right places whilst Kaito spurs her on. It's perfect. And for five beautiful minutes, I feel like me again.

And then I remember.

'Mai . . .'

'Yes?'

'Wasn't there something you wanted to tell us?'

The laughter drains away immediately, leaving a thin nervousness hanging in the air.

'Ye-es,' she sighs.

Kaito sets down his drink and leans towards her, fingers steepled in anticipation.

'Go on?'

'I . . .'

I watch her chest flutter as she inhales, and I feel like someone's scooped out my insides and left me empty. What *is* it, Mai?

'Oh, guys, it's *terrible*!'

What?

She looks at each of us in turn, and when she speaks again she's calm, but her voice carries a weight which does not fit her appearance. 'My mother, she . . . we had this big argument and she took my internet away until I'd thought about my choices. She says you're all a bad influence.'

Kaito grins. 'I mean, she isn't *entirely* wrong there, Mai.'

'Yes she is!' Mai huffs, cheeks red. 'And it gets worse. Wait till you hear why we argued . . . She wrote university applications in my name. To study law at Harvard or Oxford. Without telling me. She's made up her mind that it's what I'm going to do, and nothing I can do will stop it.'

'She can't! You can't! What about your *art*?'

'Yeah! Can't you stand up to her?'

Mai shakes her head sadly. 'I tried. My mother is determined. Once she has made up her mind, that's it. And she's already sent the applications. But I *can't* be a lawyer. I can't!'

I imagine Mai sitting at the back of an old Oxford classroom filled with wooden chairs which glow warm in the sun, and air so thick with knowledge that it wraps itself around you like a woollen blanket. But Mai is not comforted by this place. Chained to her desk, she glances up at the high windows, watches the dust motes and the clouds scudding by on the other side of the glass. She needs to be free.

'No.' I shake my head defiantly. 'You won't have to. We will think of something. Won't we, Kai?'

'Yes!' He sits up straight. 'The Gleesome never turn down a fight. And with all our superhero super-sleuthing powers, we will find a way to fix this.'

'Thanks.' She smiles, but she does not look too sure.

'It'll be OK, Mai.'

She's facing Kaito, but her eyes slide sideways to me and her shoulders sink. 'Yeah, maybe.'

Are you sure you're all right, Mai? Is something else wrong?

It just seemed like there was something you weren't saying.

No, I'm fine.

You forget, I am the High Emperor of Secrets.

Ha!

I just . . . I can't do it, Sora. I can't sit in a stuffy office all day, looking at hundred-year-old laws and fixing disputes between angry neighbours. But I can't tell her, either. The disappointment would destroy her.

I don't know that I buy it. There was more. But I can't exactly call my friend a liar.

50

Dear Sora,
Your mother tells me that you're struggling to write now.
Struggle is good for the soul, we know that, but it's not
good for the fingers. And truth be told, my old hands
are rusty too. So your illustrious grandmother went out
and bought a new-fangled contraption called a Pee See?
Perhaps you'll teach us how to use it.

We love you,
Ojiisan
(and Bah-Ba)

Ojiisan,
Computers are strange and mythical beasts, more
temperamental than the thunder god Raijin. Don't
worry if yours starts to grumble. It's their nature.
But there are things you can do which will appease
it. They like things orderly; the same requests
and orders every time. Find a way to complete
tasks that works, and stick to it. Here are some
suggestions.

Sora

I print out step-by-step instructions: how to turn on the computer, open up the browser, sign up for an email account, send mail, use the search bar. And as an afterthought I tell him where to download mah-jong. I know they can both play with real tiles, but perhaps they'll like it. And they will not argue over who is winning if the computer keeps tally.

51

What if we kidnap you?

(-: It's a nice idea, but to where?)

Um . . . I could hide you in the closet?

We're trying to free her, Kai, not condemn her.

You're right. And I don't think the police would be impressed. I'm not ready for incarceration. Not even for friendship.

I mean . . . there are CRIMINALS in there.

Hah. Thanks, boys. That's a lot of help :-p

Sorry Mai. You wouldn't want me to rot behind bars, though, would you? 0_0

Hahahaha, no.

So whatever plan we come up with, it has to be legal.

And preferably not hurt anybody.

Yeah, OK.

What if you write to the universities and tell them what has happened?

Yeah, that could work.

But I cannot bring shame upon my family like that.

She brought it upon herself, if you ask me. But I'm not sure I could do it either, so I stay silent.

OK, OK, I think I've got it!

What?

Well, these places are prestigious, yes?

Yes.

So even if they like you – I mean, your mother's picture of you – they will want to interview, right?

I think so.

So all you have to do is make them think you are a lazy student, or not interested, or less clever than they thought.

That might actually work

But . . .

What? There is NOTHING wrong with that plan. Nothing.

Except that my mother's savings, and my grandfather's, will go into the plane tickets if we have to interview.

Maybe the universities will interview by phone call?

Maybe. But then my mother will be listening.

Besides, I am a terrible, terrible liar.

Then we're back to the beginning. I still think you should tell her how you feel. It has to be better than lying.

52

'Mama?'

'Yes?'

Her breath is warm against my neck as she unbuttons my shirt.

'Would you want to know if I was unhappy?'

She smooths my collar and steps back, searching my face whilst a thousand emotions cloud hers.

'Of course.'

I wish that I could tell her about Mister Yamada. I wish I could explain how it feels to be caught in this cage of aches and limitations, how it feels to know what is to come. How I wanted so much more.

'I . . . I'm not actually talking about me. It's a friend.'

'Oh?' I do not think she believes me.

'It's Mai . . .'

'Oh, Sora, don't you think that you have troubles enough, without taking on somebody else's?' She puffs out her chest, and reaches for the last of the buttons on my shirt, moves behind me to shrug the cloth from my shoulders. 'Lift.' I lift first my right arm, then the left, as she peels the sleeves away. It is an effort.

'Please, Mama.'

She sighs. 'What is it?'

'If I wanted to do something, a big *life* something – true love, ambitions, career choice – would you try to stop me?'

She considers, and I do not think she's going to answer

me, but then: 'I'd want the best for you, Sora. Every mother does. And if your choices are not good ones, it is my job to see that you are steered right.'

But how can she *know* what's right? How can anybody know?

I scowl, and my mother's face softens. 'But if there was a chance, no, I would not stop you. Ready?'

I nod, and my mother stands before me, uses her shoulders to take the weight of my chest and lift me from the chair. And as I plop, dead weight, onto the mattress, she whispers, 'I would give you the moon, you know.'

53

After my mother said goodnight, and switched off my light, I heard her sinking to the floor outside my room, holding her breath so I would not hear her tears. But I heard the absence of them. I almost cried out, just so she'd come in, but I could not.

She would not want me to know.

But it got me thinking, about Mister Yamada, lying in his bed, in that room, trying to sleep in a place where death and despair hang in every breath of air. Alone.

It isn't right.

I lay there all night, and by the time the sun rose, I'd made up my mind.

I can't fix everything, but he does not have to be alone.

The wheels of my chair hum against the hospital floor as we approach Doctor Kobayashi's office.

There it is. The ward.

'Stop.'

'What is it?' My mother halts, panic in her voice.

'I need to go in there.'

'Where?'

'There. That room. Please.'

My mother, confused, does not question me, and as she presses the intercom buzzer, her words echo in my ears. *I would give you the moon.* My throat is sharp and tight, my face hot.

'Hello?' A woman's voice speaks through the box.

'Please, my son . . . he needs to . . .' She looks at me.

'I need to see the patient in bed one. Yamada-san.'

'He needs to see a Mister Yamada. I believe he's in this ward.'

The connection is cut, and we're left with silence.

My mother buzzes again, but nobody answers. My heart sinks.

'Sorry, Sora. Perhaps we can try again after your appointment.'

'Thanks.'

She kicks off the first of my brakes before the ward door clicks open and a nurse's face pops out.

'Hello?'

'Hello.' I bow.

'You're here for Yamada Eiji-san?' She looks worried.

'Yes.'

'I . . . I'm sorry. Are you family?'

'No. I am a friend.'

'I . . . I am afraid you are too late. Mister Yamada passed away this morning.'

No.

No. He can't have.

He can't have died alone.

I can feel the heat rising behind my eyes. But what right do I have to cry? I did not even know him.

I swallow hard before I try my voice. I am surprised to find it works. 'Was he at peace?'

She looks at my chair, and then at my mother, before she answers steadily, 'It was . . . a complex illness.'

My mother's hand finds my shoulder and squeezes until it hurts.

'What does that mean?'

'I'm sorry. I can only discuss this with family.'

'Please. I need to know. *Please.*'

'I wasn't on shift, but his breathing had been getting worse. I'm sorry, I really cannot tell you any more.'

'Thank you,' my mother says, and starts us down the hall before I can protest.

Whilst we're waiting for Doctor Kobayashi, my mother asks, 'Did you know him?'

I think about last night, and wonder whether Yamada Eiji could feel me thinking of him. Whether he knew that someone cared.

I hope so.

'Not really. I met him once.'

She nods, as though that makes it a little better. But it doesn't.

54

Mai is the first online, and I'm so glad to see her. I send her a message almost before she's properly logged in.

> **Hi**
> *Hi :)*
> *All right?*
> **Not really**

I hear the *clink* of a new message, but I cannot see the words. Tears fall down my face, wet the collar of my T-shirt, sticky and shameful.

I know Mai's asking what is wrong, but I don't know what to say.

That a man I did not know just died?

It's stupid. And I can't explain.

And it wouldn't matter even if I could because he's *dead*. Words won't change a thing.

Clink.

Clink.

CLINK.

Is it possible for those sound effects to become insistent? Louder?

I squeeze my eyes shut, to force away the tears.

> *What's wrong? Sora?*
> *All right, that's it . . .*

My cellphone rings loudly, startling me.

It's Mai.

'Hello?' My voice shakes.

'Sora! What is it?'

'I . . .'

She waits for me to answer, her breathing heavy with anticipation, and I imagine I can hear her heart beating through the phone.

'What on earth is *wrong*, Sora? Talk to me!'

'I . . . I don't want to die *alone*!' The last word comes out as a wail.

'What?' She's shocked, and I'm instantly sorry, but I cannot stop.

'I don't want to die alone, and I don't want to die like that.'

'Like what? What's happened?'

'Nothing. I just . . . I'm *scared*, Mai.'

'You are not going to die alone, Sora. I'm not going anywhere, and neither's Kaito, or your mother.'

'But I'm still going to die, aren't I? You can't stop it. And it's horrible. It's so *ugly* and *raw* and *I don't want it.*'

'I know, Sora. I know.'

We sit, saying nothing, and as I cry an ocean's worth of silent tears, I think she's crying with me.

55

What are you both doing next Sunday afternoon?

Um . . . I should be studying.

Can you study later?

Whaaat? The Great Mai of Legendary Grades wants to abandon the books?

Yes. Please. It's important.

Sora? Can you make it?

I'd have to ask Mama if she can take me wherever it is, but I think so.

We'll pick you up (:

So, 3, at Sora's apartment?

OK.

OK.

What's so important?

You'll see (:

Um, Mai . . . is this going to be a better surprise than the last time?

I promise.

OK then.

56

'Abe-san.' My friends bow in unison when my mother opens the door.

'Do you want to come in, or are you in a hurry?'

Initially, my mother forbade me from going out without her. *It isn't safe*, she argued. *What if something happens?*

But for once, I argued back, and in the end she used my cellphone to call Mai and ask where we'd be going, and what time we'd return.

She actually grinned at the answer.

'We should go.'

'Then I insist you stay for tea on your return. Sora, you have your wallet? Phone?'

'Yes, Mama.'

'OK, then.' She moves out of the doorway, and lets Kaito take the helm.

As soon as our front door is closed, Kaito starts running down the hall towards the elevator.

'Whoa! What's the hurry?'

'No hurry, just excitement,' he says, breathless, as we're forced to stop and wait for the lift.

Mai catches up with us seconds later. 'Maniacs,' she laughs.

In the elevator, Kaito flexes his muscles, posing in the mirrored walls like some sort of cartoon strongman.

'Oh yeah, like you have the physique for that!'

He reels back in mock offence, but he cannot keep up the expression, and his face breaks into a grin.

'Nerd.'

'Thank you.' He bows.

Never has the journey out of the building gone so fast, felt so light, and suddenly we're wheeling out into the autumn sunshine.

'So where are we going?' I ask.

Mai skips excitedly, and claps her hands together like a little girl on too much sugar. 'I'm taking you both out for ice cream.'

'Ice cream?' I can hear the puzzlement in Kaito's voice. 'What's so important about ice cream?'

She pirouettes on the spot, and fixes him with an intense stare. 'Kaito, Kaito, Kaito, *everything* about ice cream is important. It is a healer. A joy bringer. A magical cure-all.'

'You sound like a crazy old woman,' he laughs. 'Three sips of this lizard-oil at sundown and your health shall be restored.'

'Haha, it's exactly like that. I *dare* you to be sad after ice cream.'

'Point taken. Although . . . I'm not sad in the first place.'

Mai's eyes flick to me and I shake my head, the tiniest of movements. But she sees.

I do not want to have to explain it all again.

'Well, then it's a preventative measure. I like my friends happy.'

It really is warm out here, and the sweet, sunned air bounces off the pavement.

'I think it's a brilliant idea, Mai. And perfect weather for it too.'

'Yes!'

'So where are we going? Anywhere particular?'

'Nope. I thought we'd just walk along and pick the first place which sells ice cream that we like.'

'OK then.' Kaito marches forward, a spring in his step that I can feel in the way he pushes my chair.

Mai prances around us, almost dancing, and I watch the way her plaited hair bounces off her shoulders, the way her polka-dot skirt flares with every turn. The way her eyes crinkle at the edges when she smiles.

'There!' Mai points across the street to a small, brightly lit parlour called the Happy Cone, with a cat painted on the sign. In the window is a poster which reads EVERY FLAVOUR YOU IMAGINE.

The vendor is an old man, who nods kindly as we enter.

'What can I get you young things?'

Kaito pushes me up to the counter so I can see what's on offer. There are at least fifty flavours, and as many choices again in topping form. There's coconut, vanilla and peach-raspberry, and at the far end sweet potato, wasabi-chocolate, tea and squid ink.

'Chocolate, chocolate-chip for me, please,' Kaito says. With . . . cherry sauce.'

The old man nods, and heaps three generous scoops into a bowl.

'What would you like, Sora?' Mai asks.

'Can I mix flavours?'

The man nods.

I scan the rows again, imagining each flavour in turn as I try to decide. 'Then . . . a coffee cream, a blackberry, aaaand' – finally my eyes settle on the brightest green tub – 'lime. Thank you.'

'And I'll have strawberry please. With lemon sprinkles.'

We settle at the table by the window, and for a moment we're each lost in the sensory pleasure of sweet-tart mouthfuls, cold on the tongue, melting as we swallow.

Mai's right. Nobody can be sad over a bowl of ice cream.

'So,' she says, looking up from her dish, 'if you were an ice-cream flavour, what would you be?'

Kaito leans back in his chair, rests his arms behind his head, and drawls, 'Well, since I'll be roughly eighty per cent chocolate by the time I finish this bowl, I think that's my answer. It's probably your basic village-boy answer, but it's true. I *like* chocolate.'

'OK. Sora?'

'Errr, squid ink. I'm an acquired taste.'

'Hah. I *dare* you to try it!'

'Umm . . . maybe later. Go on, your turn.'

Mai glances at the counter with its rainbow of flavours. 'I don't even knooooow.'

'Come on, you can't ask us and not have an answer yourself!'

'But there's so many! And I don't know who I am, at all.'

'I do.' Kaito's voice is soft. 'You'd be something sweet, but fresh. Peach. With warm buttered-toast croutons on top.'

Her cheeks flare, and she bites her bottom lip, embarrassed. But he's right. That is exactly what she'd be.

'OK, next question. If you could do anything before you die' – they look at me nervously, but I continue – 'what would it be.'

'Does it have to be realistic?'

'No. Anything.'

They think for a while, and I scoop up another mouthful of ice cream – a little of each, all on the spoon together. I swirl the flavours around my tongue until, separate at first, they all melt into one another and become something new.

Mai pulls a pen from somewhere and starts doodling on a napkin as she thinks. I try not to look, but her swift, confident strokes are arresting and I cannot help it.

On the back wall, behind the old man, there is a painted mural of a smiling cat and his canary friends all dining on a giant bowl of multi-coloured, cherry-topped ice cream. But in Mai's version, they are standing not around dessert, but around a gravestone.

She sees me looking and she shelters the paper behind her arm, but she does not stop. After a while, she speaks. 'I'd travel around the world drawing everything I see, and then I'd turn my experiences into an animated film: *Little Monkey Sees the World*.'

'I'd go to see that.'

'Me too.'

She smiles shyly. 'Kai?'

'I'd join the circus. Be an acrobat, flying through the air, all muscles and dexterity and grace.' He stops, registering the disbelief on Mai's face. 'Hey! What? He said it didn't have to be real, and an acrobat is everything I'm not. Besides, it looks like fun.'

'I'm sorry.' Mai bows her head, but I think I see her trying not to laugh. 'Sora?'

I have a hundred thousand wishes, but they're too heavy for a day like this. I will not let them ruin it.

'This.' I shrug. 'Sitting in the sun over ice cream with my friends.'

'You wouldn't . . . Oh, I don't know, travel back in time to meet the samurai? Or go to Paris? Or—'

'No.'

'All right, mister.' Mai comes to my rescue. 'Let's make this day even better. Squid-ink ice cream. Do you dare?'

'What universe do you live in where squid ink makes things better?'

'Hahaha. All right. More interesting, then. Memories, Sora, it's all about forming the memories.'

'OK.'

'Really?'

'Absolutely. I will if you will.'

Her nose wrinkles all the way up, but she nods, gathers our empty bowls, and heads over to the counter.

'Three bowls of squid-ink ice cream please.'

'Three?' Kaito protests. 'I don't remember agreeing to that!'

'Oh, come *on*. We're making *memories,* Kai. You can't miss out on this.'

'I could.'

'No! You'll regret it, when we're back at home.'

He sighs, but when she brings over three bowls, he takes his without further complaint.

The ice cream is a silky grey, and sits in the bowl like smooth pebbles.

'Here we go,' I say.

The others dig their spoons into the dessert too.

I lift mine to my nose and sniff. It smells like cinder toffee and the sea. At the same time. My mouth waters.

'Are we sure about this?' Kaito asks, eyeing the lump on his spoon.

'Yes,' says Mai. 'One, two, three.'

Spoons raise, mouths open. In.

I watch the others' faces try to work around uncertainty, revulsion, shock, then pleasure. Like children with sweet lemons.

It is exactly how I imagined, and yet not at all. The saltiness of it fizzes on my tongue, and then there is the weight of sugar. Caramel.

'Hey! This is good.'

Mai giggles. And Kaito joins in. And behind the counter the old man smiles.

Yes. This is what I'd do with my last days.

57

Almost before the door is closed Doctor Kobayashi says, 'I heard about Yamada Eiji's passing. I'm sorry.'

I shrug. 'I didn't know him.'

'No.' She pauses, offers me a sympathetic smile. 'But in a way, you did.'

'I just . . .'

'Yes?'

How do I explain it?

This room, with its neatly ordered files and tiny tree, is too small for my fears. Too *safe* to set them free.

Which makes no sense, even to me, but it is true.

'I don't know.'

'It's hard, right?'

'Yes.'

She continues. 'Watching someone suffer, watching them die, it changes you.'

'Yes.'

I think she suggests strategies that I could use to cope – write poetry, or go for long walks underneath the trees – but I don't really hear.

I am too busy with one thought.

My mother.

She watches me dying a little every day. And if I feel like this after one encounter . . . I am going to destroy her.

58

I am actually maybe going insane imagining where those applications might be sitting right now. On a plane. In a sorting office. In a dean's office. Oh! It's awful.

Tell her.

I can't, Sora. I . . . I have to do this.

Right. That's it. When are you free? We're going fishing.

Fishing?

Fishing?

Yes! All three of us. As soon as we can. Fishing helps relax the mind, right?

I suppose.

No relaxing of the mind for me. My mother has my tutor coming over allll weekend, to practise interviews.

:(

Maybe next week, if I can impress her, make her think I'm ready.

You can. You're brilliant. Next weekend then. :)

59

'This is nice, huh?'

The three of us, Mai, Kaito and myself, are sitting on a roof terrace in the centre of the city. Below us are power lines and streets bustling with traffic, but we are in a tiny scrap of paradise: green, fake grass, crisscrossing a grid of deep blue pools. The silver tails and bubble-mouths of koi flick across the surface. There are a few other people here, mostly by themselves, staring deep into the water, but it doesn't matter. It might as well be our own private world.

'Yes.' Mai leans back on her hands, stretches out her legs so that they cast shadows out across the water.

A curious carp nuzzles the surface, perhaps thinking she has food.

'Yeah.' Kaito sighs, and jiggles his plastic rod.

'You won't catch anything like that.' Mai giggles.

Across the terrace a businessman cheers noisily as his catch is weighed and then released back into the pool. There is a game to be played up here – fish for prizes, and that guy just won big.

'I had you marked as the competitive type, Kai,' I say, remembering conversations about bonus levels and epic fights.

'Out here, no. This place isn't about scores. It's about the bigger catch.'

'The what?'

'The bigger catch.'

She looks across at him blankly.

'Life.'

'Oh . . . wait. Isn't it about *escaping* life for a while?'

'Yes. But I don't mean that. I mean, this, here, us . . . It's not about the game, it's the *experience* of sitting here, on fake grass, high up in the clouds, and talking to your friends.'

Mai smiles serenely and dips a toe into the water.

I imagine the Emperor-fish swimming beneath her. Although he could never live in a place like this, I think he would approve of us taking the time to *be*.

We sit for a while. Kaito sips from a soda can, and Mai leans back and stares up at the sky.

'There's a dragon!' she says, pointing to a giant fluffy cloud.

I crane to see. 'That's no dragon. It's an elephant.'

'No way!'

'It is far too plump to be a dragon! Don't you think, Kai?'

'Nooo,' Mai protests. 'It's a very well-fed dragon. He ate lots of sheep-clouds. And foolish nay-saying teenagers.'

'All right, all right. It's a dragon!' I concede.

'Thank you!' she chirps. 'And that one's a— *Aaurgh!*' She bolts upright, frantically wiping her face. 'That was *rain*!'

As I look up, the dragon-elephant is swept away, replaced by a roiling black sky, and before we have a chance to move, it falls.

Mai screams, covering her head with bare arms. Rain rumbles against concrete and water and plastic. It pockmarks skin and flattens clothes in seconds.

'Let's go!' Mai scrambles for our things as Kaito hits my brakes, and we run for the awning at the far end of the rooftop.

We huddle, along with a few sad-looking businessmen in water-heavy ties, shivering as the rain hammers at the plastic overhead. Mai hugs herself tightly, and Kai shifts from one foot to the other. We're wet, and cold, and sticky-heavy-gross. And as I watch the water bouncing off the tumultuous pools, I laugh.

'What?'

'It's just . . . it's not about the game. It's about—' I snicker, and when I finally muster the breath to speak, my friends' voices join mine: 'The *experience*.'

60

'Oh my goodness, Sora! What happened to you?'

'It rained.' I cannot keep the smile from my lips, as I remember the feel of it against my skin, and the three of us huddled together like penguins.

'I can see that. Didn't you take shelter? You're soaked right through!'

'It was fast.' I shrug.

'For goodness' sake. Come inside. You need to get out of those clothes. I'm sorry' – she nods towards my friends – 'but Sora has to go now.'

My friends step back and let her bustle me inside.

'That's all right. We'll see you soon, Sora,' Kaito mumbles. My mother is already closing the door.

'Mama!'

'You're shivering, Sora.'

She peels my jacket from my skin, and I see the gooseflesh on my arms. She's right. And I feel it, all at once, a cold that reaches right into the marrow of my bones. How did I not feel cold before?

'Come on. Let's get you to the shower.'

She wheels me to the bathroom, and turns on the water before removing my T-shirt and helping me stand. My jeans feel like they hold a lake of water, and I wonder how my mother lifts me up, but with my weight leaned against her she unbuttons my jeans and helps me out of them before setting me back into my chair and pushing me beneath the warm jets of the shower.

'Can you manage?' she asks.

Truthfully, it is getting harder. The soap is slippery, and my arms are weak and stupid. But I am not ready for that yet. Besides, all I want is to get warm.

I nod, and she steps outside.

I sit, let the water hug my skull and pour over my back until I notice just how cold my legs are, and I twist a little so the water can warm them too.

The water from the shower feels nothing like the rain. Not just warmer. Softer too. As though it's freshly laundered. I sit here, the water warming me through piece by piece, and imagine Kaito and Mai and me sitting not in the rain but in a sauna, staring at steam clouds on the ceiling.

That one is a baby! Look!'

Warm water traces the outline of my smile.

Finally, when I'm sure the shivering has stopped, I shut the water off and reach for the towel hanging on the door. I rub myself down as best I can with clumsy hands. 'Ready, Mama.'

And my mother slides back into the room, ready to help me dress.

Ten minutes later, we are in the kitchen and my mother passes me a cup of tea.

'Here. To warm you on the inside.'

'Thanks.' I take a sip. She has sweetened it with honey.

I sip, and sip, and my mother leans her head against her hands and watches me.

'Better?' she asks after a while.

'Yes. Thank you.'

'Good. You know, I was worried about you for a while, but you seem to have made good with those two.'

Even though I came back soaked and freezing? I do not think my mother knows how to be sarcastic . . .

'Yes?'

'Yes. I like them. Especially the girl.' My mother smiles extra broadly, and the air hums with the insinuation.

Oh.

'Mama, we're just friends, that's all.' I picture Mai, twirling across the street. I see her in the ice-cream shop, hiding her smile behind both hands as she laughs. But my words are true. I want nothing more from her.

'And quite right. But if you *were* to choose a girl, you should go for one like that.'

'Mother!' I protest, but I do not really mind. It is a long time since we've talked like this.

'All right, all right. Anyway, I approve. There is a colour to your cheeks tonight, and I do not think it's just the cold. I think they're good for you.'

And I think perhaps she's right.

61

It is Monday, less than twenty-four hours since I saw my friends, but I miss them already. As I wait for them to finish with their days and reappear online, I imagine us walking through school hallways side by side, sharing jokes, swapping notes. My chair wouldn't matter. Nothing would. It would be so obvious that I belonged there with them that nobody would bat an eye.

I wish.

At least we have the internet. And today Mai cheers me up the second she appears.

Hiiiii! Before we do anything else, I just want to say . . .
You guys are the best thing that's ever happened to me.
<3 <3 <3 (-:

:-) Me too.

Hi guys! Did I miss anything? Sorry I'm late – I was at a club meeting!
You're not late.

What club?

I joined the Computer Club! :D
Oooh, look at you, Mister Programmer.

I know! The Society of Gamers kicked me out, so I needed to find another club.
Ah, I'm sorry.

I'm not. They're right. I haven't been playing much. And there's no point being there if I can't argue about new releases or beat their scores.

Haha, OK. So. They kicked you out and you joined Computer Club instead?

Yep.

How was it?

I thought it would be terrible.

I thought it would be full of awkward nerds and nobody would talk to me and they'd all think I was dumb.

hehehe

WHAT? O_o

Well, it's just . . .

You ARE kind of a nerd, K. <3

Yeah, but these are SERIOUS nerds. Nerds with qualifications. They can DO stuff. But they're so cool! And none of them minded that I'm only a beginner. And they're going to show me how to make better things!

That's brilliant!

Anyway, Mai's right. If it weren't for you both, I would never have thought to go in there. Never had the confidence to either.

Awwww ^_^ <3

That's great, Kai.

Yeah :D :D :D

Oh also . . . look:

USERNAME NoFaceßoy	
TAG-LINE If it ain't broke, I didn't build it.	
AGE 17 **GENDER** Male	

INTERESTS Computers, the internet, programming, code. I want to build beautiful things from secret languages.

If you could be anything in the world, what would you be?

Me. I have great friends, and a new gameplan. An Evil Mastermind plan. I, my lovelies, am going to TAKE OVER THE WORLD (or at least the internet and gaming worlds).

I thought it was time to let the world know who I am.

To:	S ...
From:	O_K_H@ ...
Subject:	I AM S ENDIN G YOU THIS MESSAGE SITTING in the hAllway wearing my pyjamas. Not even dressed! I HOPEYOUA re well. Ojiisan/

To:	O_K_H@ ...
From:	S ...
Subject:	Your first reply!

Dear Ojiisan!

You did it! I'm emailing you from my room. I'm not in my pyjamas though. You win.

Now you've figured out how to email, we can take over the world much faster. Brilliant!

Sora

PS Have you tried the mah-jong yet?

To: S . . .

From: O_K_H@ . . .

Subject: MAH–JONG

WOW! SO FAST! I THINK MAYBE THESE ELECTRONIC MAILS ARE ACTUALLY CARRIED BY RAIJIN. THEY ARE QUICKER THAN LIGHTNING!

AND YES BUT YOUR GRANDMOTHER KEEPS YELLING THAT THE COMPUTER DOES NOT KNOW ALL THE RULES AND THAT IT'S CHEATING IN MY FAVOUR. SHE'S JUST JEALOUS BECAUSE I ALWAYS WIN.

OJIISAN

'Hey, Mama, Ojiisan's entered the twenty-first century!'

'What?'

'It's true, look.' And I pull up the emails on my phone, and hold them out to her.

'Oh *my*! Your grandfather? On a computer? On the *internet*? Do you realize what you've done, Sora? The world's a thousand times less safe than it was yesterday!' But beneath the shock and horror I think that's a grin.

'Isn't it wonderful?'

'Sure, if you like your inbox filled with questions about the air pollution and whether you've asked for a raise yet.'

'It's OK, I told him how to search too, so he can find at least half of it out himself. He'll never have to ask you!'

She smirks. 'Did I ever tell you about the time your grandfather took out the whole street's electricity?'

'No!'

'Oh yes. He bought a new electric saw for his shed. It was fast and shiny and it *whirred* when you switched it on. Absolutely lethal. But your grandfather loved the idea that he could do six times as many projects for the same amount of time . . . but that wasn't enough. He found out a way to make it *faster*.'

'Eeee!'

'Exactly. So he tinkered, and it *was* faster, but when applied to actual wood, when it had to *cut* things . . . it exploded. Took out the power for a week.'

Whoa.

She sighs. 'This is going to be like that. He'll probably break the *internet*.'

Is she joking? I can't tell.

'Oh, and Sora? I am fielding any and all tech queries to you.'

63

> *So I got an email today, from Yale.*
> **Oh Mai!**

Jealousy drops into my stomach like a stone. And then it's gone. I *can't* be jealous of Mai.

> *And they want to interview me for a place on their law programme. It's a video-conference interview, and my mother's already planning cue cards. She says she'll sit behind the web-cam and help make sure I give myself the best possible chance. I'm doomed to success!*
> *And I can't do it. I just CAN'T.*
> *Are you up for meeting? I need ice cream.*
>
> **Yes!**
> Absolutely!

...**64**

> I just don't understand why you won't tell her, Mai. I'm
> sorry.
> *You wouldn't, would you?*

I stare at the words. Stung.

> I'm sorry?
> *It's just . . . you don't have to worry about any of this.*

What?

> No. I don't. But I wish I fucking did.

Silence.

> *I'm sorry. I didn't mean that quite the way I sounded. I just . . .*
> Yes?

She hesitates again.

> *I can't do it, Sora. I can't.*
> Why?
> *Because of everything. Because my mother expects the best from
> me, and she worries, and she has invested time and money and
> she's right, it's hard, and irresponsible, and I can't do anything
> else, but every time I think of pulling out I think of you, and all*

those schools, their history and dusty stupid books, and how you should be there. You should be going and you won't, but I can and I . . . I have to go. Don't you see?

Oh, Mai.

No.

No.

Please, no.

That's my dream, not yours. And if you want to do something for me, you follow that. The last thing I want is for you to wear a dream that doesn't fit.

Please.

Ehhhhhh.

Please? If you have to do this, don't do it for me.

'Mama?'

'Hmm.'

'Have you ever been to a funeral?'

It was a long, late night for me, and I think she heard me. She peers at me with one eye open. 'Sora—'

'Have you? Please? I want to know.'

She takes a long, deep sip of coffee. 'Yes.'

'Whose was it?'

'I'm *tired*, Sora, and I have to go to work.'

'Please?'

'My Uncle Shiro. And your great-grandparents.'

'What's it like?'

'*Sora.*'

I can imagine. Of course I can. I know how they prepare the body, hold a wake, where everyone who comes gives and receives gifts. I know about the incense and the payment for the River of Three Hells. The verses that the priest recites, the renaming, the picking of the bones.

I can imagine grief. Heartache. Duty.

But I do not *know*, and Mama is not talking.

66

> **Hey you two!**
> *Hiiii*

gvh
Delete.
huy
Delete.
I try and I try, but my fingers will not work, will not operate the keys. It's like they're dead and wooden, and ten times their usual size.

> **Sora?**
> **You there?**

uydess
Three days ago, I was just a little clumsy. Tired.
Yuwsss
DAMN IT! Why won't you even type one simple word?
I hate you I hate you I hate you!
I hit the keyboard harder, as though sheer force could will the words onto my screen. But it does not. And when tears of frustration sting my cheeks, I realize this isn't helping. I need my fingers to be calm and steady. I lift my hands away from the keyboard and I breathe. In. Out. Slowly as I can.

In. Out.

In. I stretch my fingers and feel the pull of reluctant

tendons. I grab my right hand with my left and guide a
pointed finger towards the keys.

Hi

I stab out, one letter at a time.

I'm here.

Hi :)

Thought you'd gone for a moment.

No. I'm just

I hit enter, before they get bored of waiting for my
answer.

Fingers

Not

Working

(sorry)

*Oh, Sora! That's awful. Have you got some tablets or something
that will make it better?*

Dude, that's like my worst nightmare.

I know

Mine too.

I think

I'm going

To go

:(

**You sure? We could regale you with tales of woe so terribly woeful
that you'll forget all your problems?**

I'm sure. Frustrating. Better tomorrow I hope.

All right. Phone me if you want to talk rather than type.

Yeah, me too.
Otherwise, we'll see you tomorrow. Check in even if you're not feeling great, please?
OK
Thanks.
You're welcome. xxxxxx
Night dude.

Tonight, I need my mother's help to grasp the tablet-cup, to tip it back without spilling tiny pills across the floor. Her fingers feel heavy and clumsy over mine, like she cannot judge the distance to my lips.

I try not to picture her doing this every night, or at every meal, hovering over me with a spoon. Will I end up like an infant? My mother scraping puree from my chin?

67

When I woke up the next day, I lay there with my eyes squeezed shut, and willed the universe to have reset me in my sleep, to let me wake up fresh and new and able to spring out of bed.

For the longest time, I did not dare move. Because whilst I was staying still – deliberately, perfectly still – it was my choice, and I could jump out of bed, any time I wanted.

But then my side began to cramp, and as I thought of lying there for ever, suddenly it did not feel like freedom any more. It was my future prison.

I blinked in the light and tried to stretch my deadwood limbs, and when they did not move as lithely as I'd hoped, I called my mother to help me get out of my bed.

Part of me had hoped, even then, that when I properly awoke, the energy would flow back into my fingertips, that I would be all right again.

But the universe doesn't grant wishes.

> I don't think we should meet this weekend. I'm sorry.
> *Aw why? What's wrong?*
> ALS is bad
> *:(It won't be the same without you.*

It won't be the same with me, either. I am useless now.

Mai's right. Are you sure you can't manage it? We'll help!

Or we can do something different. We could come to you if you would like!

Yes! We can bring ice cream or coffee or books or ANYTHING.

I don't know

Pleaaaase? We need you.

Unless you're feeling really bad.

No. It's not that.

It's just

You shouldn't have to

Nonsense!

Dude, we're friends. That's what we do.

OK

Yes

I'll come

YES! :)

Yay! Thankyouthankyouthankyou!

But promise me . . .

What?

I remember the look on my classmates' faces when they came to visit. Strangers' pity. The first time I saw Yamada Eiji. And all I can think is: *Don't think any less of me. Please.* But I don't know how to say it, and I know they'd only take it the wrong way.

Nothing

:)

See you then!

68

When we finally leave the apartment, it is with a list of dos and don'ts and emergency numbers as long as my hopeless arms, and I half expect my mother to come chasing after us and drag me back inside.

'I'm sorry,' I say, as we step into the elevator.

Mai frowns. 'What for?'

'My mother. The safety talk.' I glance down at my skinny body, neatly turned out and folded into a chair as though dressing it up could hide its true traitorous nature. '*This*.'

Her frown deepens. 'Don't be ridiculous. She cares about you, that's all.'

'Yeah, and so do we,' adds Kaito. 'So stop brooding, and let's focus on the important thing.'

'What's that?'

'DAY TRIP!' Mai squeals, and Kaito grins at her, blushing.

The elevator dings, stopping to let someone in: an elderly woman I have seen hauling shopping up the stairs.

'So,' Mai continues, 'where do you want to go?'

Her voice is high and loud, and I think I hear the old lady draw an irritated breath, but when I look across at her she does not say a word, just smiles.

I think about all the places we could go: the cinema, the mall, a café. But everywhere will be bustling with weekend crowds, and I do not feel like having all those eyes trail after me. I don't want people; I want sky.

'Can we just go to the park? I feel as though I haven't seen anything living for about a *year*.'

* * *

They say that everything's OK, that they're not shocked or worried by my appearance, but as we walk around the lake they're quiet, and I wonder whether they are wishing themselves somewhere else.

Still, the quiet of the park gets into my lungs, and by the time we're halfway around, I worry less. I watch the clouds scud across the sky, leaving a wintry grey canvas behind, and I watch the water, the way it just touches the edge of the embankment; I imagine dumping one more fish into it, watching as the balance tips and the whole lake overflows.

When we reach the bridge, Mai points at the water. 'Oh, look! Fish! Come on. I bet we can see them better on the bridge.'

We race up the wooden ramp and stop right in the middle of the bridge, looking out at the lake.

'Looook!' Mai squeals. 'They're so pretty! And that one has a star on its head!'

'Yeah. But the one it's picking on doesn't look so good. Oh! Oh! Fish fight!'

I lean closer to the edge, peer through gaps between the railings, but I cannot see.

'Ohhh! Fishy!' wails Mai, as there is a splash below us, and a yellow flash of scales darts hastily away.

'Aaaand, Star Head is victorious!' Kai grins back at me. 'Can you see all right?'

'Yes,' I lie.

'Cool.'

I scan what I can see of the lake for a flash of gold, but all I see are reds and whites. 'Can you see the Emperor-fish?' I ask.

'The what?'

'Oh. The Emperor-fish. He's huge and black and glitter-gold all over.'

'And an emperor?' Kaito looks puzzled.

'I think so. He's special, you know? There's something . . . wise about him.'

He leans back over the bridge and scours the water. 'I can't see him. You, Mai?'

She shakes her head.

Where is he? I was *sure* he would be here, and I want to introduce them. I want to know that they will visit him when I am gone, because . . .

Why?

'When I was little,' Mai says, still gazing into the water, 'I had this game for bridges?'

'Yeah?' Kaito looks across at her, the slightest of smiles on his lips.

'Yes. We'd each – whoever I was with, and me – find a stick, and we'd drop them in on one side, and then run across the bridge to see whose came out first. Oh! Let's do it again!'

'I think,' I say, 'the water in the lake is too still for that.'

'Let's try it anyway.'

She rushes off before I have a chance to argue, but I'm not sure I would anyway.

Kaito turns, rests his back against the bridge and looks at me. 'I like her, Sora.'

'I know.'

'No, I *really* like her.'

'Yes. Your ears go red every time she speaks to you.'

He reaches up and pulls his fringe lower, as though it

will hide his embarrassment. And I'm going to tell him that I think she likes him too, but she's climbing back across the bridge towards us.

'Hold that thought,' I mutter.

'Here!' She thrusts out a hand full of sticks. 'I brought a selection. Sora gets first choice.'

I look down at the sticks; there is a tiny one which would just get lost, a thick, dark one, a twisty silver birch, and three as straight as arrows but of different lengths. Using all my concentration, I lift my arm up and out towards her, pulling against invisible elastic. I try to straighten my fingers but all they do is quiver, stiffen further. It's no use. 'I can't . . .'

'I'll drop it for you.' She pushes her hand closer. 'Go on. Choose.'

There's a note of desperation in her voice, and I cannot refuse. I force myself to smile. 'OK, then. If you promise not to cheat, I'll have the long straight one please.'

Mai places her free hand across her chest. 'I promise. I will drop your stick at the exact same second as mine. Millisecond, even.'

'I want this one!' Kaito grabs the thickest branch.

'Haha. You'll never win with that. Don't you know anything about aerodynamics?' Mai laughs.

'We'll see.' He smiles slyly.

'OK.' Mai pulls out the shortest of the straight sticks and leans out over the bridge as far as she can. 'Ready, Kai?'

He follows suit.

'Three. Two. One. GO.'

Our three sticks hit the water with a gentle *plomp*, and Mai gasps in excitement, stands on her tiptoes and leans even further. She wobbles, and Kaito's hand shoots out to steady her. 'Easy,' he says, and then, 'I don't think they're moving. At all.'

'No, look, that one is! Yours is! Oh.' Her face falls. 'There's a fish underneath it. That probably doesn't count as moving, huh?'

'No.' Kaito shoves playfully against her shoulder, and she shoves back, and for a moment I wonder whether they've forgotten that I'm here at all, but then Mai sighs and turns to face me.

'You were right, mister genius professor, the water is too still. Shall we go?'

'Sorry. Next time I'll try to be wrong.'

She giggles. 'You do that. What next?'

I know what I want to do, but . . . it's weird. Will it be the final straw that drives them both away?

We amble across the bridge and down the path until it splits into three. Kaito stops, awaiting instruction.

OK. OK. I'm going to ask.

'Can we go somewhere quiet? I want you to do something for me.'

'Sure.'

'What is it?' asks Mai.

I swallow down my nerves. 'Read to me?'

'Read to you?' She exhales loudly, 'Oh, Sora, I thought you were going to ask us something terrible!'

'No. I just . . . I miss it. I can't turn the pages any more.'

Her eyes flash with pity, but she blinks it back, and nods. 'I think we can manage that.'

Kaito takes his jacket and spreads it on the grass beneath a flame-red maple, and Mai stretches out across it, lying on her stomach. He flops beside her and rests his hands behind his head as she flits to the first page. And she begins:

'The place I like best in this world is a kitchen . . .'

The book has been sitting in my bag for a while, pulled from the shelf simply as a distraction from hospital corridors. It is not a clever, academic book which will build me into something better with each sentence. I think it may, actually, have been my mother's, but I do not care; I let Mai's voice pull the words around me like a blanket, and I settle down to listen.

She warms quickly to the task, her voice skipping lightly over passages and carrying us away into another world. And when she finally stops, I am surprised at the emptiness of the air around us.

She rolls over and sits up to look at me, a question in her eyes.

'Thank you,' I say quietly. 'That was perfect.'

Beside her, Kaito stretches, groaning. 'Mmm. Don't stop. I want to hear the rest.'

'But we're only halfway through! Anyway, I thought we'd save some for the next time.'

He opens one eye lazily. 'Next time?'

'Yes.'

'Cool . . . this is nice, you know?'

'What?'

'This. Lying here on the grass, hanging out, no pressure.'

'Yes,' she says, and I agree.

We walk back towards the gate along a narrow pathway steeped in gold from the overhead sun. After a few minutes, Mai steps in front of the wheelchair and stops.

'Does it hurt?'

My stomach drops. 'What?'

'I mean . . . when you move your arm, or all the time, or . . . does it hurt? Because,' she adds, her voice so small and sad that it rips at my heart, 'it looks like it hurts.'

I wish that I could tell her the truth: that my morphine pills have steadily increased, that sometimes I wake in the middle of the night, and it feels like knives are pinning me down to the bed, or that today, in the autumn wind, my chest feels three sizes too small. But I cannot.

'Sometimes. Yes.'

'Oh, Sora!'

'It's OK,' I say, but we both know that it's not.

Mai turns, so I cannot see her face.

What have I done? I should have lied. I shouldn't have said anything.

She storms ahead, but only gets a few steps away before she whips back round. The sadness has gone, and in its place is red, raw fury. And she lifts her head to the sky and screams.

'Aaaaaaaaaargh!'

Fear grips me; I'm sure that a hundred people will come running, and a hundred more will turn to stare at the awkward cripple boy who is so damaged that he makes his friends go mad. But when I look around, there's no one there, and I'm flooded with a relief so great that I want to laugh. But I cannot laugh at Mai and so I turn my face to the sky and scream with her.

Behind me, Kaito howls, wolf-like. And the three of us stand here, in the middle of a public park, shattering the air with our emotions. We scream and howl and scream until there's nothing left, and our hearts and lungs are empty.

'Sorry.' Mai giggles nervously.

I grin at her, and Kaito lets out a tiny wolf-howl. And everything's OK again.

We walk a little way to the nearest bench, and sit.

'So what happens next?'

'You mean, symptoms?'

'Yeah.' Kaito nods, and I can tell he really wants to hear this. Needs to. Mai too.

So I take a deep breath, and let the words come out. 'My hands are getting worse. There is a lot that I can't do for myself, and it's going to get harder.'

'So . . . you won't be able to write to us?'

I imagine day after day trapped in my own head as my computer gathers dust just a metre or so away, and my friends trapped inside it, as alone as I am.

'No.'

Mai shakes her head defiantly. 'Then we'll call you. And we will visit.'

'Yeah, we will.' He swallows, hesitant. 'What happens after your arms?'

'Eventually? It will be hard to talk, and swallow, and to breathe.'

Mai squeals, looks away. But Kaito breathes out slowly and continues. 'But you'll be . . . you'll still be *you*, right? Inside?'

'Yes.'

Was that a shudder rippling across his shoulders?

Is he totally repulsed?

'Well,' he says after a moment, 'we're just going to have

to get the most out of everything whilst you still can. Right?'

I nod.

'Right, Mai?' Kaito nudges her affectionately, and she looks up to give me a wobbly smile.

'Yes. The absolutely most! Where shall we start?'

69

'Doctor Kobayashi?' I say as soon as Mama's closed the door behind her, left us alone. I've been steeling myself to ask this question and I cannot risk losing my nerve as we settle down to our routine.

She looks at me, surprised. 'Yes?'

'What do you think happens when you die?'

'How are you this week, Sora? Are things not going well?' She barely misses a beat.

'Please, Doctor. What happens?' Every day, every symptom, brings me closer, and I have to know.

'What do you think?'

Why do the people with all the answers never want to share?

'I wouldn't ask if I knew.'

She isn't going to tell me.

'Well, there are lots of theories.'

'Yes, but . . .' I don't want theories. I want to *know*.

'Some people think that—'

'No!' I clasp a hand over my mouth. What am I doing? How could I be so rude? 'I'm sorry!'

'No, it's all right. Go on . . .'

'Eh, all right. I'm sorry, but I know the theories. I want answers. Why won't anybody *tell* me anything?'

She looks at me with that strange expression of hers, blank but not blank at all, and then her shoulders sag.

'I'm sorry, Sora, I can't give you any answers.'

I growl. It is not intentional.

'I don't have any,' she says. 'Nobody ever comes back to tell me.'

We do not say much else. There's nothing new to say. My legs hurt, and my arms. And yes, they're getting worse and no, there's nothing anyone can do. But she knows all that.

I sit there, staring at the bonsai's twisted branches, its thick, gnarled roots. It is an ugly thing, and yet it is so beautiful.

Strange, that.

And it sounds like something you might read about, in a book of ancient poems:

The most broken, bare of things,
Is the most wondrous.

Stupid.
I try again.

Outside, quiet, but there is a song within.

No.

The gnarly tree
Deadened, goes on living.

Almost, perhaps, but it is too simple. It lacks elegance.
Except . . .
Goes on living? Goes. On . . .
What about people who die and are brought back to life?

239

They must know what's out there, right?

'*Nobody ever comes back to tell me,*' she said. But I bet *they've* told *somebody*.

I think Doctor Kobayashi looks at me strangely when I smile to myself, but she does not say a word.

Finally, the clock hits target, and I'm free. I cannot wait to get home and look this up.

'Thanks,' I grin, as she escorts me out.

'What for?' She sounds confused, but there's no time on the clock left to explain.

* * *

 life after death

does not bring me any more results than the last time, but

 returned from the dead

draws up more than simply reviews of old B-movies. Halfway down the page I see, *SCIENTIST SEES THE LIGHT. LITERALLY. Professor Gregor used to believe that when you die, it's all over, until . . .*

I click.

Professor Samson Gregor, a lecturer across the sciences at the local university, would have been the first to tell you that the afterlife was nothing more than fairytale poppycock. *Would have*. But one frosty morning, in November, everything changed.

Gregor slipped on ice, hit his head and wound up in an ambulance. Where he died.

'I died,' says Gregor, 'clinically, properly died. I had no pulse, wasn't breathing. I was gone. Except I wasn't. I could hear everything that went on in that ambulance as the paramedics brought me back.' And that isn't all. Gregor goes on to explain, 'There was a shadow-figure, beckoning to me. That's when I knew I had a choice. Walk with the shadow and leave this place, or stay and finish my work here. It was an easy decision. I know now that when I'm ready, there is something waiting for me.'

Paramedics say that the professor should not have survived. 'It was a miracle; the kind we always hope will find us.' And Samson Gregor would agree.

There are more stories like his – of bright lights and watching loved ones at your bedside. Of things that people could not possibly have seen and heard and known. And there is one, nestled amongst all these tales of hope: *OUT OF BODY 'AFTERLIFE' IS NOTHING MORE THAN ENDORPHINS AND THE DEATH OF CELLS.* I bet the scientists have explanations for everything, but right now, I do not want to know.

> *Hiiiiii guys! So all the way home I was thinking, and we SHOULD be making the most of everything. All of us. You're right. So I'm starting right now, and I have something for you.*
>
> Really?
>
> **Me or him?**
>
> *Haha. Both of you (-: Here . . .*

A file appears, and I click download and wait, watching the progress bar turn blue. What is it? The filename is just a string of numbers. No clues there.

> **What is it what is it what is it?**
>
> *Heee! You'll have it in a second. Wait and see.*

The blue bar inches forward. Judders.

> *Oh! I hope you like it! :-S*

Finally!

I click, and the file expands across my screen.

A picture, in black ink. A picture of three snow monkeys, sitting beside a pond.

I can feel a smile spreading across my face, and I stare and stare at it, trying to soak up every last pen-stroke, every detail. The right-hand monkey is small and dainty, and she's gazing dreamily into the sky. It is undoubtedly Mai.

On the left, a larger monkey slouches in exactly Kaito's way as he casts a line into the water. And in the middle, on a throne of rocks, there's me, staring out directly at the viewer with eyes that hold a hundred thousand tales.

I love it!

Wow, Mai, did you DRAW that?

(-: *yes. You like?*

Yes!

Yesssssss!

blush yay. I am SO glad. I was worried you would think I was a talentless fool, or think that I was making fun.

No! Not at all!

Noooo!

Although I never pictured myself as a macaque before.

Haha. It's a compliment.

bows Thank you, kind lady.

Hmm . . . out of curiosity, what would you see yourself as?

Haha.

Promise you won't laugh?

Yes.

A leopard.

Hah. I would not have guessed that.

Hey! You said you wouldn't laugh!

I'm not, I'm just surprised.

Really? You don't see the resemblance? Sleek and muscly, powerful, mysterious?

Hahaha. Mayyybe. What d'you think, Sora?

I picture you as a racoon dog.

I type out the words slow and steady, in short bursts so my friends are not left waiting.

> Which I PROMISE
> is a good thing.
> They're brilliant.
> Smart and funny and loyal

And when she's sure I'm finished, Mai adds:

> *And they're sort of adorable.*
> **Hah. Yeah, but they wouldn't last two seconds in the ring with a leopard.**
> *OK. Sora? What's your animal?*
> I think the monkey's perfect.
> *Aww thanks ^_^*
> **It is. But if he were anything else, I think Sora would be a crane.**

I think of the crane, long-legged and beautiful, a bird around which legends are woven; a creature strong enough to carry people up into the heavens, long-lived enough to observe the world and impart happiness and wisdom. I am neither of these things. So why the crane, out of all the creatures he could choose from? I try to see myself that way, imagine myself strutting serenely through wet green pastures, offering advice to minnows, but I cannot. When I try to place myself inside the bird, it changes, shrinks into itself, feathers tousled and its wings chained to a tree.

I shake my head to rid myself of this awful image, and I change the subject.

It's GREAT Mai

You're really talented.

^_^

Yeah. Sora's right. You NEED to do this.

Has your mother SEEN these?

Does she know

How good you are?

Aww, you two! <3

I'm serious . . .

Please please please please tell her

I can't! The interview is in 3 weeks, it's all already started. I can't pull out now.

Please?

71

Between each mouthful, I watch my mother's face, the attention written over it as she waits for me to chew and swallow. Neither of us says a word, but the silence screams with meaning.

Scoop, lift, wait. *My son.*

Open, close, chew. *I'm sorry.*

Scoop, lift, wait. *I will always be here.*

Chew, swallow. *You shouldn't have to do this.*

Scoop.

Chew. *I'm sorry.*

It takes an age, and by the time we're done my mother's plate has long gone cold, but she does not complain.

She swallows hers in two bites whilst she waits for water to make tea, and then she sits back down beside me.

I watch her steady hands pouring the light green liquid into mugs, listen to the familiar sound of tea on china as it flows, and my mother's breath, slow and calm, above it. But somehow it is different tonight. The tea sounds stressed, stretched, as though it is being poured from too great a height and would rather stay inside the pot, and Mama's exhalations are tight, deliberate.

'Here.' Her voice is too loud, and there is not room for it in here with all the quiet. But if she notices, she is not saying anything. She lifts a mug up to my mouth, and I close my lips around the rim and sip.

And I recoil, but it's too late; the burning liquid is already on my tongue, blistering my palate. I splutter, spit tea all over the table, as my mother leaps up to fetch water and a cloth.

My mouth stings, and I have to swallow fast as saliva pools into it in response. My eyes water.

'I am so, so sorry, Sora,' she says, mopping up the mess, using the cloth to wipe my chin. 'I should have checked it first.'

'It's OK.'

'No, it's not. It was careless.' She sighs, wrings the cloth between her hands, spilling drops of tea back onto the table, and looks up at me with a newly serious expression. 'I should be taking better care of you.'

'It's fine, Mama. I shouldn't have drunk it.'

'No. I mean always . . . I spoke to my boss today about some proper time out of the office.'

I have only met my mother's employer once, but I cannot imagine he was pleased. 'No! You can't!'

She folds a warm hand over mine. 'Yes I can.'

'But what about your job?'

'It's fine. I'm going to work from home for a while, until . . .'

Until I do not need her.

'Anyway, I can manage the accounts from here. I am staying home, and that's the end of it.'

'But—'

'The *end* of it.'

The next day, my mother does not leave for the office. She lingers just a little over her first cup of coffee, and then she sets up her computer and a stack of papers at the kitchen table.

I should be glad of it. Glad of the company and the assistance. Grateful that my mother is both willing and able to change her schedule for me. I know this. And I *am*, but still I find myself wishing for the click of our front door closing behind her.

Everything is different now, and I wish with all my heart it weren't.

72

'Breathe in.'

I let my lungs expand until my head fizzes and my chest feels like it's going to burst, and then I close my mouth around the tube which the doctor's holding out for me.

'And out.'

I blow. Hard. And I deflate. I imagine all the bad things passing through me, out into this box where they can't harm a single thing. Silence: gone. Cramps: gone. Fear: gone. Every last faulty neuron: gone.

I wish.

'Good. All right? Right. Breathe in.'

We do the test, designed to see how strong my breathing muscles are, three times. 'Best of three,' the doctor says, loud and cheerful, as though he's doing me a giant favour, sneaking me extra turns at a fairground game.

Each time my lungs expand and then contract it hurts a little more. I'm tired, and my chest feels like I've just been punched. But he does not seem worried. He jots down numbers on my chart, and nods.

'Good. OK.'

'Am I . . . normal?'

'You are anything but normal, Sora,' he grins. Not funny. 'But your breathing's fine for now. A little low, perhaps, but nothing to be worried about.'

'Thank you.'

He sets down the chart, reaches for my fingers. 'Your

other symptoms, though . . . how are you managing? Is the pain all right?'

Is the pain all right?

When is pain ever all right?

I nod. If I go home with increased medications, my mother will worry. And I do not want to make a fuss.

'Doctor?'

'Yes.'

'What will happen when I fail the breath test?'

I've read all this a hundred thousand times, but I need to hear it from someone who knows, not an article which could, for all I know, have been written by a first-grader.

'There is no failing, Sora. It is not an exam.' He pauses, and his eyebrows sink right down over his eyes. 'But when the time comes, there are machines to help you breathe. Respirators. And there is the possibility that further down the line we might insert a trachea tube. But you're good, for now. Let's focus on that.'

73

'Heyy, Sora!' Mai slips into my room, with Kaito close behind her.

'Hi?' I was not expecting to see them, and for a moment I'm confused. Worried, even. But Kaito flashes me a red-eared, sheepish grin, and my fears dissolve.

'Sorry, I know we didn't plan to meet up, so I hope it's OK that we're here?'

I smile, try to push myself upright on the bed. 'Of course.' And I mean it. I have missed them. The last time I tried to log on, I had to call my mother in to press the power switch, and then I could not use the keys. Even the mouse felt fiddly and small against my touch, and navigating the forum was near impossible. I tried. And tried. And if I had the strength I would have thrown the whole machine out of the window.

Twice, I nearly asked my mother if she would do it for me; if she'd navigate through screens and type my words. But KyoToTeenz is *mine*, and I do not think she'd understand.

Mai perches on the bed beside me, grinning.

'We got you something.'

'You what?'

'Well, when you didn't show up online, we missed you. And we figured you'd miss us too' – she grins impishly – 'so you wouldn't be absent by choice. And we thought . . . well, here.'

She looks at Kaito, who pulls a bright pink plastic bag out from behind his back, and thrusts it towards me.

'I . . .'

'Oh right, yeah.' He pulls it back and reaches inside. 'Ta-da!' He pulls out a webcam and the biggest computer track-ball I have ever seen. 'It's a super-sensitive "one touch" thing. You've got no excuse now – you *have* to come online and listen to us whine about our teachers and parents and terrible code.'

A sharp lump rises in my throat, and I know that if I speak, my voice will croak, and crack, and break, and that will be the end. I swallow and swallow again, until finally my throat opens enough to whisper, 'Thank you.'

Mai's cheeks redden, and she shakes her head. 'We really, *really* missed you.'

'Yeah. It's not the same without you, dude.' Then, 'Shall we set it up?'

I nod. 'Yes please.'

He turns on the computer and rips open the packaging, and Mai moves up the bed, leans her head against my pillow.

'I can't work with you watching me!' Kai mutters, tugging at his fringe.

'OK, then, how about a story?' She had insisted on taking the half-finished book home with her, 'to practise', and now she pulls it from her bag and settles herself in to read some more.

74

'Hey, dude.' Kaito's face slides across my screen and settles clear.

'Hi.'

'I don't see you. Turn your camera on.'

I move the cursor to 'turn camera on' and click, and my face joins his. I look like an idiot.

'Heyyy!' he cheers. 'Looks great, huh?'

'Yes. Thanks. Best idea ever.'

He bows theatrically, and I laugh.

'How was your day?'

'Uuuuuh, Sora, I am *not good* at the pretty stuff for websites.'

'It just takes practice, surely?'

'Yeah. But it's So. Slow. And I want to be better at it noooww.'

'Hahahaha. Patience, young grasshopper.'

He pouts, but then Mai signs in and joins us, and he cannot help but grin.

'Hiiiii!' Her camera loads before she sits down, and there is a second, before she bounces into view, where there is just a chair, and cream-white walls behind it.

Kaito's walls are blue, and behind him are two posters; one is of Kirby, bright pink and jolly, and the other is dark and ominous, a shadow in the mist, with the tag *FIND HIM, BEFORE HE FINDS YOU* stamped across the bottom.

I feel like a little boy, my nose pressed up against the windows to see what is inside, to guess who lives there, what they do, imagine myself sitting at their tables, eating from their larder, lying in their beds. And it is wonderful.

75

BOY, 14, DEAD.
IS INTERNET CULT TO BLAME?

Police are investigating after 14-year-old Suzuki Haru was found dead in his father's car. The boy, once happy and hardworking, left behind a note proclaiming his dissatisfaction with 'the system', and in light of the recent rumours of large-scale suicide spam, it has to be asked – is this responsible for Haru's death?

It is difficult, at present, to be sure, but one thing is certain: as Haru's mother says, he was 'not a bad boy, or a sad one. Something has gone very, very wrong.'

I stare at the words on my screen. The smiling, goofy face printed beside the words. I do not know this boy. The article is short. It tells me nothing more than that he's dead. So why does my chest suddenly feel as though it can't expand? Why is there heat behind my eyes and guilt weighing heavy on my mind?

I close the browser quickly, erase the page history, but still those words are etched into my brain:

Happy and hardworking.
Dead.

It isn't right. And I need to know what made him do it.

To:	S . . .
From:	TheSClub
Subject:	The Club Needs You

Long have our ancestors wielded the power of life and in death.
And now it is our time.

We need your voice.
Let us stand together against injustice.
Thousands of voices, crying out. Same message. Same time.
Let us make our voices heard.

I dig out the latest email from my trash, and force myself to read it.

Is this what they sold him?

It's several hours old, and if the police are right, the link might be a dud already, but still I feel a nervous sweat covering my palms as I let the cursor hang above the link.

I click, and half close my eyes as a page loads.

WELCOME TO THE S-CLUB!

ENTER

The page is bright, and cheerful, and it might easily be thought the entrance to a school club, or a local café-bar. Which only makes it worse.

Hi! Welcome to the Samurai Club!

The Samurai Club (or Suicide Club, if you prefer) is here to take a stand against all the injustice of our times. To follow our noble tradition and make the grown-ups think about the legacy they're handing us.

Now is your chance to **really** make a difference.

We make it easy. Whatever method, whatever location you choose, alone or as a group, we're here with advice and support.

We will even provide your goodbye note, carefully crafted to leave exactly the right message for your loved ones. All you have to do is sign up, and pledge your final moments to the cause.

Together we CAN make a difference. Click 'MAKE ME A WARRIOR FOR JUSTICE' below, and we will contact you when it is time.

I skip the bright, shiny button and scroll further, to:

Helpful links:

Forum: Post an ad to form your own group! You needn't be alone.

Helpful Hints and Methodologies

Wonder what it's like? Click **here** or **here** to find out more.

What it's *like*?

How can anybody possibly report? *I killed myself today, and it was wonderful!*

No.

And that's it – suddenly I cannot take it any more. My

eyes itch with the words I've made them see, and I taste the bitterness of bile at my throat as my stomach heaves. I call out for my mother before I even know what I am doing, and I only just have time to switch off the screen before she rushes in.

I retch and retch and retch again, and my mother holds a bag before my face, and rubs my back until finally it stops.

'All right?' she says.

I nod.

'OK. I'm going to call the doctor. If you're coming down with something, I think he ought to know.'

'No, Mama, I'm fine. Honestly, much better.'

She frowns, but she hesitates.

'Please?'

She puts a hand to my forehead, and sucks her breath in through her teeth as she thinks. 'You're not warm. Perhaps you *are* all right.' She reaches for my wrist, feels for a pulse. I'm sure she does not know what she is looking for, but if it makes her feel better and means I don't have to explain or see a doctor, I am not saying anything. 'All right. But if it starts again, no arguments.'

'Yes, Mama.'

I won't think about it. I won't.

But as my mother helps me to clean up, I cannot help seeing that newsprint face, and wondering what he will be missing.

'Mama?'

'Mmmm?' She pulls my arm free of its sleeve and reaches for the other. 'Left arm.'

'When I was small, what did you dream I'd become?'

She stops, frowning, and my half-pulled sleeve flaps

gently at the end of my arm. 'I don't know.'

'A doctor? Surgeon? Pilot?'

'I don't *know*, Sora.'

'But you have to know!'

She is silent, and I know she wants to use the line which every parent gives: *As long as he is healthy, I don't care.* But I cannot even give her that.

'Please?' I say, softer this time. I don't know why it matters. It shouldn't, but I see that face inside my head, and somehow it does.

With a sigh, she perches on the bed next to my chair. She stares and stares at me, until suddenly the faintest of smiles appears on her lips, and she says, 'When you were three, your grandmother taught you to make cupcakes.'

I nod. I remember the feel of the batter as I dipped my fingers in and squelched it between my hands. I remember standing at the oven, Bah-Ba reminding me every two minutes that the door was hot, and not to open it. And I remember my excitement as I tasted the first one.

'And for *weeks* you told everyone exactly how to make them, step by step, in your impatient three-year-old voice. And I knew right then that you would teach, one way or another.'

And somehow, although she has not really answered, my mother's words are perfect. And for a moment she doesn't look sad at all, just proud, and I don't know what of, but I don't care, and I wish that I could make it last for ever.

'Mama?'

'Yes?'

'Can we have cupcakes for dinner?'

I watch as my dear, wonderful mother digs out ingredients from the back of the cupboard, and tips them all into a bowl: flour and butter and sugar and eggs, and sour-dried berries.

'Chocolate chips?' she asks, and I nod.

'Of course.'

And then she looks across the counter, and she smiles. 'Would you like to stir?' And her smile's so bright and warm that I almost forget everything else.

'Yes.' I so *want* to forget.

She rests the bowl on my knees, and folds my hand in hers just like my grandmother did, that first time, and we stir.

We do not have a proper meal tonight. We sit with mugs of tea and a whole plate of cakes between us, and we eat until our stomachs hurt.

78

I do not sleep well. And every time I wake, it is with the faces of Suzuki Haru and Yamada-san in sight, and the distant memory of dreams. They were arguing, I think, but I can't remember why.

My bones ache, and I think I must cry out because I remember Mama's face, hovering above me, and I think she slipped something onto my tongue and made me swallow, and then everything was warm, and almost safe, and somehow I ignore the shadows watching me and I go back to sleep.

When I wake again my mother has already drawn the blinds, and sunlight spills onto the bed, half blinding me.

'How are you feeling today?' My mother's voice sounds distant. I groan. 'You might feel groggy. Last night . . . I gave you extra—'

'I know. I remember.' My own voice is loud and slow and slurred.

'Here.' She pulls me upright, helps me sip at a glass of water and swallow pills which feel far too big and stick in my throat. 'Better?'

'Mmhmm.'

Everything feels heavy. My head, my neck, my tongue. The blood that slugs around my veins. And when my mother lets me go, I slump back onto my pillow and I feel like I will never move again.

My mother keeps a check on me, peering down at me as

though I am a creature laid on ice at the morning market. A squid, all sadness and ungainly limbs and slime. She peers, and makes unhappy noises, and I know that she will leave the market empty-handed. But on the fifth or sixth time that she gently slips into the room, one set of drugs is taking over from the other, and I'm starting to feel better.

'Hi,' I say.

'Hello.'

'I'm sorry. I don't mean to make you worry.'

She sits next to me, brushes my sticky squid-hair from my forehead, and I wonder, *If Haru's mother had done this, would he still be on this earth today?*

79

I switch on the monitor before I remember that yesterday's viewing is still there. The thought makes me gasp, pull back a little, but it is too late. The screen blinks into life, and there it is.

> ## Hi! Welcome to the Samurai Club!

So brazen.

False. *Warriors for Justice?* No.

I wonder what the samurai would think, seeing their name up there.

I suppose they would approve: call it *giving your life to a cause* or *standing up for those who can't.* But this isn't giving a life, it's taking it. Ten or a hundred or a thousand times. More. And what if those people are the very ones that we should be protecting?

Would you ask the wounded out onto the battlefield?

I don't know why I don't close the thing down, but I can't help it, I'm scrolling, scanning the page once more. And then I stop.

We will contact you when it is time.

But they talk of everyone standing together which, unless there are a host of deaths that are left unreported, means that it isn't time yet; that Haru's death was not a part of this.

So why?

I picture him sitting at the wheel, knowing that those were his final moments. Alone.

What was he thinking?

Did it hurt?

And I'm clicking on the last link at the bottom of the page: *Wonder what it's like? Click here.*

Good Endings

Helping people find the end they're looking for.

Considering suicide?	What is it like?	How to proceed	The Sitting Room

---

<click>

What is it like?

Endings vary. Some are quick, others slow. Some people choose to withdraw, find their own space and peace of mind, whilst others seek out company. The important thing is that it is **your** ending. You get to choose.

Your final moments can be anything you want, but we strongly recommend you think about your options before going ahead; you only want one shot at this.

Check out 'how to proceed' for more information on your choices.

I wonder, for half a second, about looking for 'CO poisoning', but I do not want to know what the boy's last breaths tasted like. I *do not want to know.* So instead, I click on 'The Sitting Room', which sounds safe and warm. Perhaps it is a place where people go to talk about their problems openly. Seek help. Maybe the *endings* are a last resort. A myth.

> **There are: 3 rooms open. Click to enter.**

Three rooms. Three slightly fuzzy photographs of individual rooms.

This . . . is not the neat-boxed forum I expected. And I *know* that this is something different. I can feel myself falling down a warren, but I cannot stop. I click on the first – a bright, clean room with a window streaming evening sun, a low coffee table and a lamp.

The same picture, larger, fills most of my screen. A video.

I click, and the progress bar ticks slowly forwards, but nothing happens in the room. It is empty; a still life.

I wait. And wait. But there is nothing.

What is this? The nothingness just makes me nervous.

I scroll down, looking for a clue, and my eyes are drawn to rolling text – a chatroom.

> **What is he doing? What are you DOING man?**
> **Nothing's happening!**
> **What is this?**
> **Yeah . . . this is a joke, right?**
> **He's not even going to show. How rude!**
> **Maybe he is having second thoughts?**
> **Yes, but he's already invited everyone . . .**
> **I just . . .**
> **I can't . . .**
> **I don't know why he would even bother, honestly, his life is pretty perfect, right?**
> **Waheyyyy, finally! You're late to your own party!**

I flick back up, and watch a man, young, maybe in his twenties, walk onto the screen. And I shrink the player so that I can see both the stream and the conversation.

He kneels at the table, and gingerly places a knife in front of him. He breathes in, deeply, and out, and then he lifts his head so that he's looking straight into the camera.

I wonder if he sees us.

With his right hand, he strokes the handle of the knife, breathes in, and out again, and the hairs on my neck stand on end.

Please? Don't do it.

Your life is yours. Don't waste it. Everything will be OK.

Ahahahahaaa, nice knife. Is it real?

I bet it's one of those play knives. Bendy rubber.

Ah, life-y, shut up, it's his choice.

Sicko; why don't you hurry up and die already. Some of us are getting bored.

He grips the handle properly.

And the silence burns my ears.

In. Out. I can see his chest move, even on the pixillated screen. I can see the weight behind his eyes. And I wish that he would look at us and smile, put the knife away and laugh, tell us that he wins, fooled us, it was all a joke.

But he does not.

Do it! Do it!

Do. It. Do. It. Do. It.

NO, PLEASE!

Yaaaaaaawn!

Once more he fills his lungs.

'I'm sorry,' he says, loud and clear, emotionless. And *slice*, before his words have died, knife meets skin across his wrist. And there is blood. A flash of pain, but then he grits his teeth and *slice*. Again.

Blood. His hands are wet with it. They glow. He tries to make a third cut, but his hands are shaking and the knife falls to the floor.

What?

Sayonara, friend.
I hope you find peace.
KETCHUP! :P
Nnoooooo! :'(
No seriously, this is all a sick joke. An actor.
You can get up now.
Ahahahahahahaaaaaa. Nice.

He lets his hands rest on the table edge, outstretched in welcome. And as all the colour drains from his face, he smiles.

Take a bow! :D
Dude, this shit is real.
No way! You couldn't put this stuff online – it's fake
Real
Fake
Real
Real
Sorry to burst your dreams. It is real.
HAHAHAHAHAHA, YOU FUNNY.
GET UP NOW.
Please.

Is it real?
Does it matter?
Whether it is real or not, I can't stop staring.
He did it.
Right there. In front of me.
He's gone.

Who was he, the man in my screen? They said he had a perfect life. Who was he, and why was he alone, and why did no one stop him?

Why?

I take an extra shower, and beneath the flow of water, all I do is cry.

That night, I'm woken from my sleep by something at the window. *Tap tap tap.* I try to blink the heaviness out of my eyes. Try to wake up enough to look.

Tap tap tap tap tap.

It's dark. The moon is barely a sliver. But as my eyes flick open I can see him standing out there, arms outstretched. Smiling. And it takes me a moment to realize I'm not awake. That we're seventeen floors up.

And later, when I wake in a tangle of sweat-sticky sheets, I lie there in a wash of calm so strong it almost makes me panic. Everything is quiet, and still. And when I close my eyes I see him there again, at the window, with the same smile on his face as the moment when he died.

I'm not doing this.

I'm not even saying I *want* to. I'm just . . .

| 🔍 **ways to die** |

I type it, and delete, and type it and delete, and type it again several times before I have the nerve to click, but every time I start to turn away, I see those faces, imagine myself in Yamada-san's bed, and I type the words again.

Still, as I hit search, I remind myself: *you're just looking.*

The first page, *50 Dumbest Ways to Die*, is filled with people who walk into meat lockers in nothing but their underwear, or try to fit three packets of rice crackers into their mouths at once. But the next is serious. And it scares me.

Some of the suggestions I can't even read. I never want to know the details, never want to think of them again.

Some are less horrific. But at the fifth one, as I ask myself for the fifth time, *What would Mama think?* I realize . . . I can barely move, and my mother is home all day. I could not do it anyway. I couldn't get tablets or tubing or whatever without somebody noticing, and I couldn't use them without help.

Even if I wanted to.

Which I'm not saying I do.

81

Mai looks up at me from her place, sprawled across my bed, her arms hanging down over the edge.

'We should do something.'

'Like what?' Kaito asks.

'I don't know. Sora?'

'I . . .'

'Ssh!' She snaps a finger to her lips. 'No arguments. We need a bucket list. Paper!' She roots around in her bag and pulls out a tattered exercise book.

I shake my head. 'No thanks.'

'Why not?' She glares.

And I explain about Wish4Life, how I know it is meant to bring hope and joy, but it just feels cruel, and everything I want to do, everything I want to achieve is long-term and impossible.

My friends are quiet for a moment, lost in their own thoughts, and part of me wishes that I could take it all back, but the rest just hopes they understand.

And then something clicks in Mai's head, brings her back to me. She grins. 'This will be different, I promise.'

'What will?'

'We are making a list. Three lists – one each. Full of anything and everything. No time, or physicality or money worries. Just things we'd like to do.'

I stare at her. Did she not hear what I said?

'Come on . . . Oh, fine. I'll start . . . I would like to visit the ocean floor, thousands of metres down. I want to find a cave to stay in for a while and meet all of the crazy things that live down there. I bet it's like space, only weirder. And I'd like to work with all the greatest animators, and be famous just like them.' She scribbles away as she talks. 'And I'd like to meet that boy in my school with the bright red guitar.'

I glance at Kaito, his ears glowing guitar-red as he chokes down jealousy.

'I'd skip forward to a time when I could write code that works,' he butts in, 'and make sites and games and every-thing to benefit the masses. And I want to invent a machine which studies for you—'

'That's cheating!' Mai squeals.

'Not the point. It would free up time for everything else.'

'Fine!' she huffs, adding it to Kaito's list.

'And I'd like to go to Hollywood. That would be cool.'

Mai nods. 'I'd like the three of us to go to Disney, or go visit the snow monkeys. A day trip.'

'And go to the moon.'

'And the desert.'

'Yes! And eat marshmallow toasts around a fire and look at the stars.'

'And learn how to make food from other countries. Hamburgers and pasta and . . . whatever they eat in the desert too.'

My friends shout out one thing after another, and Mai scribbles until several pages of her book are full, and finally, when Kaito says, 'I want to fight a simulated monster and feel as though it's really there in front of me!' I can't resist.

'All right. I'll play. On one condition.'

'What?' Mai's eyes shine bright with pleasure.

'You add "I want to study art instead of law" to yours.'

She does not answer me, but I see her turn the page from Kaito's list to hers, and write, so I say, 'I want to explore a library that takes a week to walk through, and sleep beneath an igloo made of books. And I want to teach in huge old lecture halls, with dust motes hanging in light which streams in through high windows. And drink root beer on a desert island. See the cherry blossoms fall in Yoshino and learn how to swing a bat like Tomoaki Kanemoto. And'– and I know I'm going to say it and I wish I could stop, but I cannot – 'I want to get up from this chair and run, and know that everything will be all right.'

'OK.' Mai sits up and smiles, not batting an eyelid, and if we were online I would be sending her a million text-based hearts. 'I think that's enough for now. I need a minute. Kai, can you read on from where we left off?'

She lobs the book, this one about a girl-spirit-thing who eats books instead of food, at Kaito, and he opens it, flicking the hair out of his eyes to reveal bright embarrassed cheeks. And he begins.

Kaito's voice is awkward, stumbling, and I find myself watching Mai instead of really listening. She pulls her knees up and rests the book against them, and I can see that she is concentrating, brow furrowed, chewing on her bottom lip.

Kaito sputters words about the sweet sweet taste of romance novels and the chewiness of mysteries, and Mai's pen sweeps across the page.

Finally, she looks up, stretches.

'OK. I'm done. Here.'

Kaito takes the notebook and holds it up so I can see it too.

The Brilliant Adventures of Professor Crane and Friends, she's written, at the top. And then, in a series of boxes, a comic strip.

'I wanted it to be a flick-book so that it moved, but there wasn't time.'

Kaito shakes his head. 'It's brilliant!'

'Read it?' I ask, because I want to hear it in her voice, so she shuffles around behind us so that she can see the page.

'Professor Crane was wise, but he was sad,' she said, and I let the pictures – a crane, folded awkwardly into a wheelchair, staring through the window at a gorgeous sunny day – tell the rest.

'His wings were broken, and he could not fly.'

My heart wrenches as I see his tear-filled eyes, and I do not care that birds don't cry.

'His friends came to visit him, but it was not the same. He wanted adventure. And sunlight on his feathers.' She pauses, lets us take in the scene: Professor Crane, dejected, whilst his friends – Racoon Dog and Macaque – do their best to make him smile.

'Science and medicine had tried and failed, and Old Crane was ready to give up. But his friends were not, and one day they arrived with arms full of bits and bobs and thingummies, and heads full of ideas.

'They circled him, and scratched their heads, and finally, AHA! Ideas! Snowy the monkey tried first. Taking a ruler . . . and her paint box . . . and a big roll of paper, she painted him new, magnificent wings.

'But the wet paint was heavy, and when she tried to fix the wings to the professor—'

Grinning, Kaito points at the little drawn-in noises,

stopping her mid-sentence. 'Do the sound effects!'

'*You* do the sound effects.' She laughs, digging him in the ribs.

He nods.

'The wet paint was heavy,' Mai continues, 'and when she tried to fix the wings to the professor . . .'

'Rrrrrrrrrp!' Kaito yells.

'. . . the paper sagged and tore.'

I look from my friends to the ink-strokes on Mai's page, the way she's made the paper look heavy and waterlogged, so you *know* that the poor monkey's plan could never work, and I don't know whether to laugh or cry.

But I don't have time to work it out because Mai ploughs on: 'But the friends would *not* give up.

'They scratched their heads, and frowned, and paced around in circles, until finally:

'AHA!' Mai yells.

'And Racoon Dog rushed off to find his toolbox, and he was bashing and clanking and twiddling away until finally he emerged with . . . robot wings!

'Professor Crane's friends helped him to strap the robo-wings in place, and they all held their breath as Racoon Dog switched them on . . .

'They buzzed . . .

'And beeped . . .

'And whirred . . .

'And then they twitched, and the professor stretched, and flexed his steely robo-feathers. And with a huge smile, he stood, and flapped his robo-wings.

'His friends threw open the porch windows and cheered as the professor leaped into the sky.

'And he stretched out his shiny new wings as far as they would go, and he flew!'

And Mai's voice, in those last words, is so full of wonder and promise that as I'm staring at the final panel – a vast summer sky, and in the middle, heading higher still, a tiny, glinting crane – I feel like I am flying too.

Finally, she breaks the spell.

'You see?' she whispers. 'This way, we can do anything we like.'

82

Over the next week the three animal friends go everywhere: they taste huckleberries in an old saloon whilst wearing cowboy hats and boots, see the sun set over the Sahara, and rest their weary limbs in steaming rock pools at the top of mountains. A new episode appears in my inbox every day.

They're beautiful. And each one makes me laugh, and wish that I could jump into the screen and go adventuring: taste the berries and feel the water on my skin, take my friends to wild, exotic places.

But every day it's getting harder to even get out of bed, to click the mouse and pull my face into a smile.

Today's episode sees Professor Crane and Snowy and Racoon Dog building a Super Special Time Machine, only Racoon Dog miscalculates the size of the battery, and there's only enough juice for one round trip. They argue over where to go – whether to see the dinosaurs or pharaohs, or go forward to spy on their future selves. But eventually, the promise of a little T-Rex action wins, and off they go to vast, unblemished lands to search for leathered wings and footprints big enough to stand in.

'Are you all right?' Mai asks. I stop reading, switch windows so that I can see her, and her frown spills across my screen.

'Yes.'

'You don't look it.'

'I'm just tired.'

As I say the words, I realize how deeply true they are. I'm tired. I stare harder at the screen, push the thought away because it is too big and terrible, and I do not want it. But I'm tired. And I wish that I could travel back in time to when it wasn't so.

83

'Mama!' My voice cracks the night, but I don't care. Hot pain sears my legs and spreads into my groin, and if I could move I'd curl up into a ball and die. 'Mama!'

And she's here, soothing, smoothing, asking what it is that she can do. I cannot answer. It is all I can do to squeeze the tears out of my eyes and keep from screaming.

'My son,' she says. 'My son. What can I do?'

But I do not know.

I just want it to stop.

She reaches for my tablets, and I *so* want them. All of them, until it stops. But I see her eyes, her stone-set jaw, and I cannot let her watch me float away. Somehow I shake my head, and when I part my lips my words spill out. Dry and desperate, but there. 'No. Please. I don't—'

My mother does not listen. She pops the foil, and tries to slip the small white tablets onto my tongue. But they stick to my lips and I twist my head, spit them away.

'No.'

She stands there, helpless, pill box in one hand and water in the other, and looks on as a fresh wave of pain takes hold, and I bite down so hard that I taste iron.

'Sora—'

'No.' It hurts, but it will pass.

This time, I win. She pulls me up into her arms, holds me, nestles her face in my hair. And I can feel her warm breaths, as sharp and erratic as my own, and her heart beats hard against my back, and if I'd had those pills, if I were floating away, I might think that there weren't two of us, but one.

Finally it breaks, and my breathing steadies. We stay wrapped together for a moment longer, and I let the post-storm calm wash over me, until my mother shifts beneath me and the moment's gone.

She lays me back against the pillow and crosses the room, and I'm half confused until she says, 'You're soaked,' and reaches for a fresh dry shirt. Now that she has said it, I can feel the dampness on my skin, cooling fast. I feel hot-but-cold, and sticky, and I really want a shower but the clock beside me flashes 03:00 and I cannot make my mother haul me out of bed.

She helps me into a new shirt, which catches on my clammy skin, and I wonder whether the fabric is instantly prickled with sweat. Then she kisses my forehead and steps towards the door.

'Wait!'

She stops. I know it's late, and she is tired, but I don't want her to go.

'Stay?'

She shuffles back towards me. 'Of course.'

'I'm sorry, Mama.'

'Hush.'

'No. I hate it, I hate it, I hate it. And I'm sorry.'

She stares, clenching her jaw, and I don't know whether she is angry or just trying not to cry, and then she whips round without a word and she is gone, leaving an emptiness behind.

I did this to her. Me and my stupid sickness. It's so bad that she cannot even look at me, cannot be in the same room as her own son.

But then she's back, filling up the room. She's smiling, though her eyes are heavy, and she has something in her hands. An album.

She slips onto the bed beside me, and opens it to the first page. My mother's face, younger then, stares back at me, and with her is a scowling baby.

'That was the happiest day of my life,' she says. 'The day I brought you home.'

She turns the page, and there's me, maybe two years old, on a tiny purple trike. 'You loved that thing. So proud of it. You'd go up and down Bah-Ba's yard all day.'

She turns the page again. Mama and Bah-Ba and Ojiisan, standing behind me in my first school uniform. I remember that day. It was three whole weeks before the start of term but I had begged Mama to let me wear it, show it to my grandparents. It was hot, and I should have been out chasing butterflies, but Ojiisan and I stayed inside all day, taking it in turns to play the teacher and the schoolchild.

She turns the page again and again and again, and our whole life is there – baseball games and lazy summer days, mountain hikes and festival parades, drama club and debate club and several of me curled into a chair or under tables with a book.

I laugh at a picture of my mother climbing up into a cherry tree, brandishing a wooden sword. My legs dangle from the top left corner, and I imagine yelling down at her, 'Can't catch *me*, renegade! I am Lord Sora, the greatest and most noble samurai that ever lived!'

'We've had some good times, haven't we?' I say.

'Yes.' She sighs. And her fingers pause, stop turning. 'Yes. We have. So don't you ever say you're sorry; *I'm* not.'

I'm not, either. Not for this. But every day I'm further from the boy I was, and I want *him* to be the one that she remembers.

....84

I lie awake for hours, waiting for the dawn as that thought grows inside my head.

It's selfish, leaving everyone behind to deal with the mess I've made. But I don't have a choice, I'm going to do that anyway.

Is it different, if I *choose* to go?

I watch the colour sweep across the sky as though the sun is a small child with a damp cloth, and the sky a magic-bumper-fun canvas. One touch and the picture is revealed.

Yes, it's different.

But I don't know which is worse.

Is it worse to snatch myself away, or to drag everything out, make everybody wait for the inevitable?

I try to imagine my mother walking in to find me gone, reading the words I've left behind, and I cannot. But neither can I see her stooping over me when I am nothing but two moving eyes inside a hardened shell.

I'm damning her whatever choice I make.

But I don't want to stay, not like that. I don't want to lie day after day, unable to run, go outside and see the stars or climb a tree. I don't want to watch her hovering and not be able to reach up and give her a hug, or speak the words 'I love you'.

And yes, she'll cry, she'll mourn.

But she's going to do that anyway.

* * *

Over the next few days I watch the lines around my mother's eyes, and listen to her gentle sighs, the slow, tired shuffling of her feet. She smiles, but it is strained, and I know she's only doing it for me.

I start to formulate a plan, and though it's risky, and not without pain, I am sure it's right.

85

I type *help me to die* into the search bar.

And that one word, *me*, brings it home.

This time I am not looking for theories. I want this.

And if I'm going to do it, I'll need help.

I think maybe I'll find it at the Society for Dying With Dignity, but they are careful, and they barely even mention anyone like me, focusing instead on passive death, on adequate meds and the turning off of life support.

I *hate* that.

For one brief moment I consider asking Doctor Kobayashi for my last wish from Wish4Life: a trip to the Netherlands, with Mama. The Netherlands, where the laws are different and there is help for people like me. We could have one last holiday, visit the canals and windmills, and then I could quietly slip away and Mama could come home alone. But I'd like Mama to travel when I'm gone, and . . . I do not think she would. Not after that.

Besides, I doubt I could get Wish4Life to sign off on my *death*.

I read, and I read, and I read. Of law, and court cases and human rights groups campaigning against the very thing I want to do.

It is not easy, and there are no answers. No samurai code that lays it out before me, tells me what, and where, and how, and gives society a safety net.

I'm glad it is not easy, in a way, because they're right,

those groups. In the hands of the wrong person . . .

I shudder, and the SClub emails burst into my mind. It's not the same, it's not, but . . .

Nobody should ever be coerced.

I find a set of videos recorded by a man not much older than me, with ALS, watch him waste away over two years, in ninety fast-forwarded minutes of footage.

And a woman sobbing to a news crew about her sick daughter, robbed of breath and opportunity by one well-meaning doctor who should not have drawn that needle, found that vein. He had no right to make that choice.

Twice I have to push away from the computer and wait for my tears to dry. No, it is not easy, and when I think of what I'll have to ask my friends to do, my stomach heaves.

I just hope they understand.

....86

In today's *Professor Crane and Friends*, the trio visit Ye Olde Librarium, and walk into vast halls filled with leather-bound tales, old medical journals and great tomes of history. The room is tall – ten metres or more – and shelves run to the ceiling, with rickety ladders reaching to the top.

I want to stare at it for ever, to soak in the sight of it, reach in and feel the pages, but Mai does not leave time to linger. The friends quickly discover a secret corridor, locked behind a swinging bookcase, and they're off, down a deep, dark tunnel filled with cobwebs.

Down a set of winding stairs the corridor narrows.

And there's another door. Not locked, but stiff.

It creaks.

And there are boxes, long and thin, and even though Professor Crane tries to whisper a warning, his friends are curious, and pry them open one by one.

Is it treasure? Extra-special books, older than Kojiki?

Something moans. Sits up, pushing the lid away.

AAAAAAGH!

The three friends tear back towards the library, but the ancient Library Tombs have been disturbed, and the creatures they've awakened follow.

AAAAAAGH!

Along and up, and along again they run, but the creatures behind them are quick, gaining on them.

They try to run faster, and there's the doorway, up

ahead. They're almost there, but icy fingers lie upon their necks. Can they make it?

'PROFESSOR!'

Snork 'Whut?!'

And the professor lifts his head, and he's in the library at a desk piled high with books, and there are no ghostly creatures anywhere.

Racoon Dog looks at him, one eyebrow raised. 'You were *snoring*.'

Professor Crane stretches his neck and unruffles his feathers before opening another book from his collection. 'Nonsense. Cranes don't snore. We do not have the throats for it.'

'Do you like it, do you like it?' Mai squeals, bouncing so hard that her webcam shakes.

I nod. And I *do*. But I've been working on my plan, and it's ready, I think. I think it could work, and now that I know, it is weighing down upon me, so I almost cannot think, or breathe, or anything.

'Yay! So what's next? I can't decide. The moon? Or should we just go to the fair?'

I have to tell them.

My stomach drops. But I *have* to tell them.

'Um . . . there's something I did not put on the list,' I say, so quietly that I do not know how they hear me, but they do, as though I'd yelled it through a megaphone.

'What is it?'

'Sora . . . are you all right?' asks Mai. 'You've gone . . . sort of grey.'

'There's something I did not put on my list,' I say again, and my hands are shaking.

'Sora?'

'Well?'

And I say it. The four hardest words I've ever pushed across my lips.

'I want to die.'

And I can't believe they're there, out in the open. So completely true and untrue all at once. And for a moment I just stare at nothing, and I do not even see my friends' reactions until Kaito explodes: 'WHAT?'

I can't speak. It is as though those four words have used up all of my power and there is nothing left.

'Sora! Sora? What do you mean you' – and he whispers the next bit as though the words are poison – *'want to die?'*

I open my mouth to explain, but I cannot form the words.

And then there's Mai, quiet, and oh so still. 'You . . . aren't talking about the comic, are you?'

'No.'

There are tears in her eyes, and Kaito's glaring, red-faced, muttering *no* under his breath over and over again. 'No, no, no, no, no, no, no.'

I wish that I knew how to tell them why.

'Come over tomorrow? I'll explain.'

I just need to work out how.

CULT LEADER CAUGHT

An arrest was made last night in connection with the Suicide Cult case. An unidentified female in her late twenties was apprehended at her Tokyo apartment in the early hours. Police have seized the woman's laptop, and are confident that she can answer questions as to the source of recent spam.

The woman, who was forcibly assisted to the police car, woke neighbours with her shouting, saying, 'I am not to blame. Suicide is rife. I do not point a gun at anybody's head.' And whilst this may be true, with suicide at an all-time high we certainly do not need anyone providing our young with extra encouragement, and it is good to know that she is behind bars.

KittyL<3ve: She's gone? It's over?

BambooPanda: YAAAYYYYYY!

0100110101100101: 'I do not point a gun at anybody's head'? No, darling, you just send them putrid fanatical messages every freaking day until they crack. It's like internet water torture. Ugh.

ShinigamiFanBoy: But she's GONE, dude. Caught. No more water in your inbox.

88

As soon as my bedroom door is closed, Kaito pounces.

'Does your mother know?'

'Hush! Please.'

'Well?' he demands, dropping his voice.

'No. I couldn't . . . I can't . . .'

He walks up to the window and back, pacing. 'Exactly, Sora. You *can't*. You can't *do* this.'

'I . . .'

'You what? You're sad? We're not enough for you? You're *tired*?'

'No! But . . . yes. It's difficult.'

'What's difficult? You're giving up!'

There is a bitterness in my friend's voice I would not have thought possible, and I feel lost. Trapped. I look to Mai for help but she is still by the door, and she is looking at me with the same expression that she wore on that first day, and even though they're *here*, I feel as though I have been cast onto an island all alone.

'I don't have a choice,' I say, willing them to understand.

'There's always a choice,' he snaps.

And I feel the anger rising in my chest, my throat, spilling out across my tongue in a salty, bitter wave, because there isn't. If I could choose to live, I would. If I could choose to stay, to make my mark upon the world, I would. But I am going to die, and the only thing I get to choose is *when*, and even that depends on them, because I cannot do it by myself.

'No,' I spit. 'There isn't.'

'Yes there is. What about all this, here, Sora?' He gestures, wildly. 'Why would you choose to—'

I shrug. I want to explain, to tell them everything about my fears, about Yamada-san, and the livestream guy, and what I think about when I lie awake at night. But he can't even say the words, and I do not think he'd hear me.

'What? You can't answer me?' His words get faster, more forceful. 'You expect us to let you go ahead with whatever this is and you cannot even answer? *Why*, Sora? Tell me that! *Please*, tell me that.' His eyes blaze, defiant: a challenge.

And I can't.

'Well, *fine*, if you're just giving up, I guess you won't be needing these!' He lurches across the room, swipes the books from my shelves in one movement. 'Or this!' And he's up on my bed, standing, ripping the poster from my wall and grabbing it with two fists of rage. Tearing. 'And you won't be needing *us*!' He leaps down, grabs Mai by the wrist, the left half of my poster hanging from his other hand.

I wait for the door to slam. For them to disappear, taking our memories and friendship and my one chance with them.

But Kaito stops, and turns.

I steel myself for another attack, tense up, as though my body could run if it chose to do so.

It does not come.

And he deflates, his anger gone. And as he crumples to the floor beside my bed he looks like a sad, spent balloon.

I want to laugh, to break the silence, but my throat is dry and it's all I can do to stare.

Mai lowers herself beside him, and their fingers interlace.

She takes a deep breath, leans against him just a little, and raises her eyes to mine. 'I think I get it.'

Relief pours through my veins, fast and warm. But Kaito pulls away from her and says, 'I don't. I'm sorry, Sora. I just don't.'

I wish I could make him see. Let him hear the careful sorrow lacing every conversation, let him wake up in the middle of the night with his insides screaming, let him feel every indignity and every fear.

'I'm doing this.' I make myself look at them as I say it, try to make myself sound stronger than I feel. 'But . . .'

'But what?' Mai whispers. And I'm glad it's her who asks, because I think she almost understands.

'There's something else . . .' I can tell by their faces that they don't believe I am still talking, don't believe I could throw more at them. And I wish I didn't have to but I do not have a choice. 'I'm going to need your help.'

89

'Taste?' My mother holds a steaming spoon towards me, and I suck up the red sauce.

'Wow! That's—'

'Too spicy?'

My eyes prick with tears, but then my throat warms with a chilli afterglow which slides into my chest, heats me through all over, and then I taste the tomato-lemon-peppercorns and my tongue dances. 'No. I like it.'

She smiles, and turns to stir the pot.

'I hope you're hungry.'

As she turns away, I see what it will be like when I am gone: an empty table in my mind's eye, and my mother standing here alone with a pot too big for single portions.

Will she turn, expecting me to be here? Ask the empty room to taste her food?

I picture her sitting here in the silence, listening to one less set of chopsticks against china, and I hate it. I want to scream at her to get out. Run. Sit in cafés and restaurants and sweaty, thumping nightclubs. Anything not to be here alone. I want her to promise me, right now.

But she's humming to herself, almost happy, and I can't take that away.

Mai and Kaito would not stay to hear the details of my plan. I understand, I do – it is a lot to take in, and even more to ask of them – but we have not spoken since, and I *wish* they'd come online.

What if they tell their parents? Mine? What will happen then?

Will I be locked away inside some psychiatric ward? Strapped to a bed until my body holds me prisoner all by itself?

Or maybe they won't tell, but they'll hide from me until it is too late. Until I could not swallow anything they tried to give me anyway.

Would they still come to visit?

I log into an open chatroom, try to fill my head with familiar voices, lose myself in other people's chatter: other people's chatter, but above them all my inner voice is screaming out in fear.

Meekkat: I give you: PIE. <click here to download file OoOoOoOpie.jpg>

BambooPanda: Did you MAKE that?

Chocol8pocky: WOW

Meekkat: Yup. In HomeSkills. It is chocolate cherry.

MonkECMonkEDo: *That's AMAZING Meekkat. Good work!*

Chocol8pocky: GIMMEE

BambooPanda: CHOCOLATE cherry? How do you do that?

Meekkat: Sorry, pocky, I already gave it to my sister.

Meekkat: I put in squares of chocolate with the cherries, silly.

BaSeBaLlWiNs: O_o if you could make like, a dozen of those, you'd have a whole team fighting over you.

Chocol8pocky: Awww :(

Meekkat: Hahaha, but Baseball, pie makes u fat. It is not good for athletes.

BaSeBaLlWiNs: PIE IS VERY GOOD FOR HUNGRY ATHLETES! Pie and pizzas and ice creams. Don't you know that's why we play?

BaSeBaLlWiNs: Especially THAT pie.

Meekkat: Awww, thanks ^_^ Maybe I will make some more and then invite you over sometime.

It does look exceptionally good: golden pastry and shiny purple cherries. I wish that I could make one. Three: one each for Mama, Mai and Kaito. And I'd write messages on top in extra pastry. 'I love you.' 'I'm sorry.' 'Everything will be all right.'

And, at least until they'd finished eating, they'd believe it, and everything *would* be all right. Because the pastry does not lie.

'It's not because of this cult thing, is it?' Kaito asks, before his picture's cleared.

'What? No!'

'Because that's over. It was on the news. You don't have to do it.'

'Kai, dude, it *isn't* that.'

'Then what? I just don't understand how you of all people could throw your time away.'

Me of all people? What's that supposed to mean?

'Sorry?'

'I mean, you already have limited time. It sucks. It's stupid. But why would you throw that away? Why aren't you grabbing every single second that you have and clinging on?'

'I . . .'

'You what? *Tell me, please,* because I'm trying to understand how you could do it. Even *before* you add asking your friends to commit *murder*. Fuck, dude! That's what this is. You're asking me to pull the trigger.'

'It's not like that!'

'It is! In the eyes of the law, and the blood on my hands, it is!'

He's so indignant, so *sure,* that I want to punch him, to scream at him that at least his stupid games would be useful for something then. Target practice for the real thing.

But I don't. I take a deep breath and I look him in the eye and say, 'It's not that simple, there isn't actually a legal—'

'Ugh! Not the point, even without all that, even just the you-leaving-everything-behind part, I'm *trying* to understand, Sora, but I can't. I can't, I can't, *I can't.*'

I think of Yamada-san, lying in that hospital bed, gasping, desperate, and I wonder which is worse, *arguably murder*, or that. And I have an idea.

'Let me show you?'

91

After the usual questions – *How are you? How is the pain?* – we fall quiet, and I know she's waiting for me to start the conversation. But I don't know how.

The bonsai's trunk looks pale and weak, as though the centrally heated air has sapped the life from it, and I wish that I could open a window and help it to revive.

Doctor Kobayashi shifts in her chair, half watching me, waiting.

I take a breath, and break the silence. 'I've been thinking.'

She stops her idle half-stare to really look at me.

'Yes?'

'It's about the wishes.'

'Yes?' Her eyes brighten, and I'm almost sorry for what I'm going to ask.

'There's something I want to do, but it's . . . not your normal wish.'

'What is it? The Foundation are very good. I'm sure that we could make a plan.'

'I . . . actually, I don't think Wish4Life will help me. I was hoping *you* might.'

'Oh?'

'Mister Yamada-san . . .' Something careful and guarded flickers across her face, and I know I have to watch my words, choose carefully. 'He was all alone,' I say, thinking, *And hurt and scared and it was far too late.* 'I don't want that.'

'OK?'

'But I can't let it destroy my friends. I need to prepare them.'

'Prepare them?'

'For seeing me like that. I need them to know what it will be like. What I'll be like.'

She sighs, picks up a pen I hadn't noticed from the table and twirls it in her fingers. I do not think I've ever seen her this unsettled. 'I'm not sure what you're asking.'

'I want to show them.'

'You want' – she speaks slowly, emphasizing every word as though it's foreign on her tongue – 'to bring your friends here? To the ICU?'

'Yes.'

The pen stills. She is a sika deer, caught in the hunter's lamplight. 'I'm sorry. I don't think it is possible.'

'You did it for *me*.'

'That was different. You're a patient. I'm looking after your wellbeing.'

I know I should be quiet. Bow my head, accept her answer. But I do not have the time for such politeness any more. 'And I'm still your patient. I need this. Please.'

She frowns. Was that hesitation in her eyes, or shock that I would speak against her? It is gone before I can decide, so I push further.

'*Please.* Help me? It is my dying wish.'

She does not answer right away, and I know I've got her.

I see the decision settle just behind her eyes, and then she gives me a thin smile full of duty, not of joy. 'I will see what I can do.'

92

Somehow, Doctor Kobayashi got permission from the patients and their families, and so the next weekend, instead of sitting in my room, we board a train to the hospital. My friends are nervous. Mai is chewing on a strand of hair, swinging her legs beneath her chair, and Kaito has not said a word since we left the house. I stare out of the window, try to ignore the sharp-toothed nerves battling in my stomach as the city rattles past.

We brought flowers, which sit heavy and fragrant on my lap: a huge bunch of oranges and reds that look a little like the autumn trees. I remember that room, and if we can do a little bit to brighten it, maybe I will not feel so bad for this.

Kai draws the air in through his teeth, looks at me with this sad anger, and pushes it back out again.

'I'm sorry,' I say, quietly so nobody else in the carriage can hear. 'I'm sorry I had to ask, and that you're here, but I need you to know why.'

Mai tries to smile. 'I need to too.'

'What if we say no?'

The nerves bite harder. I don't know what to say. What *if*?

'What if we see everything and we say no?' he asks again.

'I don't know.'

The doors slide open and Kaito wheels me into the familiar rancid air of hospital corridors.

Beside me, Mai's nose wrinkles and if I weren't so nervous, I would laugh.

'Which way?'

'Right.'

We walk past the reception desk, follow the brightly coloured arrows to the elevator, and along the corridor again.

'All these people,' Mai whispers. 'Are they all sick?'

'Some,' I say, as we pass a grey-haired woman slowly staggering along with a walking frame and IV stand. 'Some are probably just visiting.'

We round the final corner. Up ahead is the ICU. The door is firmly shut, but I imagine I can hear the sucking of fake lungs, beeping monitors and groans which only serve to make the overlaying silence louder. And suddenly I'm not so sure.

'We don't have to do this.'

'Yes, we do.' Kaito's voice surprises me. 'I do. I need to know how you could even think—'

Mai reaches out to squeeze my hand. 'Me too.'

We pass the door, glide on towards Doctor Kobayashi's room, where she greets us with a wide smile, too big for her face.

'Good morning. You must be Sora's friends.'

'Good morning, Kobayashi-san.' They bow.

'Come in.' She opens her door wider, gestures to two cushioned chairs which she has placed beside the coffee table.

Once we are settled, Doctor Kobayashi perches opposite. 'OK. So, I assume you both know why you are here?'

'They do,' I answer hurriedly, before my friends say something that will give my plan away.

Doctor Kobayashi ignores me and continues. 'You're going to meet some people who are . . . well, they're very sick.'

'Yes.'

'And you're OK with this? It might be shocking.'

She explains that we'll be going into ICU, where the patients are sick enough to need special care; that there will be tubes and monitors and one of the three men in the room can't speak at all. That even though they're all much older and don't have exactly the same thing as me, there is one patient who has something similar – neurodegeneration of some kind. And she tells them that some of the treatments will be much the same as I might be given in the future. 'We'll come back here when we're done, and I'll try to answer any questions that you have. OK?'

'Do they mind us visiting?'

'No.'

I wonder how many favours she pulled in, how many people did mind, until she explained, begged, promised future aid.

Mai nods, apparently reassured. 'And they're expecting us?'

'Yes.'

'Then let's do this.' She says, 'We brought flowers.'

'They're lovely. We'll get one of the nurses to put them in water.' Doctor Kobayashi stands, moves to push my chair towards the door. 'All right. If you're sure?' When Kaito hesitates, Mai reaches for his hand, clasps it in hers and pulls him to his feet.

I slip him a sly smile, watch his ears go pink even now, here, and I am glad.

The door swings open and we're met by a young male nurse who smiles warmly.

'You must be the visitors!' He practically bounces as he speaks.

'Yes they are,' says Doctor Kobayashi, her words reflecting his.

'Great!'

I wonder whether the three men lying in their beds expected this. Do they like this man? Or do they lie there wondering what there is to be so pleased about?

'Oh, flowers! Beautiful!' He reaches down and takes the bouquet from my lap, preens the petals. 'Come on in. We're just about to have some tea.'

Tea? This doesn't sound like the ICU that I remember.

It doesn't look quite like it, either. In the centre of the room, in front of the beds, is a large round table with a thermal tea jug and a stack of paper cups. A plate of sweet rice mochi. And beyond, the curtains are pulled back to reveal plumped-up pillows, and one man even has a knitted blanket spread across his knees.

But then I really look, beyond these homely touches, and I see the grey-white walls, the wires and tubes and stiff-starched sheets. The bedpans, and the sad grey sky peering through the too-high, too-small windows.

The nurse is pouring drinks. One, two, three, four, five – he keeps going – six, seven, eight.

I glance across at the beds. Three too-skinny men lie asleep, or something like it, and I wonder whether anyone has actually *asked them* if they want a drink, or if they're on a schedule. *11 a.m. increase fluid intake.*

Ugh.

'Here you go!' The nurse passes a paper cup to each of my friends.

'Aren't we going to wake them up?'

'Heyyy, a little excitement on a Sunday afternoon never hurt a soul, right?'

Mai grins at him, taken in by his loud jolly voice, but my eyes slide across to the beds, the gaping mouths and twisted limbs. Would I want strangers barging in on me?

What have I done?

I want to run, but my friends are here, and someone has gone to the trouble of arranging this. I can't.

'Are those drinks for them?' I say.

'Yes.' And he walks across to place a cup beside each bed, but he makes no attempt to wake the men. Instead, he comes back, asking, 'Do you need a hand with yours?' He picks up another cup, hovers a few inches from my face, too close, waiting for my answer. And I do, but I do not want it.

'No thanks.'

His face falls, just a little, as he slides it back onto the table.

'Mochi?' He holds out the plate, and Kaito and Mai each take one.

'Mmmm, sweet bean,' mutters Mai.

Kai turns his over in his hands, staring at the foot of the nearest bed, and I wonder whether he is trying to build courage to look further, past the old man's knees, his chest, his face.

I wish I could sidle up to my friend and ask if he's OK. Tell a joke to distract him. Lead him out of here. But I need him to confront it. I need him to *know*.

It will be worse if it is me there, in that bed. Right? I'm doing him a kindness.

Doctor Kobayashi sees him, though, and she *does* go over to him.

'It's all right. He won't bite you.'

'Couldn't even if he wanted, by the looks of things,' he mutters.

'Do you want to say hi?'

Kaito doesn't answer, still staring at the old man's feet.

I turn to Mai, who's polishing off her third bean-cake, as the nurse puts down the plate and says to her, 'Shall you and I go over there and talk to Mister Gee?'

She nods, walks boldly over to the third bed. The nurse follows.

'Goood morning, Mister Gee. I brought you a visitor!'

Mister G gasps loudly, opens one eye and says something which sounds like 'Unnnnnggsitor?'

'Yes. Mister Gee, meet Mai! She brought you *flowers*, which I'm going to put in water and set right here so you can see them.'

'Nnnkyou.'

'You're welcome.' Mai bows politely, and the old man's mouth widens into what I think is supposed to be a smile.

Beside me, Kaito still stares.

'Do you want to ask him anything?' the nurse asks, beaming.

'Umm . . .'

'That's OK. How about you tell him a bit about yourself? You'd like that, eh, Mister Gee?'

The old man nods. It looks like an effort.

'Um, OK. I'm Mai. I'm seventeen . . . I go to school on

307

the other side of the city, and . . . I like to draw.'

'You draw?' asks the nurse.

'A little.'

'Lovely! Maybe you could run an art class sometime? We're always looking for volunteers to do things in the day room.'

'Maybe.' Mai shrugs.

'So what else?'

'Huh?'

'What else do you do? What do you like? How did you three all make friends?'

'Um . . . we met online.'

'And then you met in real life. That's brave.'

She laughed. 'Not really. It was all Sora's mother's idea actually.'

The nurse raises an eyebrow. 'And now you meet up regularly?'

'Yes.' She thinks for a moment, scuffing one toe of her shoes against the floor, just softly enough that it doesn't squeak. 'Actually, I do have a question. Does he . . . Mister Gee, do you have a family? Visitors?'

The nurse sighs, shakes his head. 'He's stuck with me for company, I'm afraid. Mister Tee over there has family, a big-shot lawyer son and a daughter who's a teacher, but they're both so busy. I've met them, once, but city life does not really leave time for social calls.'

Kaito looks up decisively, sidesteps towards me, places a protective hand on the armrest of my chair. 'It's not going to be like that for us.'

I look up at him, try to work out from his face whether he means that they will come to visit, or . . .

93

'OK,' he says, as we push out into the winter air.

'OK?'

'Yes. OK. I'll do it. And it's not because . . . I'm not saying . . . I just think that maybe it should be your choice. And if you've thought about it—'

'I have. *So* much.'

'Well then.'

Mai hangs back, and for a second I think that I've lost her, but then she rushes to catch up and grabs hold of my arm. 'It's not . . . you don't want us to do anything horrible, do you? Because I'm NOT going all ninja hit woman on you, and I don't know where to get a gun.'

I laugh. I can't help it. Relief and sadness and surprise flood through me and the only place for it to go is out.

I picture Mai in a black catsuit, scaling our apartment block with a dart-gun held beneath her teeth, and I laugh.

I imagine Kaito sitting opposite a burly member of the clans, trying to look tough so they'll let him have a gun, and I laugh.

I imagine walking out of those hospital doors and never having to go back. And my skin feels ten times lighter, and I laugh.

94

'I . . . I couldn't find a good one of Katsuhiro Maekawa, and I didn't know who else you liked, so . . .' He unrolls a huge glossy poster, holds it up in front of me.

It is a floating-world print of a mountain set before the setting sun. And it is beautiful.

'Thank you.'

'I'm . . . I'm sorry. About the other poster.'

'It's OK. You were right – baseball isn't really *me*, these days.' I shrug, flash him a grin, and suddenly all the nervousness between us dissipates.

Mai giggles. 'Oh, I don't know, I can see it now, you rolling out onto the pitch wearing To-Lucky Tiger's head.'

'Not just the head; the whole costume. Sora would make an excellent mascot, don't you think?'

I grin, and roll my eyes. 'No. I don't think. And this is sounding suspiciously like one of those inspiration fantasies.'

'Suck it up, dude. You *are* an inspiration.'

'Ugh. Mai, get him for me?'

She steps closer to him, but she shakes her head, still laughing. 'Sorry, Sora. I can't do that.'

'You two!' I avert my eyes, still grinning, but not before I see Kaito's ears pinking with pride as Mai's hand rests, just for a second, on his back.

And then he pulls away. 'So. Shall I put this up?'

'No!' Mai squeals. 'Wait. It needs . . .' She pulls the poster out of his hands and a thick black pen from the back pocket of her jeans. And in moments, there's a whole new tableau at the bottom of the mountain.

A crane, dressed in full samurai armour, kneeling. And beside him, a racoon dog, a monkey and a glistening sword.

To:	S . . .
From:	TheSClub
Subject:	The Club Needs You

FRIENDS! It is time for us to make a stand, a difference.
The System would like us to stop, and let the world return to
its old and broken ways.

But we are stronger than that.
It is time.
Your Time Is NIGH.

Join us. Become a part of the biggest revolution in history.
The countdown has begun!

'Uuuuugh, I know it shouldn't upset me, but . . .' Mai
wails.

'Yeah, me too.' We're all looking at the same email, which
landed in our accounts as we talked. I imagine it sitting in
a thousand inboxes, ticking gently. I wonder how many
people have clicked, how many names have been added to
the list of 'warriors'. I shudder. 'Is it weird to feel that way,
given that I . . . ?'

'No. Your situation is completely different.'

She's right. These people – Mai and Kaito and however many others – they have choices. Choices which
I'd grab with both hands if only my hands would work.

They should not be throwing that away.

'I thought they were supposed to have stopped it; caught the culprit.' Kaito frowns.

I shrug. They *were*. But the evidence is right before our eyes. 'Maybe there were two of them? More, even.'

'Oh, don't! What if it never stops?'

'It will. They caught the first woman, right? They'll catch whoever else is doing it.'

'You read it, though. *The time is nigh* . . . what if they're too late? What if the police can't find them and everybody dies for some stupid, awful email?'

'But what can we do, Mai?'

'I don't know. Report it? At least if the police know, they can—'

'What? Fail again? I bet they haven't even got a proper tech team on the job, just some office clerk.'

'It sucks. I can't just watch everyone die!'

There is a phrase that Doctor Kobayashi used to explain grief to me when I was diagnosed. Displaced anger. And the way Mai's voice wobbles and her huge brown eyes find mine as she says those words . . .

'You might feel sad, or scared, or angry,' Doctor Kobayashi said to me, when I was diagnosed. 'Perhaps all three. And it won't always make sense. One day you might feel fine, the next you will be angry that your shoes are scuffed, or that the sun is shining. Little, silly things that shouldn't matter. Or people who have not done anything, really, to deserve it. It's normal,' she said. 'Don't worry.'

I didn't understand her, then, but now, the way Mai's voice wavers and her eyes find mine as she stabs out those words 'I can't just watch everyone die', I think maybe I do.

'Do you think they know what they're doing?' Kaito asks.

'Who?'

'The kids who sign up. D'you think they *know*? That it's for ever. That they can't go back. That . . .'

'And they're leaving everyone behind, losing every chance they have to make things happen. This club thing doesn't mention that,' Mai spits.

'Mai, I . . .'

'Not you, Sora. Never you. But . . .'

She'd be right, though. I *am* leaving everything behind. We all fall silent for a while, and I think about their lives when I am gone. Will they miss me? Will they grow up big and strong? Choose wisely?

I wish I could see it.

The next weekend we go out to the park, the three of us. We've been through the plan, on our last outing – out of Mama's earshot – in every tiny detail, but I think we all need reassurance; to know that everything will go to plan. So we walk the paths, talking in hushed voices as we go.

It's different, now. The branches have nothing to cling to, and they stand there naked, shivering in the cold winter breeze.

'All I need you to do is pop the blister-packs and help me . . . I can't lift them. But I'll do the rest.'

'The rest?'

'Yes.' I have thought long and hard about the way to do this. I want it to be easy. No mess. No stress. Done. And I do not want to leave my friends behind in pieces. I need to leave them free of blame and free of guilt.

'What will happen then?' Mai asks.

I think it will be quick. Like eating too much food on New Year's Day and falling asleep beneath a thick, warm blanket. 'Then we'll say goodbye, and you will leave.'

They protest. I knew they would, but I am firm. It has to be this way. I found a copy of the legal documents from a company that helps people like me: paperwork confirming my condition, and my competency, and I've already drafted my own, absolving my friends of responsibility. But I have to be sure. I want them halfway home before it happens.

The next day I sit in the kitchen with my mother whilst she works. I want to soak the sight of her into my heart, and I do not want to be alone.

'Do you want your headphones?' she asks. 'A book? Music?'

'No.' And it is true. I want to hear her breathing. Hear the scratching of her pen and the tapping of her fingers on the laptop keys. I want to see the way she shifts her weight from left to right, taps her foot impatiently when she answers the boss's emails.

These things matter now, because suddenly my life is one of lasts. Last week, last days, last hours, and I don't want to miss any of it.

Everything looks brighter now, sounds sharper, and I wonder, for a second, *Is it nerves, or a new lust for life?*

But when I focus on the question it's there: the muscle cramps and tightened breaths, the fear and helplessness. It's right. It's time.

'Mama,' I say, when she looks up from her work, 'what will you do when I'm gone?'

She physically recoils, pulls away from me. 'Sora!'

'I'm serious.'

She sighs. 'We'll talk about this later.'

Will we?

I wish I could tell her that it's *always* later, and there's not as much time as she thinks. But I cannot. Instead, I say, 'Those photographs . . .'

'Yes?'

'We haven't taken any in a while.'

'No. I didn't think—'

'We should.'

'OK.'

And in the evening, when she slides the laptop back into its case, that's exactly what we do. In every room. Pictures of us pulling stupid faces, grinning, arms around each other. Serious portraits of us with books, and tea, and staring through the windows. And then we bake, and we take photographs of that too. When the cakes are in the oven, my mother grabs a handful of flour and dumps it out onto my head, snapping my look of surprise amidst a cloud of white. I shake my head so hard that I see stars, and when I look up she is covered too. And the last picture of the night is of two white-haired, white-faced people with flour hanging off their eyelashes, grinning like they really mean it.

98

And then it's here. The Night Before. My final evening.

I let my breath out slowly, and switch on the camera.

This is hard.

But I have to. I can't just leave without saying goodbye. He'll understand *this*, but he would not fathom *that*.

One. Last. Letter.

'Hi, Ojiisan.

I don't even know what to say. Except, there is a reason that they limit the number of extra innings to a game. Sometimes . . . sometimes you just can't win.

I tried. I promise I tried. But this was one hell of a curveball.

But I slid into base before the other team could stop me. I'm content with that.'

I swallow hard.

'Mama will not understand at first. I know she won't. But maybe you can show her how to hold a bat again and live. Just like you taught me.

Look after each other. You're my team. I love you always.'

I sit here for what seems for ever, trying to convey everything I feel. All those memories. Every single one. And how I love him and am sorry and wish I could stay.

And yet, this is exactly right.

Then I stop recording and attach it to an email, scheduled to send out tomorrow night, when it's all over. And I sit, staring at my screen. I don't know where the week has gone, and I can't remember what I did with it. Sure, there are photographs, and memories, and when I close my eyes I see them all, up close and personal, a slideshow just for me. But what have I done? What will I leave the world except a sorry note?

'Oh, oh, oh! Yes! You're here!'

'Hi, Mai!' I laugh, baffled by her cheeriness.

'Hi?' Kaito says too.

'I did it, I did it, I did it!'

'Did . . . what?'

'I told her! I told her I want to study art, and I used you, Sora, I hope that you don't mind—'

'*Me?*'

'Yes! She looked at me like she was going to yell, and it just came out. I begged her to listen, and I told her about you, and how you taught me that dreams are important because time is short, and sometimes, even when it's hard, we have to take control of our own destinies.'

She *actually* did it?

'And?' Kaito beats me to the question.

'She went tight-lipped and quiet, and I thought that she was going to send me to my room, tell me again that I'm too young to know what the important things in life will be . . . but she didn't. She just asked to see my *art*.'

I can see Kaito on the screen, holding his breath exactly as I am.

'She looked at it all. And then we sat, and talked, and *I'm not going to law school*! I'm going to write to the dean and explain. And I'm hoping that he'll let me switch, but if he doesn't it's OK, I'll go somewhere else. I don't care. *I'm not going to be a lawyer!*'

'Yesss!' He punches the air victoriously. 'And she beats the Mega Boss. Mai takes the win!'

'You,' Mai giggles, 'are such a dork.'

I watch them, so close that even though they're halfway across town from one another, they might as well be in the same room. And I am glad.

All the way through dinner, I can feel the tears, hot and heavy just behind my eyes. Every time my mother asks, 'Is that all right?' or 'Water?' my throat cracks beneath the awful truth. This is our last evening meal. The last time I will sit, unhurried, at the table with my mother. The last time she will cook her soba broth for me. I breathe in the scent of it, rich with spinach, and I wonder whether she will ever eat the dish again, or whether it will always be our *last meal* in her mind. For ever tainted sour.

I'm glad that it is broth tonight and there are no chopsticks. I don't have to imagine my mother placing bones – my bones – into an urn.

She knows something is wrong, offers to get me extra pain relief or make me an appointment to see Doctor Kobayashi, and I almost tell her, but I do not have the words.

...99

I wake up in the dead of night, and for the briefest moment I'm confused. There is no light, no noise, no pain. Why am I awake?

And I remember. The last day. The ending.

Nerves jump like crickets on my insides. I lie here, listening to sounds that are not there: imagined wind, the ticking of time, a fox rummaging through dustbins ten storeys below. And I think of Haru – did he wake like this, the day he died? I think of him, and Yamada-san, and the man who spoke to newspapers about the things he saw the day he died.

And this:

I cannot mourn, for I have lived.
The whistle of the sword, sings;
frees me with a final kiss

I'm scared, and I'm excited, and relieved. Because today, whatever it is that will follow this, I take control. Today everything changes.

Tomorrow there will not be that awful stomach-sickening moment when my mother has to wipe me clean, or the guilt as the baggage beneath her eyes grows larger, darker, every day. There will not be the promise of a ventilator, a machine which reads your roving eyes and translates movement into t.h.e. s.l.o.w.e.s.t. e.v.e.r. w.o.r.d.s.

There will be only memories, and freedom. In the next room, my mother lies asleep as though nothing is different, but today everything changes.

I almost made her a video too, but I could not. She would play it on repeat until my image warped and my words took on meanings that were never meant.

I still don't know what I will say to her. Or how. Or when. I wish I could take Mai's victory – my part in it – and share it; make my mother proud. And I wonder about telling her at breakfast, but I do not want to bring Mai into it. Breakfast is for us and us alone.

100

We eat in almost silence, but I do not mind. I let my eyes trace her hairline, the wrinkles around her knuckles and the way she draws a breath every time I close my mouth around a bite-size square of toast, her lips mimicking mine in miniature as though she's willing me to eat. And I remember. I remember all the times she's dealt with cuts and scrapes and bruises, all the times I ran out of the door without saying goodbye.

And here I am, almost grown, doing it again.

When breakfast is over, she sets water on the stove for tea. Only this time, she does not drop tea bags into mugs. She reaches for a tin, pulls out an orange teapot I have never seen before.

'I thought,' she says, turning to me with a smile, 'that perhaps it was time you and I lingered a little.'

101

My mother kisses me goodbye and waves us off as though this were any other afternoon.

The air feels strange. It crackles as it rubs against my skin.

'Are you OK?' asks Kaito.

'Yes. Are you?'

They nod.

'So where d'you want to go?' he asks.

'I don't know.'

'Come on, man, anywhere. Your chariot awaits.'

It's cold, and my friends look as though they haven't slept and their brains need switching off, so I suggest the movies. Pure, traditional escapism.

The first movie I ever went to see was *Spirited Away*. I sat beside my mother, and the whole way through the movie I had to keep on checking she was there, that she had not been stolen by the evil witch Yubaba and turned into a pig. I *knew* she hadn't, because my mama was not a greedy, selfish thing like the little girl's parents, but still I had to check.

I loved that movie. The colours and the sounds, the tiny, clackety soot sprites. But it gave me nightmares for a week.

Today I sit here in the dark, staring at the screen, but I'm not watching really. I let the pictures flash before my eyes as I inhale the dusty-seats-and-popcorn smell and listen to the people fidgeting around us.

And then the lights come on and it is time to go.

I have not eaten with my friends since I started to need help to get the food up to my lips, but today I want to taste everything and so, when Mai suggests the food court, I happily agree.

'Your food, sir,' Mai says, bowing theatrically. She chooses, and grabs a split-tailed shrimp sitting on a small pillow of rice as the first morsel, holds it out for me to bite. Except she is too far away, cautious, and when I stretch forward to reach it she realizes her mistake and moves her hand, and in one swift effort I am stabbed in the nostril with a pointy stick, and showered in pearls of rice.

She laughs, one hand to her mouth in shocked apology. 'I'm so sorry!'

'It's OK.'

'Let me try again,' she says, and this time she is slow and steady, and I bite down on the morsel without incident.

It's fresh and sweet, and Mai grins at me sheepishly, and I wish that this could last for ever.

'How is it?' she asks.

'Good.'

If anyone walked by our table, they would think us spoiled and greedy. We have salmon rolls, and tuna, and egg rolls soaked in sticky syrup. Seaweed, and mayo, and crab with avocado. My friends take it in turns to help, exclaiming, 'Gosh, you have to try this!' and, 'Eat up!' with every bite. I eat until my stomach swells, and then Kaito looks up and says, 'Noodles.' And orders us three bowls of ramen.

Predictably, we end up in the park, wandering the paths

beneath the trees. So far, nobody has said a word about tonight, and I am glad. I want to give my friends this day, a parting gift, untainted.

But as we walk along, Mai asks, 'Are you scared?'

'No.'

She nods, but she's still frowning. 'I'd be terrified.'

I'm not scared. Not of that, the *what comes next* part, but it isn't quite true that I am not scared at all; there is a hollow pit inside me that should be squeezed out by all that sushi, but it's not.

The sun sets early in December, and it is already growing dark around the edges of the sky.

'I love the way the branches hang there in the winter,' Mai says, as I look up to see the winter canopy. 'Like someone took a brush and ink and painted them all in.'

She's right. And I imagine her going home tonight and painting half a dozen trees, each blacker than the last. 'Me too. It looks so . . . deliberate.'

'I think nature is deliberate. Only we can't see it because we are so used to chaos,' she says. 'Like . . . that tree with the pin-straight trunk.' She points ahead of us. 'You couldn't build a thing that straight.'

And she moves round in front of me, and stands on one leg, arms outstretched to greet the sky.

She wobbles, and Kai laughs. 'You'd be straighter if you planted all your roots against the ground.' And he leaves my chair and walks behind her, takes her arms in his, stretching her further upwards, and they're reaching, steadying each other. And as the half-light glows behind them so that they look like a painting too, I think that this is how I will remember them, for always. This is what life is, what makes the world so strong.

We settle here to watch the sunset, beneath the pin-straight tree. It seems as good a place as any. Kaito leans his back against the trunk, and Mai leans hers into his chest, and for a moment we are quiet.

The sky turns, the edges dimming whilst the centre glows the brightest gold.

I tear my eyes away to look at them. 'What will you both do?'

'Huh?'

'When the sun comes up tomorrow, and next week, next year . . . what do you think you'll be doing?'

'I don't know.' Kaito is the first to answer. 'Tomorrow does not feel so real, right now.'

'No,' Mai agrees sadly. 'But beyond that's easier. I'm going to study art and become famous for my work. It will be beautiful.'

I smile. 'What else?'

'I'll live in a nice house. A proper house, with a garden gate. And I will let all the neighbour's children pick plums from the trees.' She stops, and then: 'And before that, I think I might go back and volunteer at the hospital.'

'With that crazy nurse?' Kai frowns, pulling her closer.

'No! Yes. I don't know. I don't care. I just think it would be nice. Don't you?'

'Yes.'

'How about you, Kai?'

'I honestly don't know. I want to do *something*, but I don't really know what yet.'

Mai looks up at him, snuggles closer. 'You'll be taking over the whole internet before you're thirty, dork.'

'Oh! You're right! How *awful* of me to forget the master-plan!' He grins.

'It is! I want a mansion to go with my garden fence.'

The sky deepens, and it's almost time to go. And then I see it. 'Hey, look!' I say. 'The first star!'

The first star of the last night.

We watch them blink on, one by one, and I'm reminded of that night with Ojiisan.

I always used to think that the stars lived for ever, that I would too. And I can't believe it's over.

One, two, three . . . I count the shining distant lights, and Ojiisan's voice sits inside my head. Heavy. Worried. *So many of them will be burned and gone before we even notice them.*

I know exactly what he meant, now, but it's not the way he thinks. The sky is different here. I can count the stars we see upon my fingers. And as I sit beside my friends I know I'll not be cast aside unseen.

....102

As we approach my apartment block I start to get nervous. My friends have not stayed after our days out before. Will I have to beg? Come up with a reason why they have to stay? Will my mother be suspicious?

But I needn't have worried. My mother greets us with a smile, and rather than her usual 'Thank you and goodbye' she turns to my friends and says, 'Would you come in for some tea?'

Does she know?

Does she suspect?

But as she bustles round the kitchen, boiling water, setting out the teacups, scooping tea into the pot, she hums. An old tune I have not heard for years, a song about the cherry blossoms hailing spring, filling up the air.

I wish I could tell her just how right she is; that tomorrow, everything will be completely different. New.

We sit, the four of us, and sip our honey-coloured tea as though it is the most ordinary thing. And when the tea is drained, we shuffle off towards my room. We stop in the doorway and I look back. I need to see her, at the sink or clearing dishes, unaware that eyes are watching her. I need to see her one last time.

But she has not yet turned away. She smiles at me and says, 'Just an hour, OK? It's getting late.'

'Yes, Mama.'

I can't believe that this will be almost our last conversation, and the silence hurts my heart, but I don't know what to say.

I have to do this, and I hope she understands.

....103

Kaito slides the door closed, and we look at one another with nervous grins. They might be grimaces; I can't tell.

'All right,' I say, and as I hear the words, adrenalin rips through my veins. 'Let's do this.'

Mai pushes air out of her cheeks and stares at me. 'You're sure? We're really doing this?'

Not now. Please not now. I cannot *not* go through with this.

'Yes.'

'Well, then.' Shaking slightly, Kaito reaches down into his bag and pulls out a large, clear bottle. 'I brought you this.'

Sake.

'I read about it. It's supposed to help depress the central nervous system.'

'Yes.' I nod, taste the saltiness of nerves upon my tongue.

'It's not all for you, though,' he adds, unscrewing the lid and lifting the neck to his lips. He swigs. 'For courage!'

He passes it to Mai, who does the same. 'For courage!'

And she holds it out for me.

I expect it to be smooth and bitter, but it's not. It's rough and woody, and my lips and tongue buzz underneath it. I swallow, and my throat does too.

'Wow!' I say, and then, 'For friendship!'

We pass the bottle around once more and then I say, 'The tablets are in a pot beside my bed.'

'Wait.' Kai stops me.

'I have to, Kai.'

'No. It isn't that. We . . . we have a surprise for you. A parting gift.'

I imagine rice balls drenched in syrup, incense, or a dagger to protect me from the evil dead – something that will send me on my way with a full stomach and stout heart.

But Kaito moves across to my computer, and he turns it on.

'It's not . . . I hope . . .' He swallows, starts again. 'We made something. There's so much that Professor Crane and his friends never got to do, and . . . well . . .'

'You made both of us *dream*,' Mai finishes.

The desktop loads and he opens up the browser, types in something that I cannot see.

And then it loads.

A perfect tree, all twisted bark and tiny golden leaves. And hanging there, swaying to the sound of rustling canopies, are dozens of . . . what? What are they?

'It's a virtual wishing tree,' says Mai. 'You click here . . .' She clicks, and a parchment scroll pops up in the middle of the screen. 'And you type your wish. And when you're done' – she clicks the 'finished' button and the tiny scroll rolls up – 'you choose a branch and hang it in the tree.'

'We went live last night,' Kaito says excitedly, 'and I told the forum, and look, there are already people taking part!' He takes hold of the mouse and hovers over a tiny copper wish, and it expands, revealing *PEACE*. He finds another, hovers, and I read: *See the sun rise from above the world.*

'It's beautiful,' I say.

'Mai did all the art. I just made it work.'

'It's wonderful. Can we read some more?'

There's: *Please let my mother come back home. I miss her.*

And: *No More War.*

And: *I wish to be understood.*

New bike. New car. Laptop. Skates. Guitar.

Love.

Good grades.

A cure for cancer.

Visit to the moon.

And I see Mai's: *I wish to be an artist. An animator who makes things which people love, which move them, make them think.*

'At first we made it just for us. For you. We were going to input all the things we want to do, so that you could see. But then . . . it was Mai's idea.'

'I just . . . it could help so many people, don't you think?'

'What?' I look at them, their faces filled with desperate enthusiasm, but I do not understand.

And then he shows me.

Hi everyone,

I made a little thing:

WWW.THEWISHTREE.COM

We all have troubles. All of us. And we all have wishes, things we hope to have or be. Sometimes, these things seem far too hard and far away, and then the troubles and duties start to rule our lives. Today I learned that life's too short and precious to be wasted. Wishes are important. And it is *my* wish that we spread this news. Wish. Doing is born in dreams.

'It's gone viral,' he says, clapping with excitement. 'And, dude, today Big Ninja emailed me—'

'Big Ninja?'

'The best computer guy in town. He helped me make the site do everything we wanted. And today he emailed me and said he knows a guy, if we wanted, who could target every teenage forum in the country, get *this* email in everybody's hands.'

The sake has already slowed my brain, and it takes me a moment to work out what they mean. The SClub will have competition. And it might just work.

'Can I do one?'

'Of course.'

And I get Kaito to type: *I wish that everyone who has a chance would take it. That everyone who has a dream will chase it. For those of us who can't.*

And as he types, I know how to say goodbye; I know exactly what words I should leave behind. I get him to write those too. *By hand. Signed 'Your son, with love'.*

My mother pokes her head around the door at exactly eight. I knew she would. And even though I warned my friends, and this is built into the plan, even though I know that all she sees is three friends crowded round a screen, my heart drums faster and I feel as though my skin is dancing to its beat.

'Medications, Sora.'

'Mama!' I protest. 'Not now.'

'Yes, now. Your friends won't mind.'

'I . . . I could help him?' Kaito says, just like we'd planned.

'I don't know.'

'Please, Mama,' I half whisper. 'It's embarrassing. I don't want you to fuss all the time.'

She's hurt. And I want to tell her that I do not mean it, but it's kind of true, and anyway, I can't.

'Are you sure you can manage?'

'Yes. I've taken these things every day for months. We can do it.'

She sighs. 'All right. If you're sure.' And then she leaves, shuts the door behind her, and I have to stop myself from calling after her.

I shake my head to clear it. Breathe deep. And I'm back.

'OK,' I say. That one word meaning everything.

OK, I'm ready.

OK, I'm done.

OK, it is time.

Kaito helps me up and into bed, because I cannot bear the thought of being in this chair, and then I tell him that my tablets are on the shelf above my head.

'How many?'

I give him a look, and he pours all of them into the cup. A week's worth.

He picks up the sake, knocks it back, and rests the bottle on the bed beside me.

He climbs up on one side, and Mai gets on the other so that I'm sandwiched between them.

'You're sure? You're really, really sure?'

'Uh-uh.'

He half closes his eyes as he holds the meds cup up towards my lips.

'No,' I say.

He stops. 'What?'

'Let me.'

'But you can't.'

'I know. But I need to do this.' I will not leave him with that guilt. I need to leave him knowing that I told him how many pills. That *my* fingers were on the cup.

He slides the cup into my fist, wraps his hand around mine, and we lift together. I will my hands to move. To tilt the cup myself. And I know that in reality it's Kaito's muscles that drop the sugar-coated waterfall onto my tongue, not mine, but the intention was there, and I think that counts for something.

I hope Kaito thinks so too, tomorrow.

Our hands drop, and Mai is right there with the bottle, pouring me sake after them. I swallow.

And I sigh. Relieved.

'OK,' I say. 'Go.'

'You're kidding, right?'

'We're not leaving.'

'But—' If my mother walks in, sees us here? And what if I start foaming at the mouth? Convulsing? I don't really know how this will work, and no one needs to see that.

'No. We're. Not. Going. Just try to kick us out.' Kai grins. It's wobbly, but it *is* a grin.

'You know,' says Mai, wrapping her arm over me, 'I feel a whole new chapter coming on: *Professor Crane and Friends Cheat Death*.'

'Yes!' Kaito's hand meets hers, and we're interlocked in a strange three-way embrace. 'Can we visit catacombs, play chess with the devil?'

'Sure. And then we're hiking out across a rainbow to see what is on the other side.'

And these are they. My final moments. They say a warrior must always be mindful of death, but I never imagined that it would find me like this, lying on a bed beside my friends, in a room of love and laughter.

I let my mind wander over everything we've done, and talked about. Let their voices carry me along.

I slip, and their voices warp, like underwater songs, but their touch is strong, and keeps me from floating away, and I am grateful.

'I cannot hear the birds,' I say. 'The air.' And even though it's night, and cold, I feel Kaito move away, just for a moment; then he's back, carried over to me on a strong cool breeze which smells of promises and heirlooms.

My eyes grow heavy, my head heavier. There's a weight against my chest and the other Sora, the one who lies beside me and feels all the physical sensations, cannot draw a breath, but I don't care.

And I fall deeper. Tumbling. But I know that they will catch me. And in the blackness there is only me, and my last, handwritten words:

The last leaf falls
But look close and you see
The hidden buds of spring

JAPAN'S ENDEMIC HOPE

Citizens across the nation would have been forgiven for confusion when they awoke this morning to see blossom on the trees. At closer inspection, however, one would find not blossom at all, but wishes. Hundreds of thousands of tiny paper wishes. These trees have popped up everywhere, in parks and gardens, outside schools and offices.

Beneath one, outside the Metropolitan Police building in Tokyo, there rests a plaque which says, simply: LIVE.

But why? So far nobody has come forward to claim their work, but with such an air of unrest lately, perhaps this is someone's way of reminding the nation what's important. Perhaps it's a message to all of us to live, to hope, to dream.

And maybe, just maybe, it's the end of a terrible nightmare.

ACKNOWLEDGEMENTS

They say that if you fold a thousand paper cranes, a real crane will grant you a wish. I lucked out: before I'd folded a single sheet the people below pulled together to make my book-shaped wish come true. And in lieu of a sky full of origami cranes, I offer these rather inadequate words:

First, Lucy Christopher, who opened doorways, and somehow always makes me want to write more, better words. And the rest of the Bath Spa WYP team, who, between them, demystified this business without taking away the magic; Julia Green, Steve Voake, Janine Amos, John McLay – thank you.

The best critique army anyone could wish for: Tracy Hager, Carly Bennett, Lesley Taylor, Marieke Nijkamp, Kayla Whaley and KK Hendin. Thank you. For everything. Thank you for not holding back, and for thoughtful discussions; for posing difficult questions and expecting me to answer. This book is a thousand times better because of you. And thank you for letting me flail and cry and worry all over you, but never once accepting my cries of 'I give up!'

Thanks also to my fabulous readers, whose insightful feedback and encouragement have been utterly invaluable: Bridget Shepherd, Yuri Masuya, Dahlia Adler, Katerina Ray, Rosy Mercer and Mel Sylvester, and especially Niamh Taylor, Scarlett Sylvester and Mari Madigan, the first young people to see these words; you rock my world.

Thank you, Rich Oxenham, for that first spark of an idea at the start. And Kayla Whaley, for an excellent round of Spaghetti Fridge which gave me a title; they are not my strong point, and I'm so grateful that they're yours.

Super-agent Gill McLay, for advice and enthusiasm in equal measure: I'm insanely lucky to have you.

Becky Stradwick, who had me smitten well before dessert, and Kirsten Armstrong, who swept in at the last minute with grace and insight. Thank you both for making this thing even better, and making it easy. Sue Cook, whose attention to detail is incredible. And the rest of the Random House team: all of your names should be here. Thank you, for everything you do to make books happen.

Finally, thank you to all the family and friends who've indulged my crazy research questions, read, put up with me flaking on coffee/dinner plans and dragged me outdoors every once in a while. Special thanks to the friends who hold the keys to Twitter – without you, this book would never have been finished. And to my mum and dad, for all of the support, always. I love you guys.